DEAD MAN DANCING

DEAD MAN DANCING

A Hannah Ives Mystery

Marcia Talley

This first world edition published 2008
in Great Britain and the USA by
SEVERN HOUSE PUBLISHERS LTD of
9–15 High Street, Sutton, Surrey, England, SM1 1DF.
Trade paperback edition published
in Great Britain and the USA 2009 by
SEVERN HOUSE PUBLISHERS LTD

British Library Cataloguing in Publication Data

Talley, Marcia Dutton, 1943-
  Dead man dancing. - (A Hannah Ives mystery)
  1. Ives, Hannah (Fictitious character) - Fiction
  2. Detective and mystery stories
  I. Title
  813.5'4[F]

  ISBN-13: 978-0-7278-6670-7   (cased)
  ISBN-13: 978-1-84751-086-0   (trade paper)

All Severn House titles are printed on acid-free paper.

Printed and bound in Great Britain by
MPG Books Ltd., Bodmin, Cornwall.

For my sister, Katherine Emily Dutton Carstens
1957 – 2006

Where shall we see a better daughter or a kinder
sister or a truer friend?
Jane Austen, *Emma*

Acknowledgements

Thanks, as always, to my husband, Barry, who really didn't want to take ballroom dancing lessons, but did anyway. Honey, you're better than you think.

To Petre and Roxana Samoila, ballroom dance instructors and performers on the *Queen Mary 2*, who made it look easy. It isn't.

To Jennifer Gooding of the Annapolis Dance Academy in Arnold, MD, for an insider's view of a successful dance studio, and for putting up with my endless questions.

To Helen Arguello, dance show fan extraordinaire, who took the time to tell me about her favorites; and to Carol Chase, who faithfully taped British versions of the same, so I wouldn't miss a single step.

To my talented niece, Alisha Kay Robinson, who auditioned for *American Idol* and came oh-so-close, for a look behind the scenes.

To Captain George Clifford, CHC, USN Retired, and Rear Admiral Byron Holderby, CHC, USN Retired, for keeping me on the liturgically correct path, both military and otherwise.

To my sister-in-law, Camille Tracey, and my husband, Barry, who have attended more Catholic funeral services than anyone ever ought.

To my daughter, Laura Geyer, whose satirical wit and biblical knowledge gave me Jeremy Dunstan in all his evangelical glory.

To Denise Swanson, for the title.

And to Aaron Smith for the sandwiches.

If I got it wrong, it's my fault and not theirs.

To Phil and Susanne Watkins of 'Tradewinds' on idyllic Dickie's Cay, Abaco, Bahamas in a corner of whose bunkhouse nearly half of this book was written.

To my Annapolis writers' group – Janet Benrey, Trish Marshall, Mary Ellen Hughes, Ray Flynt, Sherriel Mattingly, Thomas Sprenkle, and Lyn Taylor – for tough love.

To my web diva and lunch buddy, Barbara Parker. Come see what Barbara can do at www.marciatalley.com.

To Alicia B. Sweeney, yoga instructor, dancer, choreographer, and actress, whose generous bid at a charity auction sponsored by the Friends of the Annapolis Symphony Orchestra bought her the right to play a role in this book.

To Elaine Viets, whose cat, Mysterie, will play the role of Bella de Baltimore in the movie version of *Dead Man Dancing*.

And to Kate Charles and Deborah Crombie, without whom . . .

One

She'd cropped her hair, colored it bronze, and gelled it into stylish spikes with freshly manicured fingers. Now she stood in my kitchen door, asking me what I thought.

'Who *are* you,' I said, 'and what have you done with my sister Ruth?'

Ruth grinned and executed a shaky pirouette on one toe of her platform wedges. I figured I was expected to comment on a new outfit, but it took me a few seconds to figure out what it might be. The jacket I recognized. Boiled wool. Red. Purchased at a fleece meet in central Pennsylvania, and old as the hills. She must have meant the jeans.

'Chico's?' I ventured, admiring the fit.

'Well, *yeah*,' she said, letting me know that I'd completely missed the point. 'What else, Hannah?'

'Cool belt?' I ventured, thinking that with that buckle and all the decorative studs, Ruth would cause a sensation at airport security when she and Hutch finally set off on their honeymoon.

'Size one point five,' she said, smoothing the dark denim along her hips with the palms of both hands. 'I used to wear a two.'

One point five. I loved Chico's sizing. In my post-chemo days, I wore a double zero. I remember rejoicing when I porked up to a healthier size one, but in this Super-Size-Me era, there weren't many people with whom I could share that joy.

'Congratulations, Ruth,' I said, meaning it. I reached out and patted her hair, which felt stiff as AstroTurf under my fingers. 'You look terrific. Hutch is never going to know what hit him.'

'He'll probably think aliens have landed and taken over

my body.' Ruth crossed to the refrigerator, opened the door and peered in. 'Got any iced tea?'

'What you see is what you get,' I told her. Paul and I had been surviving on Thanksgiving leftovers for a week. I hadn't been to the grocery store recently, so the pickings were mighty slim.

Ruth shuffled condiment bottles, restacked Tupperware, opened drawers and pawed around until she discovered a regular Coke my husband kept hidden from himself in the vegetable crisper. Before I could stop her, she'd popped the top. 'I'm down ten and a half pounds,' she announced, after taking a swig. 'And thank God. My wedding gown is gorgeous,' she said, 'but it's a one-off. Size eight. It. Is. Going. To. Fit,' she added, 'even if it's the last thing I do.'

'Plenty of time for that,' I commented. Hutch had proposed to my sister over a year ago, but the wedding date had only recently been set. 'If you keep losing weight at this rate, in thirteen months, the dress will be too big.'

Ruth pulled out a chair and sat down, stretched out her legs, and kicked off her shoes. 'I'm on the Eat Less Food Diet,' she laughed.

'Genius,' I said. 'You should write a book.'

'I'll call it Hippy Girl Slims Down, Spruces Up, Marries Attorney and Joins the Establishment.' She waved her can, as if writing the words in the air. 'Not necessarily in that order.' She suddenly looked lost. 'Too bad Mother never lived to see it.'

I teared up, too, and patted my sister's shoulder. 'She knows.'

'This wedding is going to be *perfect*, Hannah,' Ruth said, turning her face away from me and toward the window, struggling with tears of her own. 'Not like the first time.'

'That won't be difficult,' I commented. Ruth's wedding to Eric Gannon had been a bargain basement quickie, all bare feet and daisy chains somewhere in the mountains of New Hampshire, with only a justice of the peace and a herd of restive cows presiding. The marriage, too, had been a disaster until, weary of Eric's philandering, Ruth had kicked the bum out and set fire to his clothing in the driveway.

'I need your help with something,' Ruth, the reformed pyromaniac said after a moment.

'Oh, oh.' I felt a sense of foreboding. I folded my arms and leaned against the fridge. With Ruth, there was usually a catch.

She finished her Coke and tossed the empty can in the general direction of the sink where it tumbled into the dish drainer with a hollow *thunk-clink*. 'I've got the gown, of course, and the cake's laid on. Michaels is doing the flowers, and I'm working with The Main Ingredient on the catering.' Ruth took a deep breath. 'What would you say to a dance band?'

'A dance band? As in a real dance band, like Harry James or Glenn Miller?'

'Exactly.'

'Well,' I ventured. 'That implies actual dancing, doesn't it?'

'Uh huh.'

'Ruth, I haven't seen you dance since the Funky Chicken was all the rage.'

Ruth shrugged. 'True, but I've been practicing.'

I thought for a moment about the repercussions of actual dancing at her wedding. My husband, Paul, was a mathematical genius, but when it came to dancing, the poor boy had been out getting his diaper changed when the rhythm fairy passed by his cradle. I wasn't much better. We had a DVD somewhere – 'Brush Up Your Ballroom' – that we'd watched a couple of times before Paul's sister, Connie, married Dennis, but aside from the simple one-two-three, one-two-three of the waltz, not much of it had stuck.

'I've been watching videos,' Ruth added, 'but galumphing around the house crashing into the furniture just isn't going to cut it.'

While channel surfing, I'd caught occasional episodes of *So You Think You Can Dance, Shall We Dance?* and a couple of other dance contest shows myself – what Paul likes to call Unreality TV – but I'd rarely been inspired to rise from my comfortable chair and take a spin around my living-room carpet.

'Hutch was big into ballroom at Ithaca College,' Ruth said, 'and I think it would mean a lot to him.' She crossed her arms on the table and leaned toward me. 'I thought maybe you could recommend somebody.'

'There's the Naval Academy Band,' I said after giving it a moment's thought. 'Some of its members moonlight with combos on weekends, but other than that, I don't know any bands, Ruth.'

Ruth shook her smartly coifed head and grinned. 'A dance instructor, silly. I've already signed up the band.'

'You are scaring me, sister.'

'I'm serious, Hannah. Didn't you work with someone last year on Dance for the Cure?'

'Right,' I said, remembering. 'Kay Giannotti of J & K Studios was one of our sponsors.' The fund-raiser at Loews Hotel on West Street had been a huge success, but I'd sulked on the sidelines, a proper little wallflower. Paul had declined to go, citing finals that needed grading, assuaging his guilt by forking out a healthy check for the cure instead.

'Chloe takes lessons at J & K, too,' I added. 'I've picked her up a couple of times. The studio's off Chinquapin Round Road.'

While I bragged about my granddaughter's last dance recital, Ruth padded barefoot to the bookshelf and hauled down the Yellow Pages. She plopped the book on the table and thumbed through the pages until she got to Dance Instruction.

Yipes! The girl was serious.

Ruth snapped her fingers in my direction. 'Paper and pen?'

I yanked open the junk drawer and found a pencil stub and an old carry-out menu, then watched as she wrote down the address and phone number on a blank space above 'All You Can Eat Special - $9.99'. She handed the pencil back. 'I'll check to see what classes they offer.'

'I'm holding my breath.'

'Be serious, Hannah! Wouldn't it be great to see *everyone* waltzing around the . . .' She closed the book with a thump. 'Shit. The dance floor at the George Calvert will never handle everyone. We'll have to check out Loews. I'll lose my deposit, of course, but . . .'

She turned to me and grinned, confident that I'd be agreeable. 'You and Paul will take lessons, too, won't you?'

I thought about the grand ballroom at the Loews Hotel,

particularly the spacious atrium just off the lobby. I remembered it as it had looked for Dance for the Cure – glamorous ball gowns, sophisticated tuxedos, elegant couples tracing graceful circles around the dance floor. I imagined myself in flowing yellow chiffon, trailing feathers like Big Bird, my hair a-glitter with sequins, swirling around in Paul's arms, light as air, characters straight out of *Die Fledermaus*.

A girl can dream.

'I'll put it to Prince Charming,' I said, 'but I'm not making any promises.'

'It's easy, Hannah. Lay down the law: no dancing, no sex.'

'*Har de har har*. I better get myself to the grocery store then, and fix him something mouth-watering for dinner.'

Ruth hugged me, hard. 'He will be putty in your hands.'

'I'm not so sure about that.'

'Bull. Your meat loaf is ambrosia. Nectar of the gods.'

'Right,' I said as I returned the phone book to its proper shelf. 'Dab a little gravy behind my ears, and I'm irresistible.'

Maybe my plan would have worked better if I'd dabbed a little Chanel No.5 behind my ears rather than Eau de Boeuf.

'You're kidding me, right?' Paul mumbled around his toothbrush and a foaming mouthful of Crest as we prepared for bed that evening.

I was perched on the lid of the toilet, my knees pulled all the way up under my nightgown, watching him brush.

'You know I have two left feet,' he said after he'd rinsed and spat.

'I know that, but maybe if we took *lessons* . . .' I jabbed a finger into my husband's lean-mean stomach, emphasizing each word.

Paul laughed out loud, then grabbed my hand and pulled me off the chenille-covered seat toward him.

Standing on tiptoes, I gazed up into his face, admiring the laughter lines that creased his lightly stubbled cheeks. 'Aren't mathematicians supposed to be musical?'

'There's a high correlation between math and music, true, but there are exceptions to every rule. And sad to say, I am one.' He kissed the top of my head.

'Come on, Paul. It's only one night a week. Surely you can manage that.'

He held me at arm's length and squinted at me suspiciously. 'Which night?'

'I don't know yet,' I said, hedging my bets. 'Ruth and I are going to check out the studio tomorrow.'

'Can't we just rent a video?'

I glanced at my husband. Sneaky Paul, looking for a loophole.

'Where's the fun in that?' I explained about the orchestra, and about Ruth's plan to make hers the Annapolis wedding of the year, if not the decade, with society page coverage in the *Baltimore Sun* and *Washington Post,* even if she had to pay for it. 'Suppose I get Connie and Dennis to take lessons, too?'

Paul grunted.

'We can make it a family affair,' I added, hopefully.

'Dennis?' Paul snorted. 'Surely cops are far too busy putting away criminals to take time out for dance lessons.'

I saw my opening, and played my ace. 'If Dennis agrees, will you agree, too?'

Paul turned me around and nudged me gently in the direction of the bedroom.

'Well?' I shot a hopeful glance over my shoulder.

'I'm thinking, I'm thinking.'

In the semi-darkness of our bedroom, I slithered under the covers. 'You know what Ruth suggested, darling?'

Paul slipped between the sheets and stretched out his arm to turn off the bedside lamp. 'What?'

'No sex 'til you dance,' I said as I pulled the duvet under my chin.

'Always helpful, your sister.'

A few minutes later, Paul's kiss told me all I needed to know.

I nibbled on his ear. 'I'll take that as a yes, then, Professor Ives.'

Two

R uth burst into my kitchen the following morning, armed with a list of dance studios, if you call three a list, and printouts with information about each. She spread them out on the table in front of her.

'I thought we'd decided on J & K Studios,' I complained, setting a mug of steaming black coffee on the table beside her. 'Yesterday afternoon. Remember?' The studio had been so supportive of Dance for the Cure that I wanted to steer a little business their way.

Ruth picked up her mug and sipped carefully. 'Well, yes, but when I got home, I thought I'd better do a bit of research. Just to make sure.'

'Make sure of what?' I asked, feeling a bit miffed that my advice about J & K Studios was being ignored.

'To make sure that Hutch won't be disappointed,' she said. 'He competed in college, so I figure he's going to be a little bit picky about instructors.'

'A *serious* competitor?'

'Won all kinds of trophies.' Ruth beamed at me over the rim of her mug. 'His mother keeps calling from Nebraska to ask if he wants them.' She laughed. 'She's turning his bedroom into an office.'

'What's her hurry? Hutch hasn't lived at home for – what? – fifteen years.'

'She's threatening to give them all to Goodwill. Anyway . . .' She hurried on before I could wedge a word in. 'When I got home, I sat down and Googled all the Annapolis area dance studios. This one in Glen Burnie, for example.' She read off an address that I knew must be located in one of the clusters of car dealerships and strip malls that lined Route

2 the entire twenty-some blighted miles from Annapolis to the Baltimore beltway.

'They've got several wedding packages,' Ruth continued. 'Everything from reasonably-priced group lessons down to a one-lesson crash course for eighty-five dollars.' She looked up at me over the frames of her reading glasses. 'Even if it were worth the drive, I don't think the crash course will do.'

'And this gal –' Ruth tapped the second name on her list – 'she teaches out of her home in Annapolis, but I checked on her website, no Latin.'

'*Amo, amas, amat.*'

'Not *that* kind of Latin!' I could see Ruth wasn't in the mood for jokes.

'Well, if I can't paso doble, forget it.'

Ruth's eyes narrowed. 'Do you know more about dancing than you're letting on, Hannah Ives?'

'Just what I see on *Dancing with the Stars*,' I insisted. 'Jonathan Whatshisname dragging Marie Osmond around the dance floor by her hair.' I tried to imagine Paul in skintight pants, high heels tapping like a Flamenco dancer, his fingers entwined in the roots of my short, coffee-colored curls. I had to giggle.

'Paso doble is supposed to represent bullfighting,' Ruth explained. 'La Passe, Banderillas, Coup de Pique and all that.' She waved a hand. 'If it weren't for Hutch, I wouldn't know the cha-cha from a rumba.'

'What *is* the difference between a cha-cha and a rumba?' I asked.

Ruth ignored me. 'Hutch comes home, grabs a cold one, and watches all those dance shows, yelling beery criticism from the sofa, especially at the judges. Hutch hates the judges.' Ruth pantomimed a dramatic hair flip, batted her eyelashes furiously and gushed, 'You two are, like, just so awesome!'

'Hutch is a lawyer. He's supposed to hate judges,' I teased. When Ruth stopped laughing, I asked, 'Why don't you get Hutch to give you lessons?'

'He's offered, but I said, no. I can't take the chance that

it would wreck our relationship the same way it wrecked the relationship I had with Rusty when I took him up on his offer to teach me how to drive.'

Remembering that notorious high school incident, it was my turn to laugh. 'Well, if you hadn't gotten a whopping ticket for driving Rusty's car without a license . . .'

'We were on back roads. Who knew there'd be a road-block?'

'Or even a learner's permit,' I added.

'I was only fourteen.'

'Not to mention driving over that patrolman's foot.'

Ruth leaned back in her chair, a grin splitting her face. 'Now *that* was worth every penny!'

Ruth, the radical, then as now. Back then, our dad, a navy commander, had been stationed at the Pentagon, a fact we tried to keep secret from our friends. We were living in a rented farmhouse in rural Virginia, on the outskirts of a tiny town where every infraction, no matter how minor, was eventually published in the police blotter of the local paper. Rusty, two years ahead of Ruth and flush with cash from his after-school job at Denny's, had gallantly paid Ruth's fine, but his ardor cooled after several months of missing Thursday afternoon band practice to drive Ruth home, where she hoped to retrieve the *Woodbridge Gazette* before Mom got to it. Eventually Ruth succeeded in snatching the incriminating issue off the stoop and burning it, but she hadn't counted on the twenty-seven neighbors who telephoned Mom to clue her in. Small towns. Ya gotta love 'em.

Annapolis was like that, in some ways. Population 36,000, and the capital of Maryland, but everyone seemed to know everyone else. That's how I knew Kay Giannotti, the 'K' of J & K Studios. Even before the Dance for the Cure I kept running into Kay – Annapolis Symphony concerts, Newcomers Club, Graul's Market, the downtown post office. She didn't actually teach Chloe – one of her associates handled the under twelves – but I'd passed Kay in the studio parking lot from time to time, a friendly nod-and-wave sort of thing.

'You were right, Hannah,' Ruth said, as if eavesdropping

on my brain. 'J & K seems to have the best deal. Group lessons from seven to eight p.m. on Mondays, with an hour of free practice following.' She looked up from her notes. 'The "K" I can figure out, but what's the "J" stand for?'

'Kay's husband, Jay.'

'You're making that up.'

'No, his name is really Jay. Jay Giannotti.'

'Too cute.' She lay down her pen, picked up her mug, and began to concentrate on her coffee. 'What's Jay like?'

'I've never met the guy. If he's anything like Kay, which is to say late forties, slender, well-coifed and well-dressed, they'll make a striking couple on the dance floor. They're some sort of champions.'

Ruth zoned out for a moment, staring into the depths of her cup. 'Hutch is a really, really good dancer,' she said at last. 'But, he gave it all up when he went to law school.'

'Do you think he misses dancing, Ruth?'

My sister shrugged. 'I don't know. He doesn't talk about it much. It's all divorce, child custody, prenups, trusts and estates . . .' She rested her elbows on the table and her chin in her hands, and regarded me seriously. 'I just want to make him proud.'

'I'm sure you will, Ruth.' I gestured with my empty mug. 'More coffee?' Ruth shook her head, so I collected our empty mugs and set them in the sink.

'Paul and I might be an embarrassment, though,' I said, rinsing a mug clean under the tap. 'When we take to the dance floor, you and Hutch might want to chassé in the opposite direction. Pretend you don't know us.'

'I'm just happy you're willing to give it a shot. Paul loves you, Hannah. He won't let you down.'

'It's not me I'm worried about.' Dish towel in hand, I turned to face her. 'It's *you* I don't want to disappoint.'

'It's just Mondays for six weeks. Can't Paul manage that?' Ruth gathered the papers, folded them in half and tucked them into the pocket of her sweater.

'If he doesn't have to trim his nose hair or neuter the house plants.'

Ruth's eyes narrowed dangerously, so I raised both hands, palms out. 'Joke!'

'Seriously,' she said. 'I've already checked with Connie. She thinks she and Dennis can actually make it. Barring a jail break or hostage situation, of course.' She chewed for a moment on her bottom lip, thinking. 'We need at least three couples to get the reduced rate.'

'If Dennis bags it, I could always dance with Connie, I suppose.'

Ruth's eyes widened, as if I had suggested something radical, like showing up for her wedding wearing flip-flops, a tube top and a pair of cut-offs. 'Gosh, no. You don't want to do that. You need to practice the ladies' part while Paul learns the gentlemen's part. It makes a huge difference.'

'And the gentleman leads, I assume.'

'Always.'

Paul taking the lead. For income tax returns, car repairs and yard work, Paul at the helm was definitely A Good Thing. But ballroom dancing? Jeesh. I was in trouble.

Three

Even a freak mid-November snowstorm couldn't keep us away from the family dinner we'd planned before turning ourselves over to the trained professionals at J & K Studios.

As surprised as I was by the unexpected turn in the weather, I was completely unprepared for who was presiding at the table when Paul and I walked into China Garden, one of those all-you-can-eat oriental buffets, a few minutes after five thirty that evening.

My father.

Paul crossed from the doorway to the table in four long strides, clapped his father-in-law on the back while simultaneously pumping his hand. 'George! What brings you here all the way from the Eastern Shore?'

'Connie and Dennis are snowed in, so Ruth put the strong arm on me. Some nonsense about a quota.' My father turned to smile at the woman seated on his right. 'I actually drove over Saturday morning. Neelie and I had an *ass-ig-na-tion*.' He drew the word out into four long syllables, and wiggled both eyebrows, a sure sign that he was up to some sort of mischief.

'George! Do grow up!' Neelie tugged affectionately on Daddy's ear lobe. 'What your father is trying to say is that I invited him to spend the weekend. He's been helping me put up storage shelves in the basement.'

Neelie was Cornelia Gibbs, my widowed father's steady girlfriend both before and after his recent post-retirement assignment to a hush-hush project with a government contractor in Saudi Arabia. Daddy had leased a one-bedroom house in Snow Hill on Maryland's Eastern Shore to be close to his work at the satellite tracking station, but sometimes came back to our family home in the Providence community near the Naval Station in Annapolis. He'd rented the house out for a while, fully-furnished, but the last tenant had been transferred to San Diego and the next family wouldn't move in until June, so except for my father's pop-in-to-check-up-on-it visits, the place was now vacant.

I'd never seen Neelie dance, but she was a slim, energetic senior citizen, and my equally slim septuagenarian father had always been light on his toes. He and my mother had cut quite a rug in the early years of their marriage. It had been five years since Mom's death. Neelie was a tonic; it was good to see Dad having fun again.

'Well, here we are!' My father raised a glass of iced water and beamed like an Old Testament patriarch as Paul, Ruth and I joined him and Neelie around the table. 'A toast to the Amazing Dancing Alexanders.'

Paul helped me off with my coat, and we settled down to thaw our hands around cups of piping-hot green tea. 'Sounds like a circus act, George,' Paul remarked.

'You'll have to think of another name, Daddy,' I said, cautiously sipping, 'since you're the only official Alexander in the bunch.'

Ruth Alexander as-was Gannon soon-to-be Hutchinson, selected a crispy wonton from a bowl in the center of the table and dredged it through a sweet, orange sauce. 'It's going to be fun,' she said, gesturing with the wonton, deliciously but dangerously dripping. 'I'm just sorry Connie and Dennis got snowed in.'

The Rutherfords lived on the Ives family farm near Pearson's Corner, well south of Annapolis. It sometimes took days for the snowplow to reach them, so during inclement weather volunteers in four-wheel-drive vehicles would pick Dennis up and drive him to police headquarters. Poor Connie, though, was often stuck. 'Connie promised they'd come next week,' I said. 'Not to worry. We've got our quorum.'

'Quorum?' Neelie looked puzzled.

'The studio has a three couple minimum,' Ruth explained.

Neelie's brow crinkled, taking in the sixth chair at our table. Still empty.

'Hutch is on his way,' Ruth hastened to add. 'He called me on my cell a few minutes ago. He was just leaving his office.'

We had completed our first circuit of the enormous buffet table when Hutch arrived, whacking his cap against his leg to dislodge the fat, wet snowflakes that were clinging to it. He bent to kiss Ruth's cheek. 'Sorry I'm late, sweetheart.'

Ruth smiled up at her fiancé and used the tips of her fingers to flick water droplets out of the fringe of pale hair that flopped over his forehead. 'You smell like wet dog.'

'You want I should smell like damp polyester?' he teased, glancing around the restaurant, looking for a place to hang his overcoat – one hundred percent cashmere, unless I missed my guess.

A waiter materialized out of nowhere, relieving Hutch of his coat. 'At least I don't smell like an ashtray anymore,' Hutch quipped as he made a beeline for the buffet table.

Ruth beamed with pride. 'And he's off the patches now, too.'

After a minute or two, Hutch rejoined us. He'd heaped his plate high with spicy chicken wings and egg fu yung, then – inexplicably – smothered it all with an indifferent brown gravy that was already congealing on the rim of his plate. Chef Martin Yan would have had a coronary just looking at it. Come to think of it, anybody would.

Hutch tucked into his grub like a starving man, while I used a spoon to scoop up the dregs of my hot and sour soup, in a very ladylike way, then returned to the buffet to help myself to some Singapore rice noodles, loaded with curried vegetables and plump shrimp, and a couple of dumplings.

When I returned to the table, Hutch was saying, '. . . why I was late. It's someone you know, Hannah.'

'Oh? Who?'

'I met with her today, and she asked me to say "hi".' Hutch transferred his chopsticks to his left hand, reached into the breast pocket of his blazer, and pulled out a hot-pink

Post-it note. It made its way around the table, hand to hand. 'Eva Haberman?' Daddy squinted at the Post-it as he was handing it over to me. 'Isn't she, I mean, wasn't she, your priest, the one whose husband . . .?'

His voice trailed off. Daddy had been in Saudi Arabia when his great-grandson Timmy was kidnapped, so he'd missed the whole ugly business with Roger Haberman, even though it was splashed across every television screen and made the front page of every newspaper in the greater Baltimore/Washington area. Then Timmy'd been found, and Roger'd drowned – hard to call it a happy ending, but it did wrap things up.

While I was still trying to make sense of the news that the Reverend Eva Haberman was in communication with Hutch, of all people, Ruth said, 'But I thought Eva was in Idaho?'

Still staring at the note, I nodded. 'After all the hoo-hah over Roger, she retreated to a family cabin in the Sawtooth Range. I had an email from her just last week,' I added, really puzzled now. 'You *met* with her?'

His mouth full, Hutch grunted.

'She didn't say a word to me about returning to Annapolis.'

Hutch swallowed a bite of egg roll. 'Well, she's back now, at least temporarily, and staying with the assistant pastor at St Anne's. She wants you to call.'

I nodded, still feeling a bit stunned. 'Will do. Did she say . . .?'

Hutch waved his egg roll. 'Lawyer–client privilege, Hannah, yada yada yada.'

Paul leaned in my direction, his breath warm against my ear. 'The plot, as they say, thickens.'

Resisting the urge to power up my cell phone and call Eva right away, I tucked the Post-it into my purse. 'Very curious,' I muttered, as I picked up my chopsticks and attacked a dumpling, spearing it neatly on the first try. 'Very curious, indeed.'

Across the table, Hutch shrugged unhelpfully.

I shook my chopsticks at him. 'No fortune cookie for you, Mr Hutchinson.'

'I'm sure Eva will share her concerns with you, Hannah. It's just not my place to do so.'

'I know.' I smiled back. 'It's just that I'm dying of curiosity!'

'And I'm dying of hunger,' Neelie interjected. She picked up her empty dinner plate in both hands, and held it out to my father. 'Will you fetch me some more of those spicy green beans, George? And steamed rice.' She smiled, revealing a row of even white teeth. 'Please?'

What's the matter with you, Neelie, I thought. Legs broken?

Even though Dad still had mounds of fried rice and sweet and sour pork on his own plate, he got up from his chair, relieved Neelie of her plate and said gallantly, 'My pleasure, Cornelia.'

When he was out of earshot, Neelie touched my arm, her face serious, and I realized why she wanted to send Daddy away from the table. 'I don't want to worry you, dear, but your father is having terrible trouble with his eyes. He's seeing a specialist up at Wilmer next Monday.'

I stared slack-jawed at Neelie, thinking *damn*. I'd arisen that morning in a cheerful mood, fed my husband hot oatmeal with butter and maple syrup for breakfast, sent him off to work with a kiss, and was looking forward, really looking forward to dance lessons – and so, Paul claimed, was he. And now, well, the older I got, the less I liked surprises. First, my old friend Eva mysteriously returns to town, and now my dad was going blind. What next?

'Trouble?' I asked. 'What do you mean "trouble"?'

'His vision is blurred, reading is an effort, and he's having difficulty driving, particularly at night. We're hoping it's just cataracts.'

'Just cataracts? *Just*?'

'Oh, for heaven's sake, Hannah, ' Ruth chimed in. 'Chill. Cataract surgery is no big deal these days. Besides, Wilmer Eye Institute is the best'

'Why didn't Daddy share this with *us*?' I asked.

'He doesn't want to worry you.'

'What are families for, if it's not to worry about one another?'

'He said he was going to tell you girls all about it, but he wanted to wait until after the appointment, when he knew more about the situation.'

'So why are you telling us now?'

'I thought . . . well, I'm not as young as I used to be, girls. So if your father needs someone to drive him to his appointment . . .' Neelie put a finger to her lips. Daddy was making his way back to the table with Neelie's green beans.

I was thinking that Daddy didn't have a bit of difficulty reading Eva's Post-it note over my shoulder when the waiter returned with a fresh pot of tea. I decided to pour another cup and concentrate on clearing up the last strands of noodles from my plate.

Ten minutes later, the waiter was back with the check on a black plastic tray covered with fortune cookies. Neelie slipped the bill out from under the pile of cookies and handed it to Dad, then took charge of the tray. 'Fortune cookies, anyone?'

I love fortune cookies, especially with Chinese tea, so I grabbed first. I tore off the cellophane wrapping and, as was our family custom, prepared to read it aloud, when Ruth beat me to the punch. 'Listen to this: "A closed mouth gathers no feet".'

Paul snorted. 'Closed mouth? You, Ruth? That'll be the day.'

'Speak for yourself, Professor,' Ruth said. 'So, what does yours say?'

'Let's see here.' Paul tore open the packet with his teeth, and read, '"A member of your family will soon do something that will make you proud".' He considered each of us seated around the table in turn, grinning. 'OK, which one of you is going to make me proud. Ruth? Surely this must refer to your dancing.'

Ruth blushed. 'Aren't you forgetting something?'

It was also a family custom, appropriated from our daughter Emily, who picked it up from her classmates at Bryn Mawr College, to add the phrase 'in between the sheets' to the end of any cookie fortune.

Paul smacked his forehead with the flat of his hand. 'Duh.'

Hutch had been part of the family long enough to be

familiar with the game. He reached across the table for the fortune. 'Hey, Paul, can I see that?'

Paul surrendered the slip of paper to Hutch who made an elaborate show of putting on his glasses, clearing his throat, and reading, '"A member of your family will soon do something that will make you proud – in between the sheets."' He laughed out loud, gave Ruth an affectionate peck on the cheek. 'Now *that's* more like it.'

Neelie opened her fortune, then dissolved into giggles. 'Mine says, "Flattery will go far tonight – in between the sheets".'

Daddy slipped an arm around Neelie's shoulders, and gave her a hug, an intimate gesture, which made me wonder just how 'platonic' their relationship was. Daddy's fortune, when he held it up close to read it next, did nothing to dissuade me of the notion that when he got Neelie home, he was going to jump her bones: '"A thrilling time is in your immediate future – in between the sheets",' he read.

At least Neelie had the manners to blush attractively as she said, 'Your turn, Hutch.'

Hutch read: '"He who laughs at himself never runs out of things to laugh at . . ."' He paused, then balled up his fortune and tossed it into his empty tea cup.

'. . . in between the sheets?' Ruth added.

'I hope that's not a commentary on my, um, equipment.' Hutch raised an eyebrow.

Ruth punched him in the arm. 'As if!' Then she turned to me. 'Well?'

I'd been holding the slip of paper between my thumb and index finger thinking about its significance, hoping it wasn't an omen. '"If you want the rainbow, you must put up with the rain – in between the sheets",' I read.

Everyone laughed.

As fortunes go, though, mine turned out to be depressingly accurate, if you discounted the part about the sheets.

Four

To the casual observer, waiting for his car to be finished at JiffyLube across West Street, our mass exodus from China Garden must have resembled a bomb scare. The six of us, irresponsibly responsible (ecologically speaking) for four automobiles, pulled out of the restaurant parking lot almost simultaneously; Ruth's aged green Taurus in the lead, and Hutch's burgundy BMW just behind. The cortège turned right on to West Street, and right again at the traffic light at the intersection of West Street and Chinquapin Round Road, the busy corner where a condominium complex called 1901 West had replaced the venerable Johnson Lumber yard which had served Annapolis's home construction needs for more than seventy-five years. The developers had reserved space on the ground floor of the high-rise for retail shops, but with the exception of a lone, optimistic Starbucks, no retailers had stepped up to the plate, and the storefronts had remained vacant for more than a year.

A few blocks later, Paul pulled into one of two dozen marked parking spaces reserved for clients of J & K, where we sat, idling, listening to the end of *Marketplace* on WNPR, and waiting for Daddy and Cornelia to catch up with us. The J & K parking lot was on George Avenue, directly across from The Rapture Church. Down the street and to the left was the Harley-Davidson dealership. We'd just driven past Mr Garbage, Global Van Lines and The Air Works, light industrial businesses that were typical of this part of town.

'Air Works?' Paul asked, switching off the ignition as *Marketplace* came to an end.

I shrugged. 'I wouldn't like to speculate.'

The J & K building itself, flat-roofed and constructed of cinder blocks painted a creamy yellow, was as far removed from the modern brick, glass and steel facades of the towering condos two blocks away as a building could possibly be. In a former life, it had probably been a dark and dreary warehouse, but in converting it to a dance studio, the contractors had opened the building up to the light by replacing the cinder blocks along one wall with a row of picture windows. Through the windows, illuminated by bright overhead track lighting, I could see polished wooden floors. Mirrors covered the opposite wall, reflecting our cloaked, gloved and hooded images as we peered in.

Paul turned toward the entrance, but I tugged on his sleeve. 'Look, Paul.'

Inside the studio, two couples were circling the ballroom, dancing to music we couldn't hear. From the hopping, bobbing and quick little running steps they were doing, I guessed it must be the quickstep. One tall, impossibly slim couple was dressed almost identically in black stretch pants and white, sleeveless, high-necked tank tops. The second male dancer wore a green polo shirt with white and yellow horizontal stripes, tucked into a pair of slim black jeans. Only someone as trim as he could have gotten away with horizontal stripes, I thought. His partner was a woman I guessed to be in her early thirties looking incredibly sexy in a red leotard. A comb headband held her chestnut hair away from her forehead, and her shoulder-length curls bounced like springs as her partner led her in a series of slow-quick-quick-slow-slow steps across the dance floor. Then, after an appraising glance at the other couple, they switched seamlessly to a quick-and-quick-and-quick-quick-slow pattern that was so rapid and intricate, I marveled that their legs didn't get impossibly tangled, causing them to trip and fall down in a heap.

I squeezed Paul's arm. 'I want to learn that. Doesn't it look like fun?'

'Looks suspiciously aerobic to me,' Paul complained cheerfully.

'Aerobic, yes, but without the boring bits.'

'Wouldn't it be easier to run a couple of 800-meter dashes?'

I was about to clobber him with my handbag, when Ruth and Hutch arrived and joined us at the window.

'I can't believe how much this area has changed, Hannah. Guess I've been spending too much time in my shop.' Ruth pointed to the Rapture Church across the street. 'The last time I went into that building, I was wearing red and white shoes a half size too big, and I bowled a 120.'

With chain-store encroachment, rising rents, and the recession (whatever the economist Alan Greenspan might have had to say to the contrary), Ruth had been through a couple of tough years with Mother Earth, the New Age shop she owned on Main Street in downtown Annapolis. But with a renewed emphasis on stocking natural, eco-friendly products, she was turning a tidy profit these days, enough to hire a full-time assistant so she didn't have to shanghai relatives like me to store-sit on a regular basis.

I did my part, though. My elderly LeBaron boasted one of her 'Compost Happens' bumper stickers, and my kitchen shelves were stocked with spice jars made out of re-blown beer bottles, and bags of fair trade coffee and tea. I'd bought a hemp notebook, and a picture frame made of recycled newspapers from her shop, but I drew the line at alternative menstrual products like washable GladRags (Glad? Get real.)

As the four of us rounded the corner of the building, Daddy was waiting for us, holding open one of the glass double doors. Neelie waited inside, and we tumbled in after her, appreciating the welcoming blast of warm air. We huddled to the right of the doors waiting politely for the dancers to finish, enjoying both the warmth of the ballroom, and the impromptu exhibition. Now we were inside, I could hear the music: Cole Porter's 'It's Delovely'.

Unaccountably, my heart did a flip-flop. I grabbed Paul's hand and squeezed. 'Thanks for coming.'

Paul turned his head and grinned down at me. 'I hope neither of us will regret it, sweetie.'

The music ended and one couple made a swooping spin while the other did a death drop finish. I realized that we had been watching a private coaching session between a pair of instructors – red leotard and green shirt – and a couple of advanced pupils – the black and white twins. After giving her pupils a brief critique, the woman in red dismissed her partner and came over to us, breathless. 'You must be Ruth,' she said to me, extending her hand. 'Jay told me your group was coming. I'm Alicia Sweeney.' She nodded toward the guy in the striped shirt. 'Chance Baldwin and I will be your instructors tonight.'

I squeezed her hand. 'Hi, Alicia. I'm Hannah Ives. That spiky-haired individual over there is the bride, my sister, Ruth.'

Alicia giggled charmingly, then beamed her 1000-watt smile on Ruth. 'So you're the bride?'

Ruth's cheeks, already red from the cold, got redder. 'And this is my fiancé, Hutch,' the blushing bride said.

After introductions all round, Alicia pointed out the closet, and the dressing rooms. 'One for the boys and one for the girls. Bathrooms are in there, too.'

Alicia waited until we'd hung up our coats, then clapped her hands to get our attention. Chance had relocated to an alcove containing what appeared to be a state-of-the-art console, where he was fiddling with dials and punching buttons. Black, industrial-size EV speakers were supported on tripods on either side of the alcove.

Alicia herded us into two lines, facing one another, boys on one side and girls on the other, just like sixth grade. 'First,' she said, draping her right arm over Ruth's shoulders, 'we're going to learn the waltz. Picture yourself, Ruth, your wedding gown frothing around you, dancing in the arms of your prince.' With her left arm, she made a sweeping motion, indicating Hutch. 'Waltzing, waltzing, one-two-three, one-two-three, just like Cinderella at the ball.' She went on in relentless fairy tale mode for a minute more while across the room, Paul tried to act cute by pantomiming dabbing at his eyes with a tissue and mouthing, 'I think I'm going to cry.'

I gave him the evil eye.

Somewhere in the middle of an anecdote about Sleeping Beauty, just as *I* was about to cry, Alicia finally wound down. 'Chance. Over to you.'

'First, the man's part,' said Chance, smoothly taking over from Alicia. 'Gentlemen. Watch me.'

He raised both arms, as if holding an invisible woman. 'Think of the waltz as drawing a box on the floor. We start with our feet together, like this. Then – watch me now – left foot forward, right foot to the side, left foot closes to the right foot, right foot back, left foot side, right foot closes to the left foot. *One*-two-three, *one*-two-three, *one*-two-three, *one*-two-three. Now, you try.'

I watched with some pride as Daddy and Paul executed the steps flawlessly. Hutch, bless his heart, performed the maneuver right along with them, as if he hadn't been doing box steps all his life.

Alicia coached us ladies through our steps, which were mirror images of the guys' – right-left-right, left-right-left – until we got it perfectly, too.

'The waltz,' Alicia said, planting herself midway between our ragged boy-meets-girl lines, 'was first introduced in the early 1800s, but denounced by the church for its immorality. It was the first time polite society had seen a man holding a woman so close to his body, and in public, too! But that, of course, was what made the dance so appealing, and why the waltz is here to stay.'

'For the waltz, and for most ballroom,' she continued, 'we use the basic, closed position.' Alicia clapped her hands again. 'OK, find your partner.'

I waltzed across the room to Paul, muttering, 'One-two-three, one-two-three,' as I went. Paul gathered me into his arms, his left hand in my right, my hand and forearm resting lightly on his upper arm, and we waited for our position to be inspected and approved.

Alicia made some minor adjustments to Daddy and Neelie's posture, then turned her attention to us, moving Paul's hand from the small of my back up to my shoulder blade. 'Slightly cup your hand, Paul, don't spread your fingers out.'

Meanwhile, Chance had retreated to the control panel where he appeared to be waiting for a signal from Alicia.

'Ready?' asked Alicia. 'Go.'

Almost immediately, the music began, an electronic version of 'You Light Up My Life'. Paul waited, nodding his head in time to the music, whispering, 'One-two-three, one-two-three,' until the vocalist began crooning, '*So many nights . . .*' before we stepped out. We made it all the way down the length of the ballroom before Paul stomped hard on my toe – 'Shit!' – and I lost my concentration.

'Gosh, sorry, Hannah.'

'No problem.'

His breath was warm on my neck. 'One-two-three, left-right-left.' Paul tapped a foot for two bars, getting his bearings before setting off again, this time narrowly missing a collision with Hutch and Ruth who were quite literally floating counter-clockwise around the dance floor, eyes locked, seemingly oblivious to anyone but themselves.

As I said, I'd watched dance shows on TV, and except for the sexy, steamy numbers like the cha-cha and the paso doble, I thought it must be against the rules for couples to look at one another. In my experience, the guy'd be staring deadpan left, and the girl would be gazing at some fixed spot over his right shoulder with a crimson-lipped, full-toothed perma-grin on her face. But there was something so up close and personal going on between Hutch and Ruth on the dance floor just then, that Paul and I stopped dancing and stood transfixed.

'Jeesh,' Paul whispered in my ear, 'get a hotel room.'

I jabbed him in the ribs with my elbow.

By then, even the instructors had stopped what they were doing to watch my sister and her fiancé.

'I thought you told me Ruth hadn't danced in years,' Paul muttered under his breath.

'She hasn't,' I said, but couldn't believe it either.

While we watched, Hutch eased Ruth into an effortless six-count underarm turn.

And the music ended.

Everyone breathed a collective, 'Ahhhh.'

For a moment, nobody spoke. Then we burst into applause. Still holding Ruth's hand, Hutch made the tiniest of bows.

'Now, don't tell *me* they're beginners,' a voice behind me grumbled.

It belonged to the guy half of the black and white-clad, quick-stepping couple.

'Well, he isn't, but my sister is,' I told him. 'Or at least she's supposed to be.'

I glared in Ruth's direction. Clearly, she had been practicing, and I wanted to know what all that bullshit in my kitchen that morning had been about.

'Tom Wilson,' the guy said, extending his hand. 'This is my partner, Laurie Wainwright.'

'Nice to meet you, Tom. Laurie. You were fabulous out there, by the way.'

'Thanks,' said Laurie, adjusting the bright red scarf she wore around her neck. Her voice was low and throaty, sexy, like Lauren Bacall. Or me with a chest cold. 'We're practicing for the Sweetheart Ball International Championships in DC in mid-February. We're dancing intermediate.'

'That's gold,' Tom explained.

'Gold?'

'The competitions have several levels,' he said.

Laurie said, 'With a partner like that, your sister could go straight from Newcomer to Bronze, don't you agree, Tom?'

'God, yes. He's amazing.'

Alicia and Chance were trying to gather their far-flung sheep back into the fold for what I imagined would be another go at the waltz, when a door at the back of the room flew open, and a woman dressed in a pink tracksuit breezed out – Kay Giannotti.

I caught her eye.

She waved.

I waved.

Kay was carrying her coat, making a beeline for the door, when she stopped so suddenly that her pink-trimmed Nikes squeaked on the hardwood floor, almost as if she'd been shot.

But it wasn't a bullet that had brought the woman up short, it was Hutch. 'Hutch? I swear to God, it's Hutch Hutchinson.'

Hutch dropped Ruth's hand as if it had suddenly grown hot. He squinted at the woman bearing down on him like a diminutive, but determined tank. 'Kathleen? Kathleen O'Reilly?

Ruth moved aside as Kay pounced on Hutch, enveloping him in a hug. 'My god, it's good to see you!' Kay purred. 'What brings you here, to my studio of all places?'

'*Your* studio?' Hutch shook his head, and then the penny dropped. 'Kay? The "K" stands for Kathleen?'

Kay tucked a wayward strand of long blonde hair behind her ear. 'When Jay and I hooked up, it seemed like a good idea. Jay. Kay. The Kay kind of stuck, but my credit cards still say Kathleen.'

'How many years has it been? Twenty? Twenty-five?'

'Who the hell's counting?' Kay waved a manicured hand, setting enough silver bracelets jangling to make up a Slinky. 'After we left Ithaca, you promised we'd stay in touch. And you didn't, you naughty boy.' Kay had neatly inserted herself between Hutch and Ruth. Hutch was red-faced with embarrassment, and Ruth, red-faced, too, seemed ready to explode. 'Hutch and I were quite a team. We won the Intercollegiate Dance Spectacular three years in a row, didn't we?' She pinched his cheek with easy familiarity, as if she were an elderly aunt and Hutch were a child. 'Have you kept up with your dancing?'

Before Hutch could answer, Ruth rudely elbowed her fiancé. 'Are you going to introduce me or not, *sweetheart?*'

'Oh, sorry. Of course. Kathleen, ah, Kay O'Reilly . . . but it's Giannotti, now, isn't it? This is my fiancé, Ruth Gannon.'

Poor Hutch. If he stammered like that in the courtroom, every case he tried would be shot down in flames.

Ruth's lips were set in a grim line, barely moving as she spoke. 'Pleased to meet you.'

I could have supplied the subtext, but it would have been expletive ridden.

'G-gosh, it's good to see you,' Hutch stammered on. 'I had no idea you were here, none at all.'

Kay snapped her fingers. 'Chance! You work with Ruth for the next couple of sets, will you?' She beamed at Ruth. 'You won't mind if I borrow your fiancé for a few minutes, will you? We have a lot to catch up on.'

Without waiting for an answer, she dragged Hutch away in the direction of her office. As they disappeared through the door, I heard her say, 'Coffee?'

A few minutes? Hardly. Kay and Hutch didn't reappear until the session was nearly over and we had pretty much nailed the waltz.

Hutch had the good sense, at least, to apologize to Ruth.

'Excuse me,' Ruth practically snarled, turning her back on her fiancé. 'Will you come with me Hannah? I think I've broken a strap.'

But there was nothing wrong with Ruth's underwear. When we got to the restroom, Ruth backed up against one of the sinks and fixed me with a venomous stare. 'How *could* you?'

'Me?'

'Yes, you!' She dissolved into tears.

'Ruth, I'm sorry, but how was I to know?' I held out my hands as if I were weighing items on a balance scale. 'Kay – Kathleen. Giannotti – O'Reilly. So similar.'

Ruth dismissed my irrefutable logic with a wave of her hand. 'Did you see the way she had Hutch wrapped around her little finger?' she sniffed.

I yanked a paper towel out of the dispenser and handed it to her. 'I think Hutch was just as surprised as we were.'

Ruth dabbed at her cheeks. 'But he didn't have to go off with her, did he?' She rolled her eyes. 'Like a little lap dog.' To demonstrate, she stuck out her tongue and panted.

I grabbed my sister by the shoulders and gave her a good shake. 'Ruth, listen to me. I think it'd be a mistake to make a big deal out of this. Hutch and Kay are old friends who haven't seen each other for more than twenty years. Hutch loves you. End of story.'

Ruth didn't look convinced.

'You aren't still worried about Hutch being younger than you, are you?'

Ruth nodded miserably.

'For heaven's sake! When you get to be our age, nine years is nothing. Nothing!' I nipped off to a stall where I unrolled some toilet tissue and brought it to her. 'Here. Blow your nose, and let's get back out on the dance floor.'

Ruth turned and examined her face in the mirror over the sink. 'I can't go back out there. I look like hell.'

'But you dance like an angel.'

Ruth dampened a paper towel with warm water and pressed it against her forehead. Observing her face in the mirror, I thought I caught the barest hint of a smile. 'Pretty amazing, weren't we?'

After a moment, she turned back to me. 'I'm as ready now as I'll ever be. But, my god, Hannah, when I asked you to recommend a dance instructor, I didn't expect you to go and ruin my life.'

Five

B ack in the studio, life had gone on.
When Ruth and I emerged from the ladies' room, we
discovered Daddy and Neelie sharing a bench on the sidelines taking a break, Paul (will wonders never cease?)
waltzing with Laurie, and Hutch leading Alicia expertly
(how else?) around the dance floor. Alicia was beaming,
clearly enjoying the novelty of partnering a new student
who didn't stumble and lurch around like a drunk.

Under Chance's supervision, 'Answer Me, Oh My Love'
was drifting lazily out of the speakers when Hutch caught
sight of Ruth and me. He paused in mid-waltz, bowed
politely to Alicia, and hurried over. 'Ruth.'

She folded her arms across her bosom and pouted.

'Come here. We need to talk.'

Ruth showed no signs of budging, so I gave her a gentle
shove in Hutch's direction.

Hutch took Ruth's hand, tucked it gently under his arm,
and led her to a corner of the studio near the Deer Park
water cooler. From where I stood, I couldn't hear what was
being said, but I could tell from Ruth's body language that
his words were having some effect. Ruth's arms dropped
to her sides, her knees relaxed, and after a few minutes,
she reached up to touch Hutch's face. When he kissed her,
quickly but sweetly, I figured all had been forgiven.

Dodged that bullet.

I was still staring at Hutch and Ruth, just a teensy bit
worried about some residual rigidity I detected in Ruth's
spine, when Paul joined me. 'There you are. I was about
to send out a search party.'

'Sorry,' I said. 'I spent longer in the restroom with Ruth
than I thought.'

'Is everything OK?'

I bobbed my head in the direction of the water cooler. 'It is now.'

Alicia flitted over to remind us that our first lesson was over, and it was almost time for the practice party. For some reason, she looked at me. 'You will stay, won't you?'

I did a sideways-through-the-eyelashes silent consultation with Paul, who winked, so I said, 'Sure.'

'Good!' And she was off to greet three newcomers who stamped through the entrance knocking snow off their boots, followed by a blast of cold air.

'Tell Ruth not to take it so seriously. Kay can be a bit pushy sometimes.' Tom came off the floor where he had been practicing some dangerous-looking hip hop moves on the sidelines. Laurie, his partner, followed.

'A bit?' Laurie's delicately drawn eyebrows arched dramatically. 'She's a selfish B-I-T-C-H, if you want to know the truth. Doesn't give a sweet goddam whose toes she steps on, if you'll pardon the pun.'

'Then why on earth do you train with her, Laurie?' I asked.

Laurie shrugged a well-defined shoulder. 'Because we've been with them, like, forever . . . why else would you say, Tommy?'

Tom didn't even have to think about it. 'Because Kay and Jay are, quite simply, the best.'

'I'm certainly no judge,' Paul said, 'but you two are fantastic. Thanks for taking pity on me, Laurie. That last dance was very helpful. I think I'm finally getting the hang of it.'

'My pleasure,' she smiled. 'You're really a lot better than you think. You just need to relax. Don't think about it so much. And stop looking at your feet!'

'That's Paul,' I told the pair. 'Always analyzing things to death.'

'Which can lead to paralysis, especially in hip hop,' Tom added, wiping his face and neck with a towel. I wasn't into hip hop, and rap music tended to liquefy my brain, turning it into gray goo that threatened to trickle out my ears. I wondered aloud about the place of hip hop in competitive ballroom.

'Not in competition, per se,' Tom explained, 'but Jay is thinking about starting a beginner hip hop class, and has approached me about teaching it. Up in Boston, I worked with Jose Eric Cruz who choreographed for Paula Abdul and Janet Jackson.'

I was supposed to be impressed, I suppose, but wasn't it Paula who nodded off while judging on *American Idol*, and Janet whose famous boob, I mean, wardrobe malfunction, gave Super Bowl viewers an eyeful? Wouldn't include those gals on *my* résumé, but, as I said, I wasn't exactly hip on hip hop.

Laurie nipped off to retrieve a fleece jacket from a hook on the wall, then wandered back, easing her arms into the sleeves. 'Did you see the movie *Take the Lead* with Antonio Banderas?' she asked as she zipped.

'Oh, yeah. Banderas is *hot*.' I flapped a hand in front of my face, fanning furiously.

She gave me a high five. 'You go, girl! Remember the dance competition at the end? That was a fusion of ballroom and hip hop.'

Paul, who had seen the movie, too, laughed and said, 'As much as I'd like to set your pulses racing, ladies, those kind of moves would kill me. Years ago, I screwed up my back in a farm accident.'

Tom tucked a corner of the towel under his belt. 'You might be pleasantly surprised, Paul. Hip hop is kind of an all-purpose exercise, involving high and low impact footwork and motions that can really free up your head, neck, and shoulders. Your arms, too, come to think of it, and even your wrists.'

Paul held up a hand. 'Whoa! Let me get the hang of the pivot, promenade and slide, first,'

With an affectionate glance at Tom, Laurie said, 'What, no botting, snaking, popping, waving, tutting or dime stopping?'

'Tutting?'

'King Tut.' Laurie strutted in front of us, walking-like-an-Egyptian, gold hoop earrings bouncing against her neck.

'Too much!' Paul turned to me. 'Can you see me doing a Steve Martin imitation at Ruth's wedding? She'd *kill* me.'

I pinched his cheek. 'You're just a wild and crazy guy.'

Eventually, Tom and Laurie drifted off to work on their routine, while Paul and I migrated to the snacks table where chips and popcorn had been laid out for the practice party.

'We're eating their food, so I think we're obliged to practice, don't you?' Snagging a potato chip, I used it to scoop up a generous helping of veggie dip.

'*Smurgle splessh schlew*,' my husband commented around a mouthful of popcorn. I puckered up and gave him a big air kiss. 'I love it when you talk dirty.'

Six

W hen I got through to Eva on her cell phone the following morning, she told me she was sitting at a table in Hard Beans and Books, drinking a tall latte and using their wireless signal to catch up on email. 'I was just responding to your last about the dancing lessons,' she told me. 'I hope Ruth invites me to the wedding, because this I *gotta* see.'

Before I could chastise my friend for not letting me know that a return to Annapolis was in her plans, she apologized. 'I'm sorry I didn't give you a head's up, Hannah, but coming back was a last-minute decision for me.' In the background I could hear subdued conversations and the *whoosh* of the cappuccino machine as the popular bookstore/coffee shop, or coffee shop/bookstore – depending on your point of view – went on with its daily grind. Hard Beans occupied a storefront midway between Blanca Flor and The Gap, a prime location just across from the newly-renovated Market House, and boasting a panoramic view of the Annapolis waterfront.

'Is everything OK?' I asked my friend.

For a moment, there was silence on her end of the line, as if everyone in the bookstore had stopped talking in order to eavesdrop on our conversation. 'Yes, and no,' Eva said.

'Is it something we can talk about?'

'I'd like that, Hannah. When are you free?'

'I've checked my calendar, and you're in luck. The White House has rescheduled for Wednesday, and HRH Prince Charles isn't arriving until Friday, so . . . any time. You name it.'

Eva chuckled. 'Hannah, you are the one thing I missed

most about this place. I have an appointment in an hour . . .'

She paused, took a deep breath. I pictured her raising a hold-that-thought hand.

'More on that when I see you. But could we meet for lunch? The usual place?'

By 'usual' Eva meant Regina's Continental Deli in West Annapolis, around the corner from St Catherine Episcopal Church, Eva's West Annapolis parish, now in the hands of an interim during her sabbatical. Dining tip for Regina's: go barefoot. The German potato salad will knock your socks off. I'd never tried Regina's sauerbraten, but some folks (it is said) drive hundreds of miles just for a plate of it. My mouth was already watering for her open-face crab sandwich, so I said, 'Eleven forty-five?'

'Done.'

After hanging up the phone, I checked my watch. Two hours and twenty minutes to go. Two hours to stew about whatever was troubling Pastor Eva, and twenty minutes to get some laundry done, so I trotted upstairs for the laundry basket, and hauled it down to the basement.

Mother always claimed that sorting the white clothes from the dark calmed her nerves. Doesn't work for me. Chocolate does. I stood in my laundry room with a heap of Paul's undershirts and Y-fronts on my left, and a meager pile of colored Ts and turtlenecks on my right. So, what the hell, I tossed them all in the washer together, turned the dial to cold, added liquid Tide, and trotted upstairs to make myself a cup of hot cocoa. If Paul ended up with pink underwear, I'd worry about it in the morning.

I arrived at Regina's ten minutes early and Eva wasn't there, so I popped into Absolutely Fabulous, the consignment shop next door. Since Daddy had downsized, my sisters and I had more hand-me-down furniture than we could possibly use, so I breezed by the dressers, bookshelves and end tables that jumbled up the shop. I still had walls and surfaces that were bare enough to collect dust, however, so some of the art work and bric-a-brac looked tempting. Exhibit A: a forty-eight-piece service of blue and white china similar to my mother's wedding china. I'd lived without fine china for most of my life, so what made me think I couldn't live without it now? Feeling reckless, I wrote out a check for eighty dollars, and asked the proprietor to pack up the dishes while I ate.

An early Christmas gift. From me to me.

I was back at Regina's sitting at a table squeezing lemon into my iced tea, when Eva opened the door. Her dark bangs were longer than when I'd last seen her, caught back behind one ear, and streaked with gray. But even if she'd been bald as an egg I'd have recognized Eva by her smile, a 1000-watt grin that started at her lips, spread to her dimples, and ended up crinkling the corners of her sea-green eyes.

'Hannah!' Eva lunged and hugged me so hard that I feared for my ribs.

'Eva, I can't tell you how good it is to see you,' I said, hugging her back.

Eva shrugged off her coat and draped it over the back of her chair, while I waved for the waitress who appeared almost immediately to take our order for two crab melts with French fries.

'You've let your hair grow, Eva,' I said, handing my menu back to the waitress.

'And you haven't.' Eva grinned. 'Honestly, Hannah, you look terrific.'

I patted my curls. 'Direct your comments to Wally at Bellissima,' I said, referring to the resident hair stylist at Paradiso, the luxury spa that my daughter and her husband had opened out Bay Ridge way last summer. 'Wally's kinda weird, but a genius with color.'

'I stopped coloring my hair,' Eva said. 'Seemed an unnecessary expense with just the wolves, elk and squirrels around to appreciate the effort. And as for styling, what do you think about this?' She turned in her chair so I could see the back of her head. Eva had twisted her longer hair into an untidy rope and secured it to the crown of her head with a tortoiseshell claw clip. A far cry from the neat page boy she used to wear at St Cat's.

'If you ever get tired . . .' I paused, searching for the appropriate word. 'Of the elegant simplicity of that hairdo, Wally will take good care of you.'

'Is that your roundabout way of suggesting that I need a "professional haircut"?'

'Guilty!'

'Point taken.' Eva slipped her napkin out from under the silverware, unfolded it and spread it out on her lap. 'How's the spa doing, then?'

'Amazingly well. Dante's taking on staff, and they may be putting in tennis courts come spring.'

'And Emily?'

'I'm happy to report that she changed her mind about home-schooling the kids, and she's back running Puddle Ducks. You remember, the day care center at Paradiso?'

'I do. And that's excellent news.'

I had to agree. Emily could be intense. Cooped up with their mother all day, who knew how the kids would turn out. Paul and I had been taking bets: Nobel prize-winning physicists, or ax murderers. Fortunately, after two months' experimentation, Jake and Chloe were back in the capable hands of St Anne's Church School and the Anne Arundel County school system, respectively, working out any renegade personality quirks by participating in dance (Chloe) and the after school soccer program (Jake). As far as I knew, there were no soccer programs for two-year-olds, but even if there had been, Emily would have kept Timmy at Puddle Ducks.

'After the kidnapping, I bet Emily doesn't let Timmy out of her sight.' Eva was always good at reading my mind.

'Never, ever. She even set up an intercom so she can monitor the little guy while he's sleeping.'

Just then, the waitress made a timely appearance with Eva's Diet Coke, giving us an excuse to leave that painful topic.

'So, how are *you*, Hannah?' Eva asked as she slipped the paper off a straw and plunked it into her glass.

With friends like Eva, who knew my medical history, the usual response – 'fine, fine' – wouldn't cut it. 'Just had my annual check-up,' I told her truthfully. 'No lumps or bumps. Mammogram A-OK. CA-125 numbers steady. I'm good to go for another year.'

'Thank God.'

'Amen to that.' Now that I'd caught Eva up on news from the Ives household, I stared hard at my friend, wondering where to begin with the long list of questions I had for her.

'You're probably wondering why I'm here.' Eva again, reading my mind.

'That's an understatement.'

'And why I consulted Hutch.'

'Uh huh.'

'It's complicated.' Eva paused, twirled her straw. 'Let me start at the beginning.'

'Please!'

'I have a stalker.'

I coughed. I spluttered. Drops of iced tea decorated my placemat. 'What?'

Eva leaned over, lifted her purse off the floor, and pulled several sheets of paper from an outside pocket. 'Email can be a blessing, or a curse.' She thumbed through the pages, and handed me one of them. 'This is his first message.'

My eyes skimmed quickly over the usual To, From and Subject lines to get to the nitty-gritty of the printout in my hand.

Pastor Eva:

I know you will forgive me for intruding on your leave of absence. I'm a fellow Annapolitan and I had the PLEASURE of attending one of your services back in April last year and was I was 'MOVED' by your prophetic witness!!!! I knew the LORD was calling me to join St Catherines. I once doubted the wisdom of LADIES in orders, but GOD has shown me that I was wrong. Also, you all are easier on the EYE than old Rector BOB (*wink*). Anyway, I was moved in my SOUL about your troubles and was CALLED TO let you hear from a parishoner that you are LOVED and MISSED. God doesn't want you to be in EXILE forever.

HE hates waste.
Yours in Christ,
Jeremy Dunstan
1 Cross + 3 Nails = 4given

I gazed across the table at Eva who was munching calmly on a French fry she'd taken from a platter the waitress must have snuck on to the table while I was busy reading Jeremy Dunstan's email. 'Who the heck is Jeremy Dunstan?'

'As he says, a parishioner. Not that he can spell the word.'

I handed the printout back. 'His email is a bit creepy – what's with all those capital letters, for heaven's sake? – but it doesn't strike me as anything to worry about.'

Eva grimaced. 'It didn't to me, either, not at first. So I actually responded to the guy, in a pastoral manner, of course.'

She handed me a second printout. 'I was seduced by his turnabout on the place of women in the priesthood, I suppose.' She scowled. 'Over the next month, we exchanged a half-dozen emails, and then *this* popped into my mailbox.'

> Eva:
> I just want to thank you for your thoughts on the Gospel of JOHN. I always read 'no one comes to the Father except by me' to mean that you have to be a CHRISTIAN to get to heaven. I've never heard your reading – that Jesus just meant he was the gatekeeper and we don't really know what the requirements are. Are you SURE that's the GODLY way of reading that? I think the devil sometimes works to make us think it's all easy.
>
> Anyway, more important is I feel that the LORD is working in our correspondence. I know the SPIRIT is moving us together. I can tell you now that when I saw you preach last year, it wasn't only your godly teaching that moved me but also, your a BEAUTIFUL woman and God can't mean for you to be alone forever. You and I have become good friends but do you think

GOD is calling us to MORE? I think of you alone in the WILDERNESS being purified like so many of our great saints, but all those saints had to come back eventually!!!! Write back and let me know your thoughts SOONEST
God Bless,
Jeremy
1 Cross + 3 Nails = 4given

I could feel Saint Eva's eyes boring into me as I read. When I finished, she said, 'Your mouth is hanging open.'

'You're surprised?' I laid the printout down on the table. 'Jiminy Christmas, Eva, what did you do? Write him back, as he said, *soonest*?'

'Not soonest. I worked on my response for two whole days. Basically, I told him I was flattered by his email, but he shouldn't misinterpret our relationship as anything more than pastor to parishioner, based on our common commitment to God.' She sighed. 'And then I got this.'

She handed me a third printout.

Darling Eva
I was VERY disappointed to hear your response to my last email and I'm not the ONLY one. God is calling us to be together and you KNOW that. Are you bringing your concerns to HIM or are you relying on WORLDLY friends and thoughts?? I have PRAYED extensively and GOD told me that your unworthy husband was only a CROSS for you to bear on your path to something much BETTER. I was DESTROYED when He took my darling RHONDA last year, BUT I know when the LORD closes a door, he opens a WINDOW. His mercy is GREAT!!! We are nothing – we can't oppose HIS will for us. I just asked him to send me a word about us. I opened the Bible with my eyes closed and pointed to a section and this is what HE sent: Psalm 19:9: 'The LORD's judgments are true and righteous, every one, more to be desired than gold, pure gold in plenty, sweeter than

honey dripping from the comb. It is through them your
servant is warned; in obeying them is great reward.' I
am ready JOYFULLY to do HIS will and take you
into my heart and my arms where you BELONG!!!
Love,
Jeremy
1 Cross + 3 Nails = 4given

'Oh. My. Gawd. That sounds an awful lot like a proposal
of marriage.'

'Exactly.'

'So, what did you do?'

'I concocted an email that looked like an auto-reply. "Rev
Haberman is away from her computer and cannot respond to
your email at the present time. If this is an emergency, please
contact . . ." and then I put in the phone number of the Diocesan
Center in Baltimore, closed my eyes, and hit Send.'

'And?'

'Nothing. I'm not proud of it, but after talking with the
bishop, I decided to ignore Mr Jeremy Dunstan. Mistake,
as it turns out.'

'Why is that?'

'When Jeremy didn't hear back from me by the end of
the week, he called the parish office, and some idiot gave
him my mailing address. The next thing I know, Jeremy
shows up at the post office in Stanley, Idaho, wanting to
know where he could find the owner of Box 293.'

'Eva, no! Did they tell him?'

'They?' Eva sniggered. '"They" is Michelle, the post-
master. And, no, she didn't, praise God, but Jeremy gave
her a difficult time. Michelle had to call the police chief to
remove Jeremy from the premises.'

'Where did Jeremy go?'

'I don't know. I only heard about the incident when I
drove into town for groceries a couple of days later. Jeremy
had been staying at the Sawtooth Hotel, but by that time,
he'd checked out.'

'So I went back to the cabin,' she continued, 'but the
whole isolation thing was starting to spook me. Like any

moment Jeremy Dunstan was going to pop out of the trees holding an engagement ring in his hand.' She paused. 'Or, maybe a shotgun.'

It was hard for me to picture Eva being spooked by anything, and I told her so.

'I locked myself in, Hannah, and every morning I'd find myself staring out the window, looking for fresh footprints in the snow.'

'Jeremy, Jeremy . . . I'm trying to put a face on this guy.' I'd been one of the faithful at St Cat's since, well since Old Rector Bob, and I couldn't think of anyone in the congregation named Jeremy.

'He wasn't one of our regulars, Hannah. When he first came, he'd sit in one of the back pews, over near the baptismal font.'

'What's he look like?'

'Short, stocky, neckless. From a distance, it looks like Jeremy has an abundant head of hair, but up close, you realize it's the world's worst toupee. Like a small brown animal crawled up top of his head, and died.'

'Man of my dreams!' I chuckled.

Just then, the waitress arrived with our order. I looked at my plate, thinking I wasn't very hungry, until the irresistible aroma of Old Bay seasoning wafted up, tweaked my nose, and got those digestive juices flowing. 'Dig in,' I said, 'before it gets cold.'

'And then, just to prove there is a God,' Eva continued, waving a fork full of cheesy crab, 'I got an email from a former parishioner who works at the Maryland Hall of Records.'

I swallowed. 'And?'

'Seems there was a church over on the eastern shore that burned down in the mid-1700s. Everyone thought the records perished in the fire, but incredibly, someone just found them in an old trunk down in Dorchester County.' She popped the crab into her mouth, then rolled her eyes appreciatively. 'Religious records are often the only source of birth and death information, so this collection is a gold mine for researchers and genealogists. Anyway –' Eva dabbed at her mouth with a corner of her napkin – 'this parishioner remembered that I had a BA in History, so for the two months left on my sabbatical, I've volunteered to help update the *Guide to Maryland Religious Institutions Featuring the Collections of the Maryland State Archives.* How's that for a mouthful?'

'Footprints in the snow aside, are you going to miss Idaho?' I asked.

'Living alone in a cabin in the middle of nowhere was just what I needed, at least at first. I talked with the bishop, prayed for guidance and direction, and left plenty of room for God to toss back an answer.' She smiled. 'I wasn't expecting God to throw me a curve, of course.'

'I've never been to Idaho. All I know is potatoes. What's Stanley like?'

'Stanley's three blocks long and two blocks wide, with a population of just over one hundred. The main drag is called Ace of Diamonds Avenue. How about that?' she laughed. 'Summer was perfection. Fall was gorgeous, for the aspens turning golden, if nothing else. But, once November came around . . .' Eva put her knife and fork down, forming an X on her plate. 'Stanley's at 6200 feet, and in the winter it gets down to thirty below. When I found myself at Williams Motor Sports bundled up to the eyebrows, shivering in my boots, and seriously considering renting a snow mobile, I decided Stanley, Idaho, was a bit too much winter wonderland, even for me. So, in spite of what happened with Roger, I came back. I'm not ready yet, but by the time my sabbatical is over, I fully intend to return to St Cat's.'

'But isn't this Jeremy guy –' I patted the printout with my hand – 'I mean, doesn't he live here?'

'He does. That's why I went to see Hutch. I can't hide out in the mountains forever, so if Jeremy Dunstan finds out I'm back in Annapolis, decides to come mooning after me like a lovesick schoolboy, and can't be made to see reason, I figure I'll need a restraining order.'

'Maybe it won't come to that.' I had a wicked thought. 'Maybe Jeremy was so despondent that he walked out of the Sawtooth Hotel, wandered into the snow-covered hills, only to be set upon and devoured by wolves.'

Eva forced a smile. 'Or, maybe he's sitting in a car outside Regina's and, even as we speak, watching us through binoculars.'

'I prefer my scenario.'

Eva and I ate in silence for a while. After I had polished off the last of my crab melt, I said, 'Hutch mentioned that you're staying with the assistant pastor of St Anne's.'

Eva nodded. 'Temporarily, until I can move back into the parsonage.'

'Eva, if you need a place, you can always stay with us. It's just Paul and me now, rattling around in that big old house on Prince George Street.'

Eva reached across the table and squeezed my hand. 'Thanks, Hannah. I'll bear that in mind.'

'You can't beat the rent,' I added. 'Free.'

'Hannah, I love you, but, no.'

When Eva left Annapolis four months ago, it'd been in humiliation. 'I've failed myself, my husband, and my church,' she'd told me as I helped pack up her things, 'But most painfully of all, I've failed my God.'

As I squeezed her hand back, I thought, sometimes, even with God's help, it takes a long time to heal.

Seven

Unlike Eva, I'd never had a stalker. But Sister Ruth was starting to qualify. Before dance lessons entered our lives, we'd gotten together maybe once a week. Since getting bitten by the ballroom bug, however, Ruth stopped by almost every day, begging me to sign up for extra lessons; I hadn't seen so much of her since my chemotherapy days when she moved in for a month, whipping up tempting dishes, urging me to eat, when all I wanted was to curl up in a ball and die. When I wasn't quietly barfing, that is.

So I felt bad about saying no.

One sunny afternoon, she showed up on my doorstep with a DVD: J & K's Ballroom Basics ($50, tax included). 'Hutch is tied up in court,' she explained, as she slotted the DVD into the player. Apparently our forty-two inch plasma screen was better suited to the task than the sixty-inch behemoth in the home entertainment center in the house Hutch shared with my sister on Southgate Avenue, but far be it from me to say so. Ruth looked so determined, that I didn't even complain when she bent down and rolled up my oriental rug.

I drew the line at actually dancing with my sister. 'I will *not* dance lead,' I told her firmly. 'I have a hard enough time learning my own part.'

Ruth frowned, then scurried off to the kitchen, returning with a mop in one hand and a broom in the other. 'Lay the handle across your shoulders,' she instructed, handing me the broom, 'and drape your arms over it.' She did the same with the mop, and we practiced side-by-side for a while like demented scarecrows. 'It strengthens your core,' Ruth explained, although it seemed more like a medieval form of torture to me, an exercise (like balancing a stack of books on one's head) designed to force wicked children to stand up straight. Dancing a rumba with a broomstick across my shoulders – one, two, three, four and one, two, three, four and spot turn left and right – well, I felt insane. I had a couple of curious neighbors, and I hoped none of them happened to choose that moment to glance in through the window, proving the point.

'Core or no core, I feel like a damn fool,' I complained.

'Persistent practice of postural principles promises perfection,' Ruth chanted.

'Who says?

'Hutch says.'

Easy for him to say.

I turned toward Ruth so she could see me when I stuck out my tongue. In the process, the end of the broomstick swept a high school photograph of Emily off a bookshelf and on to the floor, smashing the glass and scattering shards every which way over my hardwood floor.

'About those extra lessons,' I said, as I set the picture back on the shelf, lowered the broomstick, and applied its business end to the shards of glass. 'Maybe we can manage one. How much?'

Ruth paused mid-spot turn right and said, 'One hundred dollars.'

'That's $1.66 a minute,' I said, calculating quickly. 'But cheaper than repairing the damage to my house.'

'Oh, thank you, Hannah!'

Damn Ruth. Once again, she'd gotten her way.

I'd learned how to waltz, foxtrot and tango before I first clapped eyes on Jay. He'd been out of town on business, according to Chance, the dishy dance instructor, who also passed on the information that Jay was looking into opening up J & K franchises nationwide. 'He wants to play with the big boys,' Chance told us when Paul, Ruth and I showed up for our supplementary lesson. 'You know, Arthur Murray and Fred Astaire.'

'Aren't they dead?' wondered Paul aloud.

Chance nodded, grinning. 'Ages ago, but their franchises

live on. Ballroom is mega big right now. Jay hired a bunch of consultants who tell him to strike while the iron is hot, so he's figuring on tap dancing all over those old fogies, pumping some new blood and new ideas into the industry.'

Riding high on that stream of clichés, Chance excused himself to cue up the music. Once it began, Ruth tangoed off with Chance, and Paul and I were practicing our progressive side step – quick, quick, slow – when a man slipped through the sliding glass doors leading from the office on to the dance floor – Jay. I recognized him from the photo on the cover of the DVD. As he headed in our direction I stumbled, and tromped all over Paul's toes.

I don't know what I expected the man to look like. Taller than Kay, certainly – he was at least 6' 2" to her 5' 8" – and supernaturally slender, of course.

But, Jay was all that, and more. Where Kay had the fair, pink skin of a porcelain doll, Jay looked like he'd just spent a month investigating franchise opportunities on a beach in Cozumel. The man was beautiful, evenly bronzed, his dark hair slicked back into a short ponytail at the nape of his neck. The quintessential Latin lover, from the dark brows, arching quizzically over eyes of liquid chocolate, all the way down to the tips of his black, highly polished dancing shoes.

Until he opened his mouth. 'Ahm pleased to meet chew,' he drawled after we introduced ourselves.

Hispanic heritage, I decided, but raised in one of the border states. Texas, maybe, although I couldn't imagine how he'd ended up with an Italian name like Giannotti.

I extended my hand, and Jay shook it firmly. His full lips parted in a smile, revealing straight, impossibly white teeth. After a moment, he turned that smile full-throttle on my sister. 'And you must be Ruth. Kay's been telling me about you.' As Jay squeezed Ruth's hand, he glanced around the studio. 'I don't suppose your fiancé is here? There's something I'd like to discuss with the two of you.'

Ruth reclaimed her hand. 'Oh? Can you tell me?'

'It concerns both of you. Is he coming tonight, then?'

'Now you are arousing my curiosity,' Ruth purred. She

stared at Jay, a sly smile on her lips, as she took in (who could help it?) his open-neck poet's shirt and slim, belt-less black pants.

Arousing. Exactly the right word, sister.

Jay turned to us. 'Are you enjoying the lessons, then?'

'Very much,' I cooed.

'More than I thought I would,' Paul added. I hoped he was being truthful.

Jay smiled, nodded in acknowledgement, and then turned back to Ruth. 'So, you never answered me, *señorita.* Will we be seeing the bridegroom tonight?'

'He was in court today, but if he's not held up by a client, I expect he'll show up for the regular session at seven.'

'Ah. That's good, then.' From his 6' 4" (two inches of it heels) Jay beamed down on her. 'Kay tells me you're a quick study. Would you honor me with a dance before class starts?'

Ruth blushed attractively. She'd been doing an inordin-ate amount of that lately. She flapped a dismissive hand. 'Me? My gosh, I couldn't!'

Jay seized Ruth's hand, tucked it under his arm and led her on to the dance floor. 'Nonsense! Chance, cue up a waltz, will you, please?'

Paul and I watched, open-mouthed, as my sister was whisked off in the arms of the handsomest man in the state of Maryland, twirling and swirling around the floor to the tune of 'Wonderful, Wonderful Copenhagen'.

Holy cow. If Hutch walked in right now, what would he make of the euphoric grin on Ruth's face? And then I remembered Kay, pouncing on Hutch like a mother lion and carrying him off, a helpless cub, to her den.

'Well, dear,' my late mother seemed to be whispering in my ear, 'isn't there an old saying? "What's good for the goose is good for the gander."'

But I was thinking goose, hell. If this keeps up, before long the proverbial fur is going to fly.

'So,' I said when Jay finally released my sister, 'I'm dying of curiosity. What does he want?'

Ruth shrugged. 'I'm not sure. Probably hopes to sweet-talk us into signing up for another package.' She grinned. 'He is a charming son-of-a-gun, isn't he?'

'I'd have thought you'd jump at the chance to continue taking lessons. I haven't seen you so nuts about anything since you took up tie-dying broomstick skirts in the seventies.'

Ruth frowned. 'I do love dancing, Hannah. It makes me feel young and alive. But I have to be realistic. I've got Mother Earth to worry about, and the wedding.' She chewed on her bottom lip thoughtfully. 'No, we bought the wedding package, and a couple of extra lessons, but that's it. All the arm-twisting and charm in the world isn't going to convince me to sign a contract for some overpriced lesson package that neither of us needs, or has the time for.'

'I've heard some of the major studio chains use high-pressure tactics to get you to join up, but Jay and Kay simply aren't like that,' I said. 'According to the J & K brochure, the next level up is the 600 package: six privates, six groups, six parties, six hundred dollars. Sounds harmless enough.'

'I'll tell you one thing,' Ruth said. 'I won't do anything without Hutch. Can you imagine the creeps who show up for lessons with ridiculous comb-overs, bad teeth and damp hands wanting to dance with you? Ugh! Six hundred dollars sounds like a deal, until you realize that any serial rapist with six hundred dollars in his pocket could sign up for dance lessons, too.'

Ruth grabbed my arm. 'Hannah, you and Paul come along when he talks to us. Keep me focused. OK?'

I laughed. 'Oh, I think you and Hutch can take care of yourselves!'

'No, I'm serious. Remember the time we won a free weekend in Virginia and they practically locked us up until we agreed to buy a timeshare in their stupid resort?'

I laughed, remembering how Ruth and I, in desperation, had staged a fight, screaming, swearing, name-calling and hurling abuse at one another until the salesman couldn't show us the door fast enough. 'It won't be like that at all,' I assured her.

Ruth didn't look convinced. 'I have a hard time saying no to *telephone* solicitors, for heaven's sake. In case you didn't notice, Jay has oodles of charm. I might find him impossible to resist.'

'Ruth!'

'Not that way, silly. But he's *soooo* charismatic. If Jay were a TV preacher, I'd be claiming Jesus as my personal saviour and singing and sweeping the ceiling with the rest of his acolytes.'

'Sweeping the ceiling?'

Ruth's arms shot ceiling-ward and she began to sway, singing, 'He is wonderful, He is merciful,' in a fluty soprano.

I had to bop her with my purse to get her to stop. 'Behave yourself!'

'OK, but only if you agree to come along. Otherwise I might have to cover my ears and go "nah-nah-nah-nah-nah-I'm-not-listening-to-you" whenever Jay's talking.'

I laughed out loud. 'It's not going to be like that at all, Ruth.'

And for once, I was right.

'Ah,' Jay said from behind his desk as Kay escorted the four of us into his office later that evening. 'I was expecting Hutch and Ruth, but I seem to have won the lottery.'

'We're family,' I said, as if that explained everything.

'Yes. I understand. Completely.' Jay shuffled through the papers on his desk, moving a page from the bottom to the top of the stack, as if Paul and my presence had changed everything. 'Have a seat, please. Kay, you, too.'

When we were all comfortably settled, Jay turned his liquid eyes on me. 'Not to denigrate the remarkable progress you and your husband have made over the course of the past several weeks . . .' He paused, while next to me, Paul beamed. 'But I have to be honest. I called you in this evening primarily to talk about Ruth.'

Ruth nearly fell out of her chair. 'Me?'

'Yes, you, *señorita*. Your advancement has been nothing short of extraordinary.'

I resisted rolling my eyes. Ruth had been right. We were in for some major league flimflam.

After a moment, Jay turned his attention to Hutch. 'Hutch,

of course, only needs a bit of brush up to get back up to speed, even after twenty-five years.'

Get back up to speed for what? I wondered.

Jay put his hands together, fingertip to fingertip and moved them up and down, like a spider doing push-ups on a mirror. He cleared his throat. 'Have you ever heard of *Shall We Dance?*'

'The TV show?' Hutch asked.

'That's the one. To get right to the point, there's a new season next year, and they're holding open auditions in Baltimore on February 8th. I think you have a chance of making it.'

Several moments of stunned silence was shattered by Paul. 'What's *Shall We Dance?*'

'It's an *American Idol*-style reality show,' Kay explained, although how that would help Paul understand is anybody's guess as he never watched *American Idol, Survivor, Big Brother* or any kind of so-called Unreality TV. 'Instead of individuals competing, though, it's dancing couples,' she continued. 'They start with twelve couples, all amateurs, and each week two are eliminated until there's only one couple remaining.'

Ruth paled. 'I couldn't. I'm not ready.'

Kay rose from her chair and laid a comforting hand on Ruth's shoulder. 'Yes you can, and we can help you. If you agree to this, Jay will coach you privately, twice a week. Then, we'll put you together with Hutch, and work up a dynamite routine.'

'Jesus.' Ruth said.

Hutch, who had been slumped in his chair like Raggedy Andy, suddenly came to life. 'I'm game if you are, sweetheart.'

Ruth wagged her head. 'This is all too sudden, I can't even think.'

'How much will it cost?' I asked, remembering my promise to help Ruth keep her head.

'Cost?' Jay puffed air out of his lips, as if I'd insulted him. 'Absolutely nothing.'

Kay smiled benevolently. 'If you make it through the

auditions and get on to the show, it will be a priceless advertisement for J & K. That is our payback. That is our hope.'

Hutch stood up, took Ruth's hand, and pulled her to her feet. 'This is all very flattering, of course, and exciting. But, it's been a long day, and I think we'll need to sleep on it.'

'Thank you,' Ruth tossed over her shoulder as Hutch put his arm around her and led her out the door.

Paul and I said our goodbyes, and followed them out to the coat rack.

As Paul held my coat and I eased my arms into the sleeves, I heard Ruth say, 'Somebody had better tell me what to do.'

Eight

As I thought about the weeks afterward, I found that I tended to identify them by the dances we studied.

The first, Waltz Week, was all about Ruth, waltzing as we were to her tune.

Cha-cha Week, the fourth one after Thanksgiving, found me multitasking – Christmas shopping, decorating, cooking, cleaning and babysitting for my grandkids while Emily and Dante managed pre-Christmas promotionals designed to lure new members into Spa Paradiso.

> A year's membership? The perfect gift.
> Gained weight during the holidays? Get rid of it, fast.
> New Year's resolution to get back into shape? Our trainers can help.

Rumba Week began normally enough until the *Shall We Dance?* bombshell exploded at our feet. The next day, Tuesday, not long before Christmas, I telephoned Ruth several times to find out what she'd decided, but her assistant at Mother Earth told me Ruth was out.

At four fifty, I dropped Chloe off at J & K for her ballet lesson and got the answer to my question. When Chloe and I walked in, Ruth was totally wrapped up in a private lesson with Jay who was wearing his trademark black pants and a maroon shirt like a second skin. I hung Chloe's coat on a hook near the door, and the two of us stood on the sidelines watching.

Chloe tugged on the hem of my sweater. 'That's Aunt Ruth.'

'Indeed, it is.'

'She's doing the rumba,' Chloe informed me sagely.

'That's true, too.' If the steps hadn't been a dead give-away, Ruth was the complete rumba picture, down to green tights under a kicky miniskirt with a beaded hem that flicked around her thighs as she moved.

We watched for a while as Chloe's classmates began to arrive for ballet.

'I want to learn ballroom,' Chloe said. 'I want to be on TV.'

My god, I thought, does everyone want to be on TV?

'Can't you be on TV dancing ballet?' I asked my grand-daughter.

Chloe turned her wide, bright eyes on me. 'Nooooh,' she said. Rough translation: *Duh, Grandma.* 'My teacher says ballet is excellent preparation for ballroom dancing.'

'It is?'

'Uh huh. You learn to do lifts and things, like on TV.'

'But don't you need a partner for ballroom, Chloe?'

'Uh huh.'

'Do you know any boys who like to dance?'

Chloe's chin nearly touched her chest. 'Nuh uh. Boys think dancing is gross. They have to, like, touch hands!'

While I was trying to come up with some words of wisdom to reassure my granddaughter that as hard as it was to believe, someday boys wouldn't mind touching hands with her, Chloe turned to me and announced, 'Tessa is taking ballroom dancing lessons.' She rose on tiptoe, whispered in my ear. 'They're private.'

Chloe's hand shot out, index finger extended. She was pointing to the women's dressing room from which a munchkin of a girl was just emerging. She had cascades of ebony curls drawn up into a high ponytail and fastened at the crown of her head with a pink carnation. She wore a pink leotard and matching tights, and pink ballet slippers. I squinted, not quite believing my eyes. And lipstick?

'Tessa has pink leotards, and blue ones, and yellow ones, too. I want purple leotards for Christmas, Grandma.'

'Have you talked to Santa about that?'

Chloe nodded. 'Can I ask you something, Grandma?'

'Sure.'

'Is there really a Santa Claus?'

'What do you think, Chloe?'

'I don't know. Mommy says that if you don't believe in him, Santa won't come.'

Chloe's normally smooth brow wrinkled in concentration. 'I want a purple tutu, too.'

'Then I think you should write to Santa about that.'

'OK,' she agreed. 'But if Santa doesn't bring me purple leotards this year, that's it. I'll never trust him again. And I'll tell Jake and Timmy not to believe in him either!'

The ultimate threat. Exposure! Poor Santa.

The rest of Chloe's little classmates began arriving, hanging up coats, flitting in and out of the dressing room, scurrying over to the barre preparing to exercise. A woman I took to be Tessa's mother fussed over her daughter's hair for a moment, then shoved the girl in the direction of the barre with the flat of a hand placed squarely on the child's back. Chloe and I watched as Tessa raised her left leg, rested it on the barre, then slowly lowered her head until it touched her knee, as easily as a contortionist from *Cirque de Soleil*. Little show-off.

Chloe noticed me watching. 'I can do that, Grandma.'

'You can? Show me.'

Chloe skipped over to the barre, her golden hair flopping. Using both hands, she lifted her leg to the barre, then lowered her head a few inches, missing her knee by a mile. She turned her head slowly toward me, a grin splitting her face.

I clapped my hands silently.

'She's got to keep her leg perfectly straight,' somebody behind me whined.

I turned to the speaker. Tessa's mother.

'Do you mean Chloe?'

'Goodness, no, Chloe's just a beginner. I mean Tessa. If I've told her once, I've told her a thousand times.'

'How old is Tessa? Ten?'

'Nine.'

'Plenty of time for her to practice, then.'

Tessa's mother stared at me as if I'd just told her that President Bush had declared the War on Terror a terrible mistake, and ordered all our troops home from Iraq. 'For Chloe, maybe, but Tessa is trying out for *Tiny Ballroom*.'

I'd actually seen promos for *Tiny Ballroom*, an American

spin-off of a popular British show featuring eight to eleven-year-old dancers that would make its debut on cable TV in the US this coming summer. When I first saw the ads, I cringed, having a major JonBenet Ramsey moment. 'Ballroom? I thought we were talking about ballet?'

'Tessa's been studying ballet since she was five. She's been taking ballroom privately from Alicia for about a year. We're stepping it up a bit, because the *Tiny Ballroom* auditions are in three months.'

I watched as Tessa, Chloe and several other girls began their barre exercises. 'Who's Tessa's partner, then?'

'Oh my god, was *that* a production! When Joey retired, we had to put an ad in the paper. That's how we found Henry. Tessa dances with him twice a week after school. He's ten.'

'Tessa's partner *retired*? At ten?' I was glad this woman wasn't my mother.

'Eleven. Apparently Joey preferred playing Little League.' She sniffed, as if the child had declared himself a conscientious objector.

'Tessa must like dancing,' I said.

'Loves it! Tessa's a self-starter. She practices all the time. Link's built a studio for her in the garage, fully-equipped. We'd schedule lessons three times a week, but Alicia's only free on Tuesday, Thursday and Saturday, and Henry has to be with his dad on Saturday. So Saturday Tessa does tap.'

I watched Tessa exercise and wondered if the little girl ever slept. But then, I didn't suppose her schedule was any more taxing than that of any Little League or Youth Soccer fanatic. I pictured Henry as a serious kid with wire-rimmed glasses; a child of divorce, struggling to please. I wondered if he had a life, either.

Tessa spun away from the barre in a series of spot spins that made me dizzy just watching. She staggered to a halt in front of her mother. 'What do you think about that? Good, huh?'

I hated seeing a little girl sweat.

Before her mother could answer, Alicia appeared, clapped her hands and said, 'C'mon little sugarplum fairies! Time for your exercises!'

Ten little figures scrambled to the barre, rested their left hands lightly upon it, lined up like sparrows on a telephone wire. 'Position one!' Alicia shouted as the music began. 'Plié. One, two, three, four, five, six, seven, eight.'

'That's so sad.'

Tessa's mother couldn't have been talking about the barre exercise. 'What's sad?' I asked.

'Tessa was going to dance a sugarplum fairy in *The Nutcracker* this year, but Annapolis Ballet Theater decided to team up with another studio. Idiots! Tessa was *so* disappointed.'

'Demi plié!' cried Alicia. 'One, two . . .'

Across the room, Tessa raised a graceful arm and bent her knees, stealing a moment to glance at her mother who nodded in approval.

'I was disappointed, too,' Tessa's mom continued. 'I even considered taking Tessa out of class, but in the end, I just couldn't do it. I've always been loyal to Jay and Kay.' She turned to me and beamed. 'But it's just as well, isn't it, because now there's nothing to conflict with preparing Tessa and Henry for *Tiny Ballroom*!'

'I guess not,' I said, disliking the woman intensely. I'd taken dancing lessons as a kid, too, but prancing around the Rec Center – step, together, step, kick – to the Beatles' 'Yellow Submarine' at one dollar a lesson was just plain fun. Nobody expected to turn me into Ginger Rogers. And when I said I'd rather swim, please, my parents just smiled and said, sure, no problem. Maybe if they'd cajoled and wheedled and bribed me a bit, I'd have been just as accomplished as Tessa at nine.

But without the fake tan and hair extensions.

'If you'll excuse me, now,' I said, 'I need to go powder my nose.'

It wasn't until I got into the dressing room, and locked the door of the toilet stall behind me, that I realized I never asked Tessa's mother her name.

But, since I never planned to talk to her again if I could help it, what did it matter?

Nine

Four days before Christmas, Ruth left a message on my cell, asking if I'd stop by J & K to critique the routine she and Hutch had been practicing for *Shall We Dance?* Paul was working late at the Academy, getting finals marked and end of semester grades turned in to the academic dean, so I thought, why not.

On the way, I braved the icy roads, stopped off at Graul's Market to buy a pound of coffee and a pint of half and half, so I got to J & K a little late, only to discover that Hutch had beaten both me and Ruth to the studio. 'How's it going, Hutch?' I asked, peeling off my hat, gloves and scarf as I entered the studio and the air enveloped me in a super-heated wave.

Hutch tapped his watch, as if it might be broken. 'Ruth's late, and she didn't call. With the icy roads and all, I'm a little worried.'

I shrugged out of my coat. 'She's probably delayed in traffic.' I hoped I sounded more reassuring than I felt. In point of fact, Ruth would be coming from downtown and using the same roads I had, and there had been absolutely no traffic problems for me. 'She'll be along.'

'I tried her cell phone,' Hutch said, 'but it goes straight to her voicemail.'

Now that was odd. Ruth never turned her cell phone off. By the worried look on Hutch's face, I realized he knew that, too. 'Maybe the battery died,' I suggested.

'Maybe.' But he didn't sound convinced.

'Are Jay and Kay here?'

'No. We're working with them tomorrow. Just Chance.'

'Let's sit down,' I suggested, casting about wildly for ways to distract the man. 'There's something I've been meaning to ask you.' We settled ourselves comfortably on one of the spectator benches, then I patted Hutch's knee and said, 'So, truth or consequences. Where are you taking Ruth on your honeymoon?'

Hutch brightened. 'I'm not sure if I'm supposed to tell.'

'Ruth's been a bit cagey, but she's got everything else organized within an inch of its life, so I figured the honeymoon was laid on, too.'

'I'll give you a hint, Hannah. It's warmer than Annapolis in the wintertime.'

'Surprise, surprise, surprise!'

'If you won't tell Ruth that I spilled the beans . . .'

I pantomimed locking my lips and throwing away the key.

'We're booked into a resort called Maya Tulum on the Yucatan peninsula. Alicia taught yoga there and recommends it highly. Alicia says it's perfect for us, a modern resort, but with New Age sensitivities. Eco tours, beach front cabanas, vegetarian cuisine, the whole mind-body-spirit sort of thing.

'Sounds very Ruth,' I said sincerely. Ruth would love it.

'It is.' Hutch hopped to his feet. 'So, where the hell is she?'

'Car trouble?' I offered, hopefully. Ruth drove a clunker, a battered green Ford circa 1990. 'I didn't see her Taurus in the lot.'

'Damn thing died. Not worth fixing. She's driving a rental until we can replace that old heap.'

'What kind of car is she renting, Hutch?'

'A Ford Focus.'

Suddenly I could hardly breathe. I could picture the car clearly. I'd just seen it outside, a red Focus, bright as lipstick against the snow bank that had been plowed up into piles all around the parking lot. 'Is it red?' I asked, praying that it wasn't.

'Yes. Why?'

'Oh my god! There's a red Focus in the lot. Come with me.'

Without taking time to grab our coats, Hutch and I flew

out the door. 'This way!' I yelled. We raced around the building and through the lot, slipping on patches of black ice where the day's run-off had refrozen on the tarmac. 'That's it, that's the car,' Hutch shouted, pointing wildly. By that time, I was close enough to the vehicle to see through the window on the passenger side. 'No one's inside.' I paused, breathing hard. 'Maybe it's someone else's car.' 'No. That's Ruth's. See that striped hat in the back window? That's hers.' Hutch swerved to avoid a pothole, tripped, arms pinwheeling to keep his balance. By some miracle, he managed not to fall.

I recognized the hat, too, so I pumped my legs harder, rounding the rear of the vehicle and arriving at the driver's side.

Ruth lay sprawled on the ice, face up, whimpering. At first, I thought my sister had slipped on the ice and fallen. Until I saw the blood.

I knelt on the cold ground beside her. 'Ruth! What happened?'

She simply moaned.

Hutch screeched to a halt behind me, his arms dangling helplessly at his sides. 'Ruth. Oh, god. You're hurt.'

'He stole my purse,' she sobbed. 'It had the cash receipts for the day in it. I couldn't let him . . . Ow!' she cried as I touched her leg.

'Screw the money, Ruth.' I looked up at Hutch. 'I think her leg is broken.'

Ruth sucked in her lips and rocked her head from side to side.

Hutch knelt beside me and squeezed my arm. He jerked his head in the direction of Ruth's leg, and I saw what he saw. A piece of metal – Glass? Bone? – poking through the fabric of Ruth's blood-soaked tights.

'Hutch is here,' I told my sister as her fiancé and I, via some form of telepathy, agreed to exchange places. Hutch lifted Ruth's head to his thigh and pillowed it there. 'You'll be fine, Ruth,' he soothed.

'The son of a bitch stole my money! Eleven hundred dollars!'

'It doesn't matter, Ruth. It's only money.'

While Hutch tried to calm Ruth down, I walked around to the other side of the car and dialed 9-1-1.

'9-1-1. What is your emergency?'

'There's been a mugging,' I told the operator. 'We need police and an ambulance.' I gave the woman our address, then went back to see about my sister.

'Hand me her scarf,' I told Hutch.

I was afraid to touch Ruth's wound, but I used her scarf as a makeshift tourniquet, wrapped it as tightly as I dared around her thigh and twisted it tight, hoping to stop the flow of blood that continued to ooze from her calf and on to the pavement. 'How did you break your leg,' I asked as I worked. 'Did you fall? Did he push you down?'

'He whacked me with a baseball bat.'

'Oh, love, why didn't you just let him have the stupid purse?' Hutch said desperately.

'No way that motherfucker was going to get my purse,' Ruth said.

'I suppose you told him that.'

'Uh huh.'

Hutch rolled his eyes. 'Why didn't you call me on your cell phone?'

'He smashed that, too.' Ruth raised an arm, then let it drop to the pavement. 'It's around here somewhere.'

'I see it,' I said. 'It's under the next car.'

And it was, if you could call a scattering of plastic shards, circuit boards, SIM cards and batteries a cell phone. 'The good news is, I think you'll be getting that iPhone you wanted for Christmas.'

In spite of everything, Ruth managed a weak smile. 'I'm cold,' she said after a few seconds.

'Don't worry. The ambulance is on the way,' I said, willing it to hurry.

Hutch had already pulled the flaps of Ruth's jacket together and buttoned them up to her neck, but he cradled her more closely to the warmth of his chest. She gazed into his face, and burst into tears. 'Oh, Hutch, I'm so sorry. We won't be able to audition for the TV show, will we?'

Hutch lowered his cheek to her cheek and stroked her wet and matted hair. 'Shhhhh. It doesn't matter, sweetheart. The only thing that matters to me is you.'

Ruth's face was white as the fresh snow that covered the snow banks behind her, and she started to sob, gasping uncontrollably. 'She's hyperventilating, Hutch,' I said as calmly as I could. 'She may be going into shock. Lower her head, and we'll need to keep her warm.'

'Shit. Why did we leave our coats inside?' Hutch raised up on one hip, eased a hand into his pocket and withdrew a fist full of car keys. 'There's a football blanket in the back seat of my Beemer.'

When I returned with the blanket, Hutch helped me wrap it tightly around my sister. She shuddered, air hissed raggedly in and out between her clenched teeth as we waited together for the welcoming wail of an approaching siren.

Ten

Feeling like fifth wheels, Hutch and I followed the ambulance in his car, running traffic lights willy-nilly until I expected the cop who was riding in the ambulance with Ruth to pop out the back doors, waving his ticket book.

Hutch made a right turn against the light on to West Street, then veered immediately left on Admiral Drive, following the old back road to the hospital. He took the left at Jennifer Road on two wheels, ran a red light at the firehouse, nearly knocked into a pedestrian in the crosswalk of the County Detention Center, then ran another red light before turning off on to Medical Drive.

'Drive around to the ER,' I ordered. 'You get out there, and I'll take the car into the parking garage.'

The ambulance was offloading Ruth on a stretcher when we pulled up under the 'Emergency' portico. An oxygen mask covered her nose and mouth, and an IV dripped clear fluid into a vein in her arm. Poor Ruth! I hurried around to the driver's door and gave Hutch a reassuring pat on the cheek as he climbed out of the driver's seat and hurried after the stretcher. 'Stay with her,' I called as I eased behind the wheel. 'I'll be back as soon as I can.'

It took forever, of course, to find a parking space. I scoured the garage, spiraling upward ever upward until I managed to squeeze Hutch's BMW 750 sedan into a space on the roof clearly designed for a compact. Once I'd wormed my way out of the narrow space between the BMW and the SUV next door, I punched the lock button on the keyless fob, and made a mad dash for the elevator, which took me down eight floors and spit me out into the main lobby. I turned right, straight-armed the swinging door, rushed past the visitors' desk – I knew my way around Anne Arundel

Medical Center so well I could draw a map from memory – and hustled down the long hallway that led to the ER waiting room. When I got there, Hutch was standing at the reception desk, filling out a form.

'They've taken her to X-ray,' he told me. 'The policeman is with her.'

When I next saw my sister, she was in a treatment cubicle, half-sitting/half-lying on a gurney, with a blue surgical dressing draped lightly over her leg. Someone had stuffed her clothing, including the torn and bloody tights, in a plastic bag and stuck it on a shelf underneath the gurney. There was no sign of the policeman.

'It wasn't bone,' Hutch informed me, relief written all over his face. I knew he was referring to the object we'd seen sticking out of Ruth's leg. 'It was a fragment of wood from the bat. They've cleaned out the wound, and stitched it up.'

'How many stitches?' asked Ruth, sounding competitive and more like her usual self.

'Only three,' her fiancé teased, 'so don't expect any sympathy from me.' Hutch turned to face me. 'But her tibia is definitely broken, Hannah. A clean break, thank goodness. They're going to start her on antibiotics, pump some fluids into her, and keep her overnight for observation. They'll set the bone in the morning.'

'Tibia,' I said, scrambling to remember the litany of bones I'd had to memorize for some long-ago zoology class at Oberlin College. 'That's the shin, isn't it?'

'That's correct.' A nurse wearing white pants and a colorful surgical top decorated with teddy bears stuck her head into the room. 'We'll be admitting you shortly, Mrs Gannon, so don't go anywhere, OK?'

Ruth smiled. 'As if.'

'The policeman told me to tell you he'll be right back,' the nurse said, and then she disappeared as mysteriously as she had arrived.

Thinking about the policeman, I asked, 'What were you able to tell him, Ruth?'

Ruth rested her head against the pillow and sighed. 'Not

much. He seemed to think that the guy followed me from the store, that he knew I had the receipts with me. But, I don't think so. The creep came out of the parking lot of the Rapture Church.'

'Did you hear anything? A getaway car starting up, for example, or a motorcycle?'

As tired as she was, Ruth still managed to follow my train of thought: the Harley-Davidson motorcycle dealership was next door to J & K. 'Harleys are popular with badass dudes in their 50s and 60s,' she said. 'This guy didn't look the type. Black, maybe sixteen or seventeen. I doubt he could afford a Kawasaki, let alone a Harley.'

'What'd he look like?'

My sister shrugged. 'Like any other African-American teenager on *America's Most Wanted*.' She held up an index finger. 'But when they find him, he'll have an ugly scratch on his neck.' She examined her fingernail carefully for a moment. 'Wait a minute! Can't they get some DNA from under this?'

'Maybe they'll take a scraping,' I suggested, 'but I doubt the police will place a high priority on DNA analysis for a simple robbery and assault. It'd be expensive, and even then it'd take months for the results to come back.' I sidled up to the gurney and patted her good leg. 'Not likely a petty crook will be in the CODIS database anyway.'

'What? No fancy machines, no flashing lights, no instantaneous test results like you see on TV?'

'No, ma'am.' The policeman had returned. 'No designer suits and two-hundred-dollar haircuts, either. But, we're sending a sketch artist over in the morning.'

'Thank you,' Ruth said, and closed her eyes.

In less than a minute, she was asleep. Leaving Hutch sitting by her side, holding her hand, I took the long walk down to the cafeteria – where the use of cell phones was allowed – to telephone Paul and let him know what the bloody blazes was going on.

Eleven

Two days before Christmas, sporting a festive, holly-green cast on her leg, Ruth went home. Hutch installed his bride-to-be in the first-floor guest room periodically used by his mother so Ruth wouldn't have to cope with the stairs.

Christmas came and went; a joyous time. Santa delivered the necklace I'd been hinting for, Ruth's iPhone, and Chloe found lavender leotards, a matching tutu, and a glittery 'amethyst' tiara under the tree. Santa'd got the message. The old elf was no fool.

As usual, 193 Prince George was Holiday Central with feasting and merriment practically 24/7. Thank goodness for large-screen TVs, Christmas DVDs, and microwave popcorn to keep everyone occupied between unwrapping presents and eating until they could only waddle.

When Hutch returned to the business of running a law firm, I volunteered for Ruth detail. I arrived mid-morning on the twenty-sixth to find Ruth stumping around on crutches, determined to drive herself to the Safeway.

'The hell you are!' I said. 'You can't even get down the front steps.'

'I can, too. On my butt. And it's my left leg, Hannah. I don't need it to drive.'

I put my own (very healthy) foot down, and drove Ruth to the grocery where she embraced her newfound freedom by speeding down the cereal aisle in an electric Mart Cart, terrifying the other shoppers. Backing up at the deli case to take another look at the potato salad – *beep, beep, beep*, like a heavy construction vehicle – she bumped into a pyramid of party crackers, and they all came tumbling down.

'Ooops, sorry.' But she didn't seem very – sorry, that is.

That night I stayed on at Ruth's to help with dinner, while Paul relaxed at Emily's. Frankly, I'd rather be watching *Ratatouille* with my husband and the grandchildren than hovering over a hot stove in my sister's kitchen, steaming plum puddings, even though it was my specialty, a secret recipe handed down from my grandmother and steamed in her tin pudding molds.

J & K Studio was closed between Christmas and New Years, so we were surprised when Jay showed up at Hutch's around eight in the company of a woman – not Kay – who I guessed to be in her early thirties. Her blonde hair was feathered attractively around her cheeks, falling in layers to her shoulders, a hip and modern do, but with a salute to the eighties.

Hutch invited them in.

We'd just sat down in the living room to eat dessert, so I asked, 'Coffee? Plum pudding?'

'If it's decaf,' Jay replied.

'A Diet Coke, if you have it,' the girl replied.

'This is Melanie Fosher,' Jay said, as he helped Melanie out of her coat and handed it to Hutch. 'A private student.'

'Pleased to meet you,' Melanie said, in an accent that was hard to place. Boston?

I raised a finger – hold that thought – and went out to the kitchen to fetch their drinks. As I fussed with the glassware, I wondered where I'd met the girl before – she looked vaguely familiar – but what the heck was she was doing in my sister's living room with Jay Giannotti?

When I returned to our guests, mug in one hand and a highball glass in another, everyone was seated comfortably (although Jay had taken my chair) and Jay was saying, 'I have a proposition for you.'

Melanie, I noticed, was watching her teacher closely, her bright blue eyes intent.

Hutch raised a suspicious, lawyerly eyebrow. 'Yes?' he said in a tone that was usually reserved for the big 'but' that came after 'Congratulations! You are the winner of a new laptop computer!'

'It concerns the *Shall We Dance?* auditions.'

'That,' Hutch said, acknowledging Ruth's predicament, 'is ancient history.'

Jay raised a hand. 'Hear me out.'

'I'm listening.'

'Melanie, here, is one of my best dancers. She's been studying with me privately for two years.'

I'd assumed Melanie was single, but then I noticed a platinum wedding band and a diamond the size of a plump raisin on the ring finger of her left hand.

As I watched, Jay picked up that hand, and gave it a gentle squeeze. 'Her husband is her usual partner, but he's in the army, and his unit's been sent to Iraq.'

At the mention of Iraq my sister stiffened. She hated the war, but in contrast to her usual outbursts, she knew to behave around an army wife with a husband in Iraq.

'I'm so sorry,' Ruth interjected. 'Will he be there long?'

'Thirteen months,' Jay replied, before poor Melanie could get a word in edgewise.

'You must be terribly worried,' I said to Melanie as I handed her a coaster so her glass wouldn't leave a water ring on Hutch's expensive, highly-polished end table.

Melanie set the coaster on the table, and centered her glass on it. 'We thought we were pretty safe being stationed at Fort Meade, but then Don was cross-leveled.'

I thought I'd misheard. 'Cross what?'

'Leveled. When there's a shortfall of a specific skill in another unit, the army can transfer you just about anywhere. Don's in military intelligence,' she explained. 'He must have some super-secret skill that they're dying to have.'

'Is he fluent in Farsi?' asked Hutch.

Melanie grinned, and we suspected Hutch had scored a bull's eye. 'If I told you, I'd have to kill you, then, wouldn't I?'

'Well, anyway,' Jay said, in a transparent attempt to steer the conversation back to the topic with which he'd begun. 'With Ruth incapacitated – how are you feeling, by the way, Ruth?'

The man couldn't have cared all that much about the

state of Ruth's health, because he paused only a fraction of a second before barreling on. 'Melanie is a superb dancer, Hutch, and you're a great lead. I'm suggesting you partner Melanie for the *Shall We Dance?* auditions.'

I nearly choked on my coffee.

Ruth sucked in air.

Hutch rose from the sofa and went over to sit on the arm of Ruth's chair. She looked as if she'd been tasered, a smile – a grimace, rather – frozen on her face.

Melanie leaned forward, resting her hands on her knees. 'I certainly understand your reluctance to partner with a complete stranger, Hutch, but I'm in the same position as you are. Don and I were going to audition for the show and then, boom, he's shipped off to Iraq.' Melanie looked as disappointed as if she'd been dumped by the star quarterback at the senior prom.

'The show's very popular,' Hutch argued. 'I'm sure it'll be cluttering up the airways for several seasons to come. Ruth and I can put off auditioning to another year.'

Ruth's expression suddenly softened. She shifted in her chair and rose (figuratively speaking) to the occasion. She lifted her chin and looked into Hutch's eyes. 'I don't mind, really, I don't. Next year we'll be married and have other concerns.' She turned back to Melanie. 'Thank you, this means a lot to him.'

'And to me, too, Ruth.'

Jay rubbed his hands together rapidly. 'Excellent!'

'Hutch and I have been working on this routine,' Ruth began, but Jay raised a hand and cut her off.

'Are you free next Friday?'

Everyone nodded, including Ruth. I knew my sister, and could translate that lower lip quiver. She'd shown courage by agreeing to Jay's plan, but she wasn't going to sit on the sidelines like a wallflower. Ruth would attend every rehearsal, cheering her fiancé on, and since I was her *de facto* chauffeur, it appeared that I wouldn't miss a single rehearsal either.

'Well, OK, then.' Jay exhaled noisily, as if he'd been holding his breath, waiting for the go-ahead. 'Perhaps I can have some of that plum pudding now?'

Melanie smiled – apparently the arrangement suited her, too – but as I rose to get the cake, she surprised me by getting up from her chair. 'Here, let me help. I'd also like some pudding, if you don't mind.'

Melanie followed me down the hall. While I uncovered the steamer to remove a fresh hot pudding, she wandered around the kitchen, touching Hutch's state-of-the-art appliances with reverence and awe. 'This under the counter wine cooler is amazing!'

I had to agree. My wine cooler was a quick twenty minutes in the ice cube bin of my refrigerator's freezer compartment, and Lord help me if I forgot and left the bottle in there to freeze, as often happened by bottle three, or maybe four.

When Melanie tilted her head for a closer look at Hutch's 'cellar', her hair shifted, and I noticed that she wore one of those newfangled ear bud phones. If I had an ear bud phone, I would have taken it off to go visiting, but perhaps she was expecting a call from her husband in Iraq. IEDs to avoid, suicide bombers to steer clear of; who knew when a call would come in.

'The forks are in the drawer next to the stove,' I told her as I scrabbled in the cupboard, reaching way back for the last of the hand-painted plates that matched the ones I'd used earlier. Call me a perfectionist.

'Please turn around,' Melanie said. 'I can't see what you're saying.'

I had the plates in hand by then, and nearly dropped them. I turned to face her. 'You're deaf?'

'As a post,' Melanie said. 'I lost my hearing to meningitis when I was five. That's why I talk funny.'

'I never would have guessed,' I laughed. 'I thought you were from Boston.'

'Cleveland, actually. They talk funny there, too.'

I realized then that what I had taken for a cell phone hooked around her ear, was actually an industrial-strength hearing aide. And she wore two of them.

While Melanie held the plates, I served up generous spoonfuls of the cake-like pudding, and topped each with a dollop of hard sauce. While the hard sauce melted and drizzled deliciously down the pudding mounds, I asked, 'Do you sign, too?'

'I know how,' Melanie told me, 'but I don't use sign language very often since I lip-read so well.'

'I studied ASL at AACC,' I signed, finger-spelling the letters clumsily. It'd been several years since I'd taken the class, and I was a little rusty.

'Good to know,' she signed back.

'But, how . . .?' I began, then paused, searching for the right way to ask what might be an embarrassing question.

Melanie interrupted me. 'How do I dance if I can't hear the music?'

'Exactly. Do you feel vibrations through the floor or something?'

'I wish. No, you're moving around too much for that.' She pointed to one of the plates. 'Forks?'

'Oh, sorry. I intended to tell you. They're in the drawer by the stove.'

Melanie picked out a couple of salad forks and arranged one on the side of each dessert plate. 'My hearing aides help with the bass notes,' she continued, 'and I've been told that I have a good inner sense of timing.' She smiled. 'But do you want to know the real secret?'

I nodded.

'A good partner. All I have to do is follow his lead.'

'Well, you've certainly got that in Hutch.'

Melanie and I returned to the living room with the dessert, interrupting Jay in mid-sentence. From the startled looks on Ruth and Hutch's faces, I suspected Jay had taken our absence in the kitchen as an opportunity to tell them about Melanie's 'handicap'.

Melanie served Jay his pudding with a smile, then settled down in her chair to sample her own. 'Delicious' she said after a moment.

'Ditto,' said Jay. Once he'd swallowed, he turned his back on Melanie (deliberately, I was sure), waved his fork in the air and continued. 'As I was saying, handicapped contestants have a leg-up with the producers, if you know what I mean. Remember Heather Mills on *Dancing with the Stars*?'

Hutch nodded.

'She went a long way on that artificial leg. Big sympathy vote from the fans.' He took another bite of pudding. 'And *So You Think You Can Dance* had a gal with an artificial arm, and a pint-sized dancer with rheumatoid arthritis or spina bifida or something. Judges love 'em. Melanie's deafness could be a real asset. Trust me on that.'

I was embarrassed for Melanie, who kept glancing in Jay's direction, clearly suspecting that he was talking about her.

I was about to say something, when Jay turned to look at us. His face could have been flushed with embarrassment, I suppose, but it was hard to tell what might be going on under all that tan. 'Sorry, Melanie,' Jay said, tap dancing as fast as he could. 'You're so normal in every other way, I keep forgetting you can't hear.'

Melanie managed a sugary smile. 'If that's a compliment, Jay, I'll accept it.'

When Jay turned his attention back to Hutch, Melanie flapped a hand to get my attention, then began signing. 'A-S-S-H-O . . .'

If anyone wondered why the two of us began laughing hysterically, they never asked.

Twelve

The following Wednesday, while I was sorting laundry, Eva called. 'I got your Christmas card today, and the delightful surprise that was inside.'

I'd sent my friend a gift certificate for Spa Paradiso. 'I thought you could use some pampering, Eva.'

'That was very thoughtful and generous.'

'Special deal,' I chuckled. 'Seems I know the owners.' I folded a washcloth and set it on top of a stack of towels. 'Are you going to cash it in any time soon?'

'I'd love it if you'd go with me, Hannah. Any chance of that?'

I frowned at the laundry basket, a sink full of dirty dishes, two loaves of bread rising in their pans on the countertop and said, 'How about tomorrow?'

Eva and I arranged to meet at the reception desk of the spa at nine, but I pulled into the parking lot a bit late. I had taken my time getting there, enjoying the drive through Eastport and out Bay Ridge as the road narrowed, snaked through woods, topped a hill, until there it was, spread out before me in all its ice-blue winter beauty – the Chesapeake Bay. Built on the site of a former restaurant, Spa Paradiso had inherited its landscaping and spectacular view, including a generous front lawn sloping gently down to end at a sandy beach gently lapped by the water. I smiled as I drove through the spa gates, up a short drive and pulled into one of the two parking spaces reserved for 'Family'.

Eva was waiting, dressed for the occasion in a gray U.S.N.A. tracksuit, her shaggy hair pulled back into a ponytail. She'd been reading one of the wellness brochures the staff had tucked into acrylic holders arranged along the countertop.

'Did you bring a bathing suit?' I asked.

Eva returned the brochure to its holder, then tugged up on the hem of her top, revealing an expanse of bright red Lycra.

'That will do nicely,' I said.

We signed in together, consulted briefly with Heather, our spa guide, and reached an easy agreement on the plan of the day: hot tub, full body massage, lunch by the pool, and haircuts, in that order. Heather escorted us to the luxurious dressing room – a far cry from the one used by the ladies at J & K – where we stripped off our clothes, hung them in a locker, and wrapped ourselves in the plush pink spa robes.

'Ready?' I asked Eva, who was wandering trance-like around the dressing room, running her fingertips over the lockers (walnut), the countertops (polished marble), and poking her head into the multi-jet shower stalls where state-of-the-art dispensers held body wash (lavender), shampoo (aloe and honey), and conditioner (peach). 'Remind me to look out for bees after this,' Eva said.

'It is wonderful, isn't it? Dante hired the same architect who designed the spa at Pinehurst, North Carolina and a number of other fancy spas.'

Eva followed me into the hot-tub room where we padded in our terry cloth spa slippers over to the drinks bar which was kept stocked with a constant supply of fruit juice, herbal teas, and water. I brewed myself a cup of lemon-ginger tea, but noticed that Eva thumbed lackadaisically through the tea bag selection. Perhaps she wasn't in the mood for tea. 'When Heather comes to check on us in a couple of minutes, you can order a fruit smoothie, if you prefer.'

'Strawberry?' she asked.

'Oh, yeah,' I said, remembering Dante's decadent recipe for smoothies.

A few short minutes later, tea and smoothie in hand, Eva and I eased into the hot tub, submerging ourselves gradually as our bodies adjusted to the heat. When we were both neck-deep, Eva closed her eyes and leaned her head back against the rubber head support that Heather had positioned for each of us along the tiled edge of the tub. 'Ah! Jesus, take me now, because I have died and gone to heaven.' She sucked a bit of smoothie through a straw. 'This may be the last moment of peace I have the rest of my life.'

Until that point, I'd been blissed out, with only my head and the hand holding my tea cup out of the water. My eyes flew open and I stared at Eva. 'What do you mean?'

Eva sighed. 'I wanted to get comfortable before I told you.'

'Told me what?'

'Jeremy knows I'm no longer in Utah.'

'Shit.'

'I would have said hell's bells.'

'Same difference. How did he find out?'

Eva closed her eyes and sank until the water bubbled over her shoulders. 'Some helpful parishioner, I imagine. I've run into a few people from St Cat's at the grocery store.' She took another sip of smoothie. 'But I haven't actually laid eyes on the guy.'

'How do you know he's found you?'

'Two weeks ago the van from Flowers by James pulled up to the St Anne's Parish office and dropped off a dozen long-stemmed roses.'

'From Jeremy?'

'Uh huh. The card said: To Eva. You are the Rose of Sharon and the lily of MY valley.' She groaned. 'Lord help me I can remember every word.'

Holding my cup aloft, I slid down until my head was completely under water, my cry of *argh*! making bubbles in the water. When I came up for air, Eva was giggling just a bit hysterically, making me wonder what they'd put into her smoothie. I said, 'So, did you keep the flowers?'

'I did not. I took them over when I visited Bessie Brelsford at Manresa,' she said, naming one of Annapolis's high-end assisted living facilities. Manresa, a former Jesuit retreat, boasted a panoramic view of the Severn River from the Naval Academy all the way down to where the river spilled into the Chesapeake Bay.

'Has the creep shown up to see how you liked the flowers?'

'No, thank goodness. I haven't seen him at all, so I was counting my blessings, until yesterday.'

'What happened yesterday?'

'The UPS man paid a visit.' Eva sipped her smoothie and didn't say anything for what seemed like five minutes, but was probably only five seconds. The silence drove me nuts.

'Eva! Don't torture me!'

'Jeremy'd sent a box of See's chocolates. Dark chocolate-covered caramels, to be precise. This time the card said: Dear Eva, Your words are sweeter than honey to my mouth.'

'Who'd you give the candy to?'

'Are you kidding? I love See's chocolates. I ate them all, practically in one sitting, while feeling sorry for myself and watching a *Monk* marathon on USA.' She set her empty tumbler on the tiled floor next to the tub. 'I've been catching up with Hollywood since I didn't have TV in Utah,' she said by way of explanation.

That wasn't the explanation I was looking for. 'Have you talked to Hutch about this?' I asked, growing concerned.

Eva nodded. 'Sort of. I called his office and left a message. But if Jeremy isn't actually harassing me, I'm not sure there's anything Hutch or the police or anybody can do.' She sighed, hoisted herself out of the water with both arms, and perched on the side of the tub, legs dangling. She retrieved her towel and started wiping her forehead. 'I'll have to face Jeremy eventually when I go back to St Cat's. There he'll be, sitting out in the congregation and gazing at me as if I were Mother Theresa.'

'Jeremy or no Jeremy, I can't wait for you to come back,' I said. 'St Cat's has really missed you. The interim, Rory Chase, is a good man – and quite a fine preacher, by the way – but it's just not the same without you.'

'You can't exactly forbid someone from coming to church, can you?' Eva mused, obviously referring to Jeremy Dunstan and not the good Reverend Chase.

Not like keeping pedophiles away from schools. The thought leaped into my head, but I kept it to myself. Eva had troubles enough without being reminded of her late husband.

Eva slipped the rubber band off her ponytail, shook her

head and used her fingers to fluff out her hair. 'In anticipation of going back to St Cat's in two months' time, I'm counting on Wally to give me that professional cut you were talking about.'

'Have you decided whether to color it?'

'No, I find I'm rather liking the gray. I'm planning to ask Wally to cut off everything that's *not* gray, so my head doesn't look like a piece of candy corn.'

She noticed me staring at her hair: dark brown at the ends, reddish brown in the middle, with about three inches of white where it emerged from her scalp. 'Don't ask how it got that way,' Eva said with a grin. 'It's what happens when you do-it-yourself with products well past their sell-by date, bought over the counter at a combination pharmacy and farm supply store in rural Utah.

'It'll be kind of short, Eva.'

'I don't care if it is short. Although, that could set the man off.'

'Who? Wally?'

'No, Jeremy Dunstan. I can hear him now: "But if a woman have long hair, it is a glory to her." First Corinthians, chapter eleven, verse fifteen.' She snorted. 'Right now it's closer to something from the Song of Solomon: "Thy hair is as a flock of goats."' She gathered the offending tresses together at the nape of her neck, wrapped the rubber band haphazardly around it, then rejoined me in the spa.

'If Hutch or one of his associates doesn't call you back by tomorrow, you let me know. Promise? He won't intentionally ignore you, but he's had a lot on his mind lately. Have you heard what he's up to?'

'He's an attorney. That can cover a lot of territory. Are you going to make me guess?'

'No, sorry. Here's the thing: Hutch has been encouraged by his dance instructor to audition for a reality show on television, something called *Shall We Dance?* Have you heard of it?'

She raised a hand, dripping water. 'No TV, remember?'

'It's like *American Idol* meets *So You Think You Can Dance.*'

'Hannah, you might as well be speaking Serbo-Croatian. Explain, please.'

'Couples audition to be chosen as one of twelve pairs who compete for the title of best dancers. The winners each get $10,000, a Chrysler Crossfire Roadster, and the use of an apartment in New York City for a year.'

Eva sat up straight, adjusted the headrest. 'Sounds wonderful, but when are the auditions, and will Ruth's leg be healed in time?'

'Alas, no. With Ruth out of commission, Hutch has agreed to enter the try-outs with another one of Jay's students, a young dancer named Melanie.'

'And Ruth's OK with that?'

'She seems to be.'

Eva closed her eyes, apparently mulling that over. After a few minutes had ticked away, she spoke. 'What's Hutch going to do with an apartment in New York City? Commute to Annapolis?'

'I guess he'll cross that bridge when he comes to it,' I said. Just like everyone else in our family, though, I was already mentally planning museum excursions and theater weekends to New York City.

Like Momma always said, It pays to plan ahead.

Thirteen

'I've been thinking,' Ruth announced from the depths of her recliner when I showed up the following day to help her survive yet another day on crutches.

'Call the *New York Times*!' I quipped.

'Hannah, be serious, for once.'

I put down the clothes hamper I'd been in the process of lugging to the basement and gave Ruth my full attention. 'OK, I'm listening.'

'I don't think the attack on me was just a simple mugging.'

'You don't? Is that what the police told you?'

'No. They're still working on the theory that the punk followed me from Mother Earth, thinking I'd be taking the receipts to the BB&T night deposit like I normally do. When I went straight to J & K, they believe he followed me and waited until I got out of the car before he pounced.'

The police's theory sounded plausible to me. 'What makes you think the police are wrong?'

Ruth adjusted a knitted afghan over her knees. 'Remember what Tanya Harding did to Nancy Kerrigan?'

'Vaguely. Wasn't Harding the Olympic ice skater who hired a hit man to kneecap her rival?'

'Uh huh. Then there was that Texas cheerleader-murdering mom, Wanda somebody-or-other, who asked her brother-in-law to hire a hit man to murder the mother of her daughter's cheerleading rival.'

'Ruth, surely you're not suggesting . . .'

'That's exactly what I'm suggesting, Hannah. Somebody didn't want me to audition for *Shall We Dance?* and that someone made damn certain of it.'

My sister had always been spacey in a superannuated

flower child sort of way, but this cockamamie idea was a bit far out, even for her. Right-wing nuts went in for conspiracy theories, not citizens of the Woodstock Nation. Or so I always thought.

'Since when did you start believing in conspiracy theories, Ruth? The next thing I know, you'll be telling me that NASA faked the moon landing, Bill Gates designed Wingding fonts to deliver subversive messages, and that Paul McCartney is really dead.'

Ruth flapped a hand. 'Hear me out, Hannah. Jay may think I'm stupid, but I can see right through that smarmy veneer. He never thought I was a good dancer. *Never*. You know what he had us doing, Hutch and me?'

I shook my head.

'It's called a showcase move. You teach a beginner – that would be me – some simple steps, and then the expert – that would be Hutch – dances fancy all around me.'

If that was a problem, I simply wasn't getting it. 'So, what's wrong with that?'

'Nothing, *per se*. But did you notice how quick Jay was to cut me off last night when I started to tell Melanie about our routine.'

'Sorry, I didn't.'

'Well, he did, and that's because it's a shit routine, Hannah. It's not going to impress anyone except my nearest and dearest – that would be you. It's certainly not going to impress any judges!'

'Ruth . . .'

'So when Melanie suddenly became *free* . . .' Ruth's voice trailed off.

Before she could launch another sentence, I made a time-out sign with my hands. 'Whoa! You're going way too fast for me.'

'Think about it, Hannah. Jay's been teaching Don and Melanie Fosher for two years, and they're really, really good. He knows that the Foshers had a good chance of acing the auditions, right?'

I had to agree with that.

'Hutch and me . . . well, I don't know what he was

thinking about us. Maybe Jay thought I could be brought up to speed, and then – ta-dah – he'd have *two* couples in the show . . .'

Ruth swung her legs from the footrest to the floor and reached for her crutches which were propped against a folding tray table. 'I need a cup of coffee. You?'

I stepped forward. 'I'll get it.'

Ruth waved me aside with the tip of a crutch. 'No, my butt will go to sleep if I sit in that chair a minute longer.' She turned and clumped her way into the kitchen. Since the laundry room was on the way, I picked up the basket and followed close behind.

When Ruth got to the coffee pot, she turned to face me, resting the aforementioned butt against a kitchen cabinet. 'With Don suddenly gone, Melanie's out of the running, and it's just Hutch and old Twinkle Toes here.' Ruth used her crutch to tap lightly on her cast.

'So, if I hear you right, you're suggesting Jay hired somebody to make sure you'd be out of the competition so Melanie could partner with Hutch?'

Ruth sucked in her lower lip thoughtfully. 'Or, maybe *Melanie* hired somebody to do the deed, and then talked Jay into teaming her up with Hutch.'

'Oh, for heaven's sake!' I'd just met Melanie, but we'd bonded instantly. If she was the type to put out a contract on somebody, well, move over Elizabeth, I'm the Queen of England.

Ruth's eyes narrowed. 'You saw how buddy-buddy Jay and Melanie were last night.'

I had to admit that I had, but I'd thought the relationship more of a proud teacher/talented protégé kind of thing. 'Ruth, all you had to do was say no when Jay asked Hutch if he'd partner with Melanie. Hutch would have bowed out in an instant.'

A fat tear ran down my sister's cheek. 'I couldn't do that to him, Hannah. You should have seen him after everyone left last night. Flying high as a kite, up until the wee hours researching dance costumes on the Internet.'

'Oh, so what's he wearing?' I asked, welcoming the opportunity to steer the conversation in a safer direction.

'They're doing a tango, so he's been looking at Latin pants with gold stripes, and one of those shirts that's slashed to the waist.' She grinned. 'He's tentatively picked out a velvet devoré animal print.' She fanned her face rapidly with her hand. 'It's going to be hot, Hannah. I won't be able to keep my hands off the man.' She tapped her crutch on the floor, emphasizing every word. 'And little Miss Marlee Matlin better keep her hands off him, too.'

'Hard to do that when you're tangoing with somebody,' I said reasonably. 'What's Melanie wearing, then?'

Ruth shrugged. 'Dunno. They'll be meeting with Jay about it on Friday when they start working on the choreography.'

Ruth finally remembered what she'd come to the kitchen for. She located two clean mugs in the dishwasher, and poured us each a cup of . . . sludge. If Hutch had made the coffee, as I suspected he had, the pot had to have been sitting on the warming plate for at least three hours.

She took a sip of coffee, grimaced. 'So, I take it you don't think much of my theory.'

'Look, Sis, what I think isn't important. Have you shared your theory with the police?'

'They'll just think I'm crazy.'

'Think about what you've just said.'

'I know, I know, but I just can't shake the feeling, Hannah. I swear, when the police catch that little creep and shake him down, when it all comes out in the wash, they'll find that somebody *did* hire the guy to do this to me.'

'And speaking of wash,' I said, hoisting the laundry basket, 'I'd better get this load into the washing machine, or your live-in lover is going to appear in court tomorrow with a ring around the collar.'

Fourteen

'Thanks for taking charge of Chloe, Mom.' Emily had turned my granddaughter over to me at J & K for her ballet lesson with every intention of turning around and heading right back out the door. 'I'm simply frazzled. Except for Christmas itself, I haven't had a single day without a whole raft of rug rats in the nursery. I swear to God, their mothers were checking in for massages, dropping off their kids, and nipping out the back door to go do their Christmas shopping.'

'When did you get to be such a cynic, my dear? They probably *need* the massages after fighting tooth-and-nail for parking spaces, then lugging all those packages around the mall.'

'Ahh! Don't I know it. It's gotten so I avoid the mall altogether between Thanksgiving and New Years. I did all my shopping on Maryland Avenue and Main Street this year, which, being the great detective that you are, you probably deduced since I picked up those earrings you had Jean set aside for you at Aurora Gallery.' She grinned. 'Next year, I think I'll shop over in Chestertown or Easton,' she said, naming two delightful small towns on Maryland's still largely unspoiled eastern shore.

'The only thing I wanted that I didn't get this year you can't exactly ask Santa to pop into his sack and haul down the chimney,' she continued.

'Oh? What's that?'

'A full-time nanny.'

'Seriously?'

'Or maybe an *au pair*. The spa's doing really well, Mother. So well, in fact, that we may be able to pay off our investors next year.' She rolled her eyes theatrically. 'Honestly, it will be a huge relief to get that obnoxiously tweedy Mrs Strother off our backs.'

'Ooooh,' I said. 'Does that mean your father and I will be rich beyond our wildest dreams?' Paul and I had invested in Spa Paradiso, too. Five percent. Enough to finance a space the size of your average bathroom.

Emily grinned. 'Of course.' She wrapped her scarf around her neck, and took another step toward the door. 'I love managing Puddle Ducks, but Dante wants me to be involved in the day-to-day operations of the business, too. He's got me interviewing candidates for office manager, and we need a secretary.'

'I know what that's like,' I chuckled, recalling all the misspellings and unintentional howlers in the résumés I'd reviewed for my son-in-law before the spa opened last year: 'I was the manger of $2,000,000 in pubic funds.'

I'd been wrapped up in résumés the day Timmy was kidnapped.

Don't go there, Hannah, I was warning myself, when Chloe bounced out of the dressing room, reminding me that all my grandchildren were home, happy and healthy.

I bent down and kissed the top of Chloe's golden head. 'So, how's my little sugarplum fairy?'

Chloe pulled away, more important things on her mind. She tugged on her mother's coat sleeve. 'Can I have a pair of toe shoes, Mommy?'

'Toe shoes?' Emily knelt down so she could converse with her daughter eye to eye. 'You have to be at least ten years old for toe shoes, Chloe.'

Chloe's lower lip curled out. 'Tessa got toe shoes for Christmas.'

'If Tessa jumped off a cliff, would you jump off a cliff, too?' Emily smiled and patted her daughter's cheek. 'We'll talk about it later. Now, run along to the barre, sweetie, and after your lesson, maybe grandmother will take you to KFC.' Emily sent a please-don't-make-a-liar-out-of-me glance in my direction.

'Absolutely,' I said, thinking I could pick up a family

bucket and save myself from having to cook dinner. Never mind about the cholesterol.

'Yay! Chicken wings!' Chloe cheered, toe shoes apparently forgotten, as she skipped over to join her classmates at the barre.

'I swear, Mom, I could just kill Shirley!' Emily said when Chloe was out of earshot.

'Shirley? Who's Shirley?'

'Shirley Douglas. Tessa's mother. She's a B-I-T-C-H on wheels. Tessa is only a year older than Chloe, but to hear her mother talk, you'd think Tessa's been dancing *en pointe* since she emerged, red-faced and squalling, from the womb. Shirley's always complaining and asking special favors for her little darlin'.' Emily gestured toward the wall of neatly labeled plastic bins that held the studio's extensive collection of show costumes and dance accessories such as feathers, fans and boas. 'Nothing's ever good enough for that woman. You think Tessa could wear one of the studio's cowgirl costumes? No way. Shirley had one specially made. When they put on the *Annie Get Your Gun* review last year, it looked like –' Emily put both hands to her mouth, like a megaphone – 'J & K Studios present Annie Oakley and her little dancing hayseeds.'

'It wasn't that bad,' I said, having actually seen the show.

Emily huffed. 'I know for a fact that Kay can't stand Shirley, so I don't know why they put up with her. It's not like there aren't other dance studios in Annapolis.'

'What about Tessa's dad?'

'Link?' Emily snorted. 'He's a wuss. Yes, Shirley, no Shirley, now may I kiss your butt, Shirley. Did you know she hired a specialist to design a dance studio right in their garage?'

'So I heard.'

Emily's face softened. 'I suppose Link's an OK guy. Just can't imagine what he sees in Shirley. Then again, he's a lobbyist in DC, so he probably doesn't spend enough time at home to get tired of her.'

'I'm trying to remember if I've met him.'

'Probably. Five foot nine or ten, impeccably tailored suits, beer gut, receding hairline? He shows up for all Tessa's recitals, grinning and clapping like all the other proud papas.'

I had to smile. Emily's description fit just about every lobbyist I'd ever met on Capitol Hill. But I sympathized with the guy. The commute – one hour each way during the lightest of traffic – could be a killer. The night I got stuck in a snowstorm and ended up sleeping on a sofa at a Holiday Inn in Bowie, stranded there with a bunch of truckers, had been a turning point for me. I had just about decided to quit, when my RIF notice came, taking the decision out of my hands.

Emily brushed her lips against my cheek. 'Bye, Mom. And thanks!'

'Not a problem. Chloe'll have dinner with us? I promise to have her home by bedtime.'

Emily waggled a finger. 'No videos, now!'

I held up three fingers. 'Girl Scout's honor.'

But my other hand stayed behind my back, fingers crossed. I still hadn't found time to see *Ratatouille*, after all.

Waiting for Chloe's ballet lesson to finish was an exercise in How Many Ways Can Hannah Avoid Talking to Shirley. I went to the restroom, spent a long time washing my hands, combed my hair, checked my teeth for signs that the Crest Whitestrips I'd been using were working – brighter teeth in five days! – but it'd only been three, so there wasn't much to see.

I'd run out of things one normally does in a restroom, and was considering fashioning carnations out of Kleenex tissues like I did in junior high, when Laurie drifted in, wearing her usual white and black practice outfit, but carrying a garment on a hanger in a long plastic bag. Suddenly, all I wanted to do was talk to Laurie about her clothes.

'That looks beautiful,' I said following Laurie into the dressing room side of the dual purpose area.

Laurie hung the gown on a hook on the wall, carefully spreading out the bottom of the bag where it trailed along the floor. 'Wait 'til you *see*,' she gushed.

I watched while Laurie stripped to her underwear – pink, lace-waist hipsters and a matching push-up bra. Under my sweater and jeans I wore Lollipop cotton briefs and a sports bra from Sears. I was glad I didn't have to change in front of Laurie. Fashion-wise, it'd be embarrassing.

Laurie unzipped the bag and withdrew a ball gown, a frothy long-sleeved, high-necked peaches and cream confection slathered with Swarovski crystal beads. She stepped into it and raised an arm, 'Zip please.' After I obliged, she smoothed out the fabric, swaying from side to side while checking her reflection in the mirror.

'That's gorgeous,' I said, admiring her reflection in the mirror, too, twinkling like ten thousand tiny stars. 'Absolutely stunning.'

She turned around. 'And check out the back.'

'What back?' I asked, laughing. Except for four narrow bands that formed a tentative connection between the neckband and each side of the dress, there was no back. The gown plunged nearly to her, um, tan line.

'May I?' I reached out to touch the fabric. First I lifted a sleeve, then a bit of the voluminous skirt. 'How do you dance in this?' I asked, goggle-eyed. 'It weighs a ton!'

'You get used to it,' she said. 'You should have seen the gown I wore last year for the Yuletide Ball Championships in Washington, DC Fire-engine red, but it weighed ten pounds. I felt like I was dragging a small child around the dance floor with me.' She beamed. 'Tom and I got firsts in tango and rumba, though, so who's complaining?'

I watched while Laurie carefully stepped out of the gown, returned it to its protective covering and lovingly zipped the bag shut. When she finished, she waggled her fingers at me. 'I'm trying out a new color. What do you think? She fanned her fingers and held them a little closer to my face. 'This is called My Chihuahua Bites!'

'Get out!'

'No, seriously. OPI has the *craziest* names for their nail colors. I thought about Los Cabos Coral, but that was too match-y, if you know what I mean.'

I was familiar with OPI colors. I'd been painting my toes

with Twenty Candles on My Cake for a couple of years, although the last time I got a pedicure, I considered a red called I'm Not Really a Waitress simply because the name intrigued me. 'Well, whatever it's called, I think it's perfect with the gown.'

'Thanks.' Laurie's cheeks turned the same peachy shade as her gown. 'Tom thinks so, too.'

Laurie pulled a tube of lipstick out of her handbag. 'Revlon Moondrops, Peach Silk,' she announced, then leaned close to the mirror and began repairing her lips. She mashed her lips together, checked the results, and said, 'The dress I had specially made. Cost the earth! This –' she waved the tube and grinned – 'I buy at the grocery store!'

Christmas had passed, so I wondered if the Yuletide Ball had, too. 'Yuletide Ball, you said? Did you and Tom compete again this year?'

'Yuletide's not until December 28th, but we're not doing it this year. Decided to wait until the Sweetheart International Ballroom Competition in February when we'll really be prepared. We're competing international standard advanced.' When I looked puzzled, she went on to explain, 'That's the gold syllabus.'

I knew from hanging around J & K for more than a month that ballroom dancing competitions had a series of experience levels – bronze, silver, and gold – each with its own syllabus. When a couple got to the pre-championship level, there was no syllabus; presumably they just danced to their own razzle-dazzle choreography until their feet dropped off. If they did well at the Sweetheart Ball, taking away firsts in gold, Tom and Laurie would be advancing to the pre-championship level the next time they competed.

'Which dances?' I asked, knowing that there would be a separate charge to compete in each heat, so some couples decided to pick and choose.

'All of them – waltz, foxtrot, tango, quickstep and Viennese. Tom and I are going for broke.' Laurie chortled in a very unladylike way. 'Shit, Hannah, by the time it's all said and done, I'll bet we'll have dropped five grand.'

'Five thousand dollars for a single dance competition?'

I couldn't believe it. Paul and I'd spent less than that on a ten-day cruise to the western Caribbean. In a stateroom. With a balcony.

Laurie ticked them off on her fingers. 'Costumes, shoes . . .' She stuck out a foot on which she wore a bright red, vampy T-strap. 'These babies cost $175! Jewelry, photographs, video taping. It never ends. And you have to pay for it all upfront.'

'Golly.'

Laurie raised both hands, palm out. 'Oh, let me show you something!' She scrabbled around in her purse, and after a few seconds came up with a small plastic box. Inside the box, each nestled in its own semicircular slot, were false eyelashes. But not your ordinary, run-of-the-mill false eyelashes. Where these lush, fringy lashes attached to your eyelids there marched a single row of peach-colored rhinestones.

'Just what I need for the office,' I said, examining the lashes up closely.

'Exactly!' Laurie hooted. She tucked the box back into her purse. 'Eight dollars, and they're yours, in a color to coordinate with every outfit.'

'Cheap at twice the price,' I laughed.

Suddenly, Laurie cocked her head to one side. 'Do you hear that?'

'What?' I stood quietly for a moment, but all I heard was the sound of the furnace kicking in. 'I don't hear anything.'

'Exactly. That means ballet class is over and we're soon to be overrun by munchkins in leotards. Eek! Gotta change.'

More quickly than I thought possible, Laurie slipped into her usual black and white practice outfit. She tucked her handbag into a locker, twirled the dial on the combination lock, stroked the plastic bag containing her gown and said, 'I'm outa' here.'

I followed Laurie into the studio where we found Alicia issuing final instructions to her students, lined up in a row before her like good little Radio City Music Hall Rockettes. 'Next time we work on your *ronds de jambe á terre*!' She clapped her hands together quickly three times. 'Class dismissed!'

Chloe and her classmates broke formation as quickly as if a grenade had been thrown in their midst, streaming past me, giggling and screaming, on their way to the dressing room.

At the same instant, Jay emerged from the men's dressing room and padded across the floor to his office in stocking feet, leaving a trail of white footprints behind. I was puzzling over this – talcum powder? – when I heard an exasperated sigh from behind me.

'He *always* does that,' Alicia moaned. 'The man sweats like a stevedore.'

'Other than sweaty feet, Jay strikes me as pretty fastidious,' I said when Alicia returned with a janitor's broom and began erasing the telltale powder marks from the floor.

'Oh, he is,' she said, furiously scrubbing. She stopped work for a moment and leaned on the broom handle. 'Those eyebrows, for instance.'

I remembered the dark, lush, perfectly shaped brows he'd artfully arched and charmed me with.

'He's got a personal uni-brow prevention program,' Alicia continued. 'A Vietnamese gal down on Riva twirls a bit of string around her fingers – *whish, whish, whish* – goodbye hair. It's called threading.'

'Expensive?' I wondered.

Alicia shrugged and continued sweeping. 'Don't know. Never tried it. Tweezers have always been good enough for me.'

Eventually Alicia disappeared with the broom, and while I waited for Chloe, I watched Tom and Laurie practice a Viennese waltz. As '*Que Sera Sera*' played softly in the background, the pair whirled gaily around the floor, rising a little on the first beat, holding the second beat a little longer than the first so that they appeared to be floating, and then taking a quick step three, almost as if they were falling. And again, and again, and again, a whirl in black and white, with Laurie's trademark red scarf floating behind her like a banner. I was entranced.

It wasn't until the music stopped that I realized, except for Tom, Laurie, and me – and Shirley Douglas who I could see talking to Jay on the other side of the glass doors of his office – everyone had gone home. Where the heck was Chloe?

Before I had time to panic, Chloe shot out of the dressing-room door, ran over to me, grabbed my hand and tugged. 'Grandma, I need you to come.' Her normally smooth forehead was creased with worry, and she seemed on the verge of tears.

'What is it, Chloe? What's wrong?'

She tugged harder, throwing her whole body weight into it. 'Just come!'

Chloe led me through the women's dressing room and into the bathroom. She stopped in front of a stall at the end of a row of five. 'In there.'

From behind the door came the sound of quiet sobbing. 'Who's in there?' I whispered to my granddaughter.

'It's Tessa.'

I pushed on the door to the stall, but Tessa had it locked. 'Tessa,' I said in as soothing a voice as I could manage. 'It's Chloe's grandmother. Will you open the door for me, sweetie?'

'Nooooh!'

'Please?'

'I don't want to!' Tessa wailed.

'If you don't open the door, I'm going to ask Chloe to crawl under and unlock it for me. Do you hear me, Tessa?'

The sobbing continued for a long moment, and then I heard the latch slide open. Inside the stall, I found Tessa hunched over the toilet where she'd clearly been throwing up. I wrapped my arms around the little girl, supporting her until the worst of the retching had passed.

'Chloe, go get a paper towel and put cold water on it, please.'

When Chloe returned with the dampened towel I used it to wipe Tessa's cheeks and chin. 'Run get Tessa's mother, Chloe. She's in the office talking to Jay.'

Tessa stiffened. 'Nooooh! Don't get my mom!'

'What on earth is wrong, Tessa?'

'She'll be mad at me.'

'No, she won't.'

'My mommy and daddy are fighting all the time,' Tessa sobbed. 'I'm afraid they're going to get a divorce.'

'Sometimes parents don't agree on things,' I reassured her. 'It doesn't mean that they don't love one another any more.' I smoothed some unruly strands of long, dark hair out of her eyes. 'Chloe's daddy and mommy sometimes yell at each other, don't they Chloe?'

From the doorway of the stall, Chloe nodded solemnly. 'And then they hug and kiss.'

Tessa snuffled noisily. 'My mommy and daddy don't hug and kiss.'

'Maybe they hug and kiss after you go to bed,' I suggested a little desperately, offering her a wad of toilet tissue with which to blow her nose.

Tessa took the tissue and blew, a honking A-flat that echoed from stall to stall. She smiled wanly. 'If I'm very, very good, maybe they won't fight any more.'

Poor Tessa. Suddenly all I wanted to do was pick her up and take her to my house. When I got her there I'd dress her in jeans and a T-shirt, let her get sticky making Rice Krispie Treats and allow her to eat them all in a single sitting while watching *Shreck* on DVD.

'Tessa,' I said. 'Your mommy and daddy will love you no matter what.'

'They will?'

'Yes, they will.'

I sent Chloe and Tessa out to wash their hands, and had just flushed away the evidence, when I heard Shirley call from the dressing room. 'Tessa! Are you in there? Don't keep me waiting, little miss!'

When I got out into the dressing room, Tessa and her mother were gone, no surprise, and Chloe was waiting for me, a strap of her Angelina Ballerina backpack looped over one shoulder. 'Can we go to KFC now, Grandma?'

'Of course we can.' I took Chloe's hand, and we walked out the door together with Chloe chanting, 'Chicken wings and fries, chicken wings and fries.'

Wouldn't it be wonderful if a bucket of chicken from KFC could solve all the world's problems that easily?

A few minutes later, as we waited for our order at the drive-thru, Chloe said, 'Tessa can't eat French fries, Grandma.'

'Why not?'

'Because dancers can't be fat.'

'That's true, I suppose, but your friend Tessa isn't fat, is she?'

Chloe shook her head.

'Well, I wouldn't recommend eating French fries every day, Chloe, but there's nothing wrong having a French fry every once in a while.'

I pulled up to the window, paid for our order, and set the hot, aromatic bag on the front seat between us.

I put the car in drive, but before I could pull away, Chloe said, 'What's wrong with Tessa's nose?'

'Her nose?' I closed my eyes, trying to recall any imperfections in the little girl's face as I was wiping it. 'Why, nothing's wrong with Tessa's nose, Sweet Pea. Why do you ask?'

'Because back there in the bathroom, Tessa told me she has to get her nose fixed.'

Fifteen

'A nose job on a nine-year-old, can you believe it?'
'Stop sputtering, Hannah, and hand me the pliers, will you?'

I handed Paul the pliers with one hand while steadying the ladder he was standing on with the other. 'And you know what else?'

'What?' he mumbled around a mouthful of screws.

'I always thought Tessa's hair was improbably thick. Well, yesterday I found out why.'

Paul lowered his hand and snapped his fingers silently. 'Bulb.'

I handed him a 100-watt bulb.

'OK, I give up, why?' He tucked the new bulb under his arm and handed me the dead one.

'Hair extensions, and a really first-rate job of it, too,' I said, grasping the old bulb gingerly by the screw end where it wasn't so generously encrusted with fried insect carcasses.

Paul finished screwing the fresh bulb into the socket of the light fixture in the ceiling of our entrance hall, replaced the globe, then climbed carefully down from the ladder. 'Don't get your undies in a twist about the hair extensions, Hannah. Hair extensions are reversible. The nose job, though, is another matter.' He collapsed the ladder and started lugging it toward the basement. 'But, what reputable plastic surgeon is going to perform a nose job on a child?'

'I've heard there are surgeons in Brazil who'll do anything.'

In fact, I had a friend who took a 'cosmetic vacation' to Rio de Janeiro – the Face Lift and Tango Package – and came home with a new face and a Brazilian boyfriend, all for less than five thousand dollars.

Paul leaned the ladder against the wall, and locked his

dark brown, no-nonsense eyes on mine. 'Tessa is not your child, Hannah. This is not your problem.'

'I know I need to let it go,' I admitted. 'But nothing's going to stop me from composing letters to Child Protective Services in my head.'

'My advice, sweetheart? Put it out of your mind.'

But I couldn't.

That night I dreamed the mother of one of Tessa's pint-sized rivals hired a hit man to bump off Shirley, believing that Tessa would be so upset about her mother's death that she would bag the *Tiny Ballroom* competition. Instead, Tessa, in the weird, meandering way of dreams, ended up waltzing with a miniature Hutch for the *Shall We Dance?* auditions, while Melanie and Tom eloped to Vegas in an airplane piloted by Kay, leaving Jay to comfort Laurie in her tear-stained peach gown.

Ancient Romans sometimes submitted their dreams to the Senate for analysis and interpretation, believing dreams were messages from the gods.

If that was the case, I was keeping this dream entirely to myself.

Epiphany.

The Three Wise Men.

The true gift of the Magi, Pastor Eva once preached, was the revelation that the child born of Mary in Bethlehem was the Son of God, His gift to all the world. As Christians, she said, we are reminded to seek enlightenment during this season.

I was all for enlightenment, but no amount of study or thought had thrown any light on who had attacked Ruth and why. So while I waited for an epiphany, either my own or on the part of the police, I used the day like everyone else to take down the Christmas decorations and burn the tree.

The following day – Tango Monday – was lesson five. After a family dinner *chez moi* of Hurry-Up Chili and tossed salad, we shoehorned Ruth into the car – front passenger seat slid way back, left leg fully extended – Daddy, Neelie, and I climbed into the back, and Paul drove us to J & K. Hutch had gone ahead to get in some practice time with Melanie. It was only a ten-minute drive, but long enough that sand-wiched as I was in the back directly behind Ruth with my knees folded up to my chin like an accordion I feared I wouldn't be able to walk when I got out, let alone dance.

Feet all pins and needles, I limped in.

Something was out of whack; I sensed it. The studio looked normal enough, I suppose, but it felt as if I'd inter-rupted something, like 'OK folks, knock it off, company coming, everyone look natural'.

Chance, looking very bodybuilder slash surfer dude in a Blue Man Group T-shirt tucked into Levi slims, had cued up a waltz – 'Are You Lonesome Tonight?' – but nobody was dancing.

I hadn't laid eyes on Kay for weeks so I was pleasantly surprised to see her there. She was dressed for success in a dark blue business suit, an ivory-colored blouse, dark hose and Ferragamo pumps. Clipboard in hand, she leaned against one of the EV speakers while talking with Hutch and with Melanie, who wasn't paying attention.

I'd have expected to find Tom and Laurie perfecting their waltz, but they were sprawled on a mat in the corner, doing stretches, acting cool.

And sitting on a bench near the office, bookended by Shirley and Jay, was Tessa looking sulky, her little legs dangling, knocking the heels of her silver Capezios together. In contrast, the grown-ups on both sides laughed, Jay's head thrown back in full-blown, open-mouthed guffaw; Shirley, more modest, head down, shoulders quietly shaking.

I handed Paul my coat to hang up along with his, then wandered casually over for a second look at Tessa, which confirmed my first impression. No lumps, no bumps, not tip-tilted, crooked or pug. Tessa's nose was perfectly aquiline, with the merest hint of a tilt at its tip. Miley Cyrus should be paying a plastic surgeon for a nose half as fine as Tessa's and not the other way around. Perhaps Chloe had misunderstood.

Whatever I imagined had been going on just minutes

before in the studio, our group's arrival seemed to have broken the spell. Tom and Laurie, wearing their trademark black and white, rolled up the exercise mats and quickly took the floor. Laurie had replaced her red scarf with one in iridescent green, selected to coordinate (I felt certain) with her bright emerald shoes. As they waltzed, the scarf billowed behind her, like an ocean wave.

Daddy and Neelie were waltzing expertly, too, gazing into each other's eyes. Daddy was singing along to the words, '*Do the chairs in your parlor seem empty and bare* . . .' and I gulped, trying to swallow the lump that had risen in my throat. It had been several long years since my mother's death. Daddy'd met Cornelia at my sister's shop and they'd been dating semi-steadily ever since. He responded to her offbeat sense of humor; my sisters and I liked her, too. Whether marriage was in the future or not, nobody knew. We were simply glad to see him happy.

While I waited for Paul, who had nipped into the restroom, I decided to say hello to Kay. 'I hope I'm not interrupting anything important.'

Kay smiled back. 'We're just getting our ducks in a row for the *Shall We Dance?* casting call.' She tipped the clipboard in my direction so I could see the sheaf of forms attached to it. 'Fortunately, both our candidates seem to qualify.'

'You have to be a US citizen or legal resident,' Melanie explained. 'They had some trouble last year with a finalist whose green card had expired.' She laughed. 'No problem with that here.'

Hutch frowned. 'As I was saying, Kay, I'd like to take those forms home and go over them, particularly the release. If I'm reading it correctly, it gives the CNT producers permission to do anything they want with our audition, even if it embarrasses the hell out of us.'

Kay stared. 'I don't think that's negotiable, Hutch. You either sign the release or forget about auditioning.'

'Once a lawyer, always a lawyer,' I cut in.

Melanie wrinkled her nose. 'Last season they videotaped this couple, and the girl was so nervous she threw up all over her partner! You'd think the producers would edit that out of the tape, but *no*! They actually showed her throwing up.' She stuck out her tongue. 'Then they further humiliated the poor thing by blasting her lack of experience.' She tapped Kay's arm. 'You saw it, Kay. What'd that awful judge say? Something like how it made him sick to his stomach to watch her lousy dancing?'

'Seems like a cheap way to get a laugh,' I said.

Hutch agreed. 'Well, neither Melanie nor I is going to throw up, I assure you. And they're certainly not going to say we're lousy dancers. We might not make the cut, but if you have to act like an nincompoop in order to see yourself on television . . . well, we'll just say thanks, grab the souvenir T-shirt and get outa' there.'

Kay squeezed the clip, slid the application forms off her clipboard and handed them to Hutch. 'Remember, you need to set aside three days for this. If you make it through day one, there may be a call back.'

Hutch fanned through the pages, divided them, and gave half to Melanie. 'That's not a problem for me. Melanie?'

Melanie shook her head.

Kay blew a sigh of relief. 'Well, that's it then. The only thing left to talk about is your costumes.'

I had hoped that by arriving early, we'd get a sneak preview of Hutch and Melanie's routine. Hutch had been maddeningly hush-hush about it, forming a cross with his index fingers when I asked, and saying, 'Jinx, jinx!' What with maneuvering Ruth and her unresponsive leg into the car, we'd arrived too late for a preview, of course, but if I managed to get Melanie alone, I planned to pump her.

They'd be dancing a tango, that's all we knew.

In the alcove behind us, Chance flipped a couple of switches and 'Hello Young Lovers' came wafting out of the nearby speakers, presumably the last selection of the practice session before Alicia arrived to turn us into tangoing fools. I felt a hand on my shoulder, Paul's breath warm on my ear. 'May I have this dance?'

I slid into my husband's arms and waited, counting along with him – one-two-three, one-two-three – until, whoosh, we were off, whirling in a surprisingly competent way counter-clockwise around the floor. 'You've been practicing,' I accused Paul as he expertly avoided a collision with Daddy and Neelie who were, quite frankly, paying more attention to one another than to the line of the dance.

'Not really,' Paul said a bit breathlessly. 'It just suddenly clicked. I think I've got it.'

I locked my jaw and said, 'Oy think he's gaw'tit.'

'At least until Mizz Alicia shows up to browbeat us into the tango,' Paul panted, leading me gracefully around the next corner.

'I feel like Cinderella at the ball!' I giggled as we spun past Tessa's mother, circled around Daddy and Neelie again, then took off on a diagonal, following Tom and Laurie. It was exhilarating and, like Cinderella, I didn't want the ball to end.

I was so preoccupied that I didn't even wonder what had happened to Tessa, until I saw her, and stumbled.

'What's the matter?' asked Paul as he skipped a beat to catch up.

'Over there,' I muttered without moving my lips. 'Tessa and Jay.'

It was just like my dream, but instead of dancing with Hutch, Tessa was dancing with Jay. As Paul continued waltzing me around, I thought I'd get whiplash trying to keep my eyes on the pair.

Jay towered over the girl, but bent himself almost double in order to take her right hand in his left; Tessa's left hand rested gracefully on his right forearm. As they waltzed, Jay adjusted his steps to match hers, taking mincing steps, as if his pants were too tight. It looked painful.

As I watched them dance, I had to admit that Tessa was good, really good. Shirley Douglas had every right to sit on the sidelines and beam, as I could see she was doing out of the corner of my eye.

As the music ended, Jay twirled Tessa several times under his arm, then keeping a firm grip on her hand, escorted Tessa back to her mother.

'Was I good, Mommy?' Tessa chirped.

I couldn't hear Shirley's reply, but she patted her daughter's cheek. A split second later, Tessa turned and flounced off to the dressing room, her plaid skirt swishing around her thighs.

Jay, still standing with his back to me, began talking to Shirley, whose face grew suddenly serious.

I was trying to decide whether to eavesdrop on Jay and Shirley or dash off to the dressing room and corner a guileless nine-year-old when Kay popped out of the office, clipboard clutched to her chest. If looks had been arrows, Jay would have been instantly dead, pierced through head, neck and heart, and bleeding profusely. Kay turned on her sensible heels and stalked back into the office.

'What's that all about?' I asked Hutch who had come up to join us.

'I don't know. Melanie was here earlier. Why don't you ask her?'

I looked around. 'Where'd she go?'

Hutch pointed toward the dressing room.

I was in luck. Tessa and Melanie. Two birds with one stone?

I trotted off to the dressing room where I found Tessa exchanging her Capezios for black and white saddle shoes. Since Melanie couldn't escape from the ladies' room without passing us by, I plopped down on the bench next to Tessa and watched silently while with tongue-protruding concentration, Tessa tightened the laces, tied her shoes.

'I like those silver shoes,' I said as Tessa tucked them into her dance bag. 'And the red ones you wore last week were also very pretty.'

Tessa grinned. 'I have silver jazz shoes, too, and pink Latin salsas.' She stuck out a foot. 'These look like my hip hop shoes, but they don't have split soles.'

'What's a split sole?' I asked, smiling, picturing the devil perched on my left shoulder arguing with an angel hovering over my right.

'It's in two parts. You can point easier.'

'Oh, I see,' I said, although I didn't really. 'Laurie

Wainwright has a lot of gorgeous shoes. Did you see the green ones she's wearing today?'

Tessa's eyes narrowed and she said in a conspiratorial tone, 'My mommy says a girl can never have too many pairs of dancing shoes.'

Words to live by.

'Well, bye!' Tessa snatched up her bag and before I could say 'bye-bye' myself, she'd disappeared through the door.

I was sitting on the bench cataloging my shoe collection – which didn't take long – when Melanie came out of the bathroom, drying her hands on a paper towel. 'Are you all right, Hannah? You look lost in thought.'

'I was,' I said, being careful to face Melanie head on. 'I was just wondering why women are so enamored of shoes. My grandfather used to say, what's the point, Hannah? You can wear only one pair at a time.'

'By that logic, you should own only one light bulb and simply carry it around the house, screwing it in wherever you need it to see.'

'Or one chair!' I hooted. I patted the bench next to me. 'Speaking of chairs, sit down for a minute. There's something I want to ask you.'

Melanie sat and raised a curious eyebrow.

'Out there a minute ago? Kay came out of the office and cut Jay dead. And earlier, when we first came in, I thought the atmosphere was a bit, um, thick?'

'I didn't catch all of it,' Melanie explained, 'but while Hutch and I were waiting for Kay to bring out the forms, she got hung up in the office with Jay. I could see only her part of the conversation, but I think they were having an argument.'

'About what?'

Melanie shrugged. 'I'm not sure; depends upon what was on the printout Kay balled up and tossed at his head. I saw her say, "How do you explain this?" If it was a bank statement or spreadsheet or something, then they might have been arguing about money.' Melanie paused, wrinkling her nose in concentration. 'But it could just as easily have been an anonymous email.' She laughed. 'You know, "If you wonder what your husband is doing on Wednesday nights when you think he's at choir practice, check out Room 221 of the Quality Inn in Glen Burnie. Signed, A Friend."'

'Sometimes I wish I had taken a class in lip-reading rather than ASL,' I chuckled. 'It's a skill that could come in handy.'

'Yes, indeed.' Melanie's eyes went on scan, as if checking the room for bugs. 'Ever curious about what Hillary Clinton said to her aide before stepping up to the podium at the debates?'

I nodded vigorously.

She leaned toward me and whispered. 'Find Bill in whatever hotel room he's in and hide him somewhere until the fucking campaign is over!'

I laughed so hard I was gasping for breath. 'You're making that up!'

Melanie grinned. 'I am, alas. But it could happen.'

Melanie and I were still giggling when Laurie burst through the door, breathing heavily. She bowed at the waist, and rested her hands on her knees. 'Anybody who tells me it's the guy who does all the work in a lift, I'm going to pop 'em one on the side of the head.'

I'd watched Laurie and Tom practice 'swallow' lifts – she'd take a running leap into his arms and he'd raise her overhead with her back arched, legs straight, arms extended like wings. If Tommy miscalculated . . . well, it was a long way for Laurie to fall.

'I remember that move from the end of *Dirty Dancing*,' I said. 'Looks dangerous. Baby and Johnny practiced in a lake.'

'I wish,' Laurie panted. She crossed to her locker and wrenched the door open. Using both hands, she grabbed the hem of her shirt, whipped it off over her head, and used it to wipe the sweat from her face. 'Whew! I'm ripe!'

'Not so you'd notice,' I said, taking a moment to loosen the buckles on the T-strap heels I'd bought especially for dancing.

'Shower free?'

'Think so. Want me to look?'

Next to me Melanie said, 'I'll check.'

In a moment Melanie was back. 'Someone's just finishing up in there, but the communal shower room is free and clear.'

Laurie groaned. 'Not for me, girl. I've never bought into that Save Water, Shower with a Friend gig.' She removed a fresh towel from her locker and draped it around her neck. 'I've seen all the pitiful tits, asses, thongs and tattoos I need to in life, thank you very much.'

As I considered Laurie's remark, I realized I hadn't used a communal shower since sometime before my mastectomy. The plastic surgeon had done a masterful job of recreating my missing breast, considering the limited material he had to work with. But, outside the confines of my underwear, I was more than a bit lopsided, and my reconstructed nipple tended to point north rather than south.

Needless to say, *Playboy* magazine wouldn't be calling to set up a photo shoot any time soon, and I didn't think anyone else would appreciate a close-up view of my off-kilter anatomy either. Thankfully, Paul didn't seem to mind.

Laurie padded past me barefoot in her underwear – blue denim boxer-style briefs and a matching lace-trimmed bra – and leaned against the tiles next to the private shower-room door. 'Besides,' she caroled back, her voice echoing hollowly from wall to wall, 'in a minute I'll be surrounded by munchkins in tutus, and I'm not going to strip off in front of *them*.'

Melanie, who had been quiet up to this point, screwed up her mouth. 'I don't like community showers much, either. You can pick up all kinds of diseases in there. Legionnaires', athletes' foot, plantar warts, ringworm . . .'

Alicia poked her head into the room, a welcome interruption to Melanie's litany of disease. 'Ladies, we're waiting for you!'

'Why?' Melanie wanted to know.

I stood up and tapped my heels together experimentally. 'They want us to tango.'

'Oh, good! Hutch and I will be practicing with you tonight.' Melanie leapt to her feet. 'You'll love the tango, Hannah. It's so sexy! Let me show you.' She demonstrated the steps, dancing slowly around the dressing room. 'Slow, slow, quick-quick, slow. Slow, slow, quick-quick, slow!'

I copied her as closely as I could, but stumbled on the last quick-quick-slow.

'It might help to remember it this way: walk, walk, tango-close,' Melanie said, demonstrating the steps as she talked.

Alicia opened the door and sing-songed, 'La-dies, we are wait-ing!'

'OK,' I yelled, and the two of us scurried out.

I found Paul, Melanie found Hutch, Daddy and Neelie were holding hands, ready to go. Ruth still sat on a bench, her broken leg propped up on a chair, drinking a Diet Coke from a can, and there was no sign of Shirley or her daughter.

I expected Alicia to be teaching the session with Chance, but when Chance cued up '*Olé Guapa*' and hurried out on to the floor, Jay materialized out of nowhere and waved him aside.

'*Caminar es todo!* The walk is everything,' Jay announced, taking Alicia's hand.

I watched Chance back off the dance floor, darkly scowling. When Jay wasn't looking, he shot a bird at his back.

'What's that all about?' Paul wondered aloud.

I squeezed his hand. 'Tonight it appears we're getting the A-team.'

Sixteen

I was throwing together a quick dinner for Paul and myself involving a combination of Campbell's Golden Mushroom soup, sour cream and chicken breasts, when the phone rang. Using my free hand, I continued layering paper-thin slices of chipped beef in the bottom of a glass baking dish, picked up the phone with the other.

'Eva! How's it going? Any more gifts or visits from the persistent Jeremy?'

'None, thank goodness. But, I've been attending the seven thirty service at St Anne's,' she continued, 'so perhaps that's why. Jeremy isn't exactly the Rite One type.'

'I'm surprised. You'd think he'd be right on board with "Ye who do truly and earnestly repent you of your sins". How's it going at the Hall of Records?'

'Splendidly. I'm anticipating being finished with the project by mid-March, which is one of the reasons I called you today. Rev Chase and I have been talking to the bishop, and we've agreed that I will resume my duties at St Cat's on the first Sunday after Easter.'

Feeling so happy about this news that I thought my heart would beat its way clean out of my chest, I turned to the calendar hanging on the cabinet next to my kitchen phone. I flipped up the page for February (Glacier National Park in winter) and turned to March (The Dry Tortugas, Florida). 'That'll be March 30th?' I asked, picking up a pencil.

'Yes.'

'Eva, I'm marking it down on my calendar right now, and Paul and I will be there with bells on.'

'I know you and Paul will, Hannah, but I worried about the rest of my congregation. You remember how nasty it got when Roger . . .' Her voice trailed off.

How could I forget? When Roger Haberman was unmasked as an Internet pedophile on network TV, half the congregation stood by Pastor Eva staunchly, while the other half petitioned for her resignation. And half of *them* were picking up stones. I was casting about for words of encouragement to send Eva's way, but coming up short.

'Your friends will be there, Eva. And some of your detractors, too, if only to satisfy their curiosity.'

'I'll bet. Does she still have horns? Where's she hiding her forked tail?'

'Don't be silly. Once the service starts, you'll have them in the palm of your hands. Certainly by the time the sermon is over. I'm sure of it.'

There was silence on the other end of the line as Eva considered what I had said. While I waited, I stretched out my arm and set the oven to 350°F. Eventually Eva sighed, then said, 'I was wondering if you're free for lunch on Friday.'

'You're not going to believe why I'm not.'

'I knew I should have asked you sooner. What's up, if you don't mind my asking.'

'Remember that dance show I was telling you about, the one that Hutch is going to participate in?'

'*Shall We Dance?* I do. How's Ruth's leg doing, by the way?'

'Fine, if you measure rate of recovery in inverse proportion to shortness of temper.'

Eva chuckled. 'Sounds like our Ruth. So, how is Ruth handling the idea that Hutch is competing with someone else? What's her name?'

'Melanie.'

'Right. So, what's that got to do with you standing me up for lunch on Friday?'

I explained about Hutch and Melanie's schedule, then said, 'CNT is taping the auditions, and Hutch has managed to snag a few tickets. On Friday, I'll be standing in line at the Hippodrome Theater in Baltimore, waiting to be part of the studio audience.'

In fact, Hutch had five tickets. I counted off quickly on my fingers. Paul, me, Ruth, Chloe . . . 'Eva, if Hutch hasn't already given it away, we have an extra ticket. I'd love it if you could come, too.'

'Sounds like fun. I've never been to the taping of a TV show before.'

'There's usually a lot of hurry up and wait, but if that's a yes, great. You can spell me with Ruth and her blasted wheelchair.'

'It must be hard for Ruth to see someone take her place in the competition, and with her fiancé, no less.'

'As cranky as she is sometimes, Ruth's resigned to it, and she and Melanie have actually become friends. Melanie is a no-nonsense, stick-to-the-rules kind of person, very disciplined when it comes to her dancing. Like Hutch. When they're together it's all about the dance. Work, work, work. Blood, sweat and tears. I'd be surprised if Ruth perceived Melanie as a threat.'

'Did you say Melanie's an army wife? May account for the discipline.'

'Too true. But Ruth's been rock-solid, too.' I chuckled. 'She's appointed herself team manager, videotaping the practice sessions, advising on costumes.'

'What do you think of their routine?'

'I hear their tango is so hot it may set the Hippodrome on fire. Jay's been doing the choreography and Ruth says it's brilliant.' I stretched out the phone cord as far as it would go, opened the oven, and slid the baking dish in. 'But you'll see it soon enough. We're leaving early in the morning, around six a.m.'

'Assuming Hutch still has the free ticket, I'll bring a Thermos of hot coffee and a bag of donuts and be at your house by five forty-five.'

'Sounds like a plan.'

Seventeen

On Thursday night, Hutch called a summit.

It was well past midnight, and we were still gathered around my dining-room table, in the center of which sat a straw placemat and a box of day-old donuts from Carlson's. Day-olds from Carlson's were better than oven-fresh from just about anywhere else.

'I haven't been up this late since college,' I said, stifling a yawn. 'One semester I pulled two all-nighters in a row, and ended up falling asleep in the stairwell of my dorm.'

'Exams or papers?' Melanie wanted to know. At what – mid-twenties? – she wasn't that far removed from her own college days.

'Papers,' I said. 'Scrambled my brain. As I recall, there was a treatise grandly entitled *La Vie de Stendhal dans ses oeuvres* and a cultural anthropology paper on the Jibaro Indians of Eastern Ecuador. The Jibaro were headhunters,' I explained. 'You can imagine the nightmares.'

At that moment, Paul appeared from the kitchen carrying a fresh pot of coffee, which he set down on the placemat in front of me. 'Nightmares? What did I miss?'

'We're just going over the schedule,' I said. 'Hutch and Melanie are leaving . . .' I checked my watch. 'They're leaving in an hour.'

Hutch kneaded his eyes with his fingers. 'Jay thinks if we're standing in line by two a.m., we'll be among the first group to get in.'

'Coats, hats, gloves, and long underwear?' I asked.

Hutch shot me a withering, sleep-deprived look, and I raised an apologetic hand. 'Sorry. Once a mother, always a mother.'

Melanie smiled sweetly. 'I'm wearing so many layers I can barely walk.'

'OK, then,' Hutch said, consulting his notes. 'We're taking

Melanie's car. Paul, tomorrow morning you're taking Ruth, Chloe, Hannah and Hannah's friend Eva, and driving my car.'

'Why not use my car?' Paul asked.

'Because I'm an Inner Circle subscriber, so I've got a prepaid parking pass for the Hippodrome Atrium Garage.' He tapped a map I'd printed out from the *Shall We Dance?* website. 'You go in here, on Eutaw Street.' He looked up. 'It'll be easier to navigate to the theater from there with Ruth in her wheelchair.'

'Agreed. But where will you park?'

'In one of the Inner Harbor hotel garages.' Hutch flapped a hand. 'Don't worry about us.'

He patted the breast pocket of his sports jacket, stuck his hand inside and pulled out a small, yellow envelope. 'Here are your tickets.' He opened the envelope and dealt out each of the tickets like playing cards. 'You're supposed to enter on Baltimore Street, that's the south side of the theater near the ticket office. Even with tickets, I'd advise you to arrive early so you'll get the best seats.'

'Where will you and Melanie be?' Ruth asked.

'According to Jay, contestants are required to line up out front, under the marquee. It'll be clearly marked.'

'It's going to be so C-O-L-D!' Melanie rubbed her hands together rapidly. 'I hope Jay and Kay don't have to stand outside very long. He's been feeling achy lately. Thinks he may be coming down with the flu.'

Paul raised an eyebrow. 'Are the Giannottis *competing*?'

'Not exactly. One of the producers thought it'd be a brilliant idea to have dance exhibitions during the taping breaks. So they've tapped a few of the local professionals for the honor. Jay and Kay are brushing up the paso doble they took to the Internationals last year. I was there,' continued Melanie. 'They are *amazing*!'

I cringed as Hutch tipped my grandmother's antique walnut dining-room chair back on its two hind legs. 'I think it would be easier to plan a military invasion of a Third World country.' He ran a hand through his thinning hair. 'Sometimes I wonder why the hell I'm doing this.'

Ruth laid a hand on his arm. 'Because you could have in

college, but didn't. Now there will be no regrets.' Using both hands, she wheeled her chair back a few inches from the table, angling it slightly to face me. 'I'll always regret I stayed home that Easter instead of coming over to visit you in France, Hannah.' She laughed bitterly. 'I missed La Sorbonne, can you imagine? In *Paris*! But what did I know? I thought I'd *die* if I couldn't spend that vacation break with Eric. What a mistake that turned out to be!' Tears welled in her eyes.

Hutch picked up Ruth's hand, brought it to his lips and held it there. 'I love you, Ruth.'

At that, Ruth began to cry in earnest, tears trickling down both cheeks, leaving dark spots on her pink cashmere sweater. She banged on her cast with her fist. 'Oh, hell! With this stupid cast on my leg I can't even be a drama queen and race out of the room in tears!'

At that point, everyone started to cackle, even Ruth.

When he got himself under control, Hutch stood up, clasped his hands together. 'Is everyone clear?' When we all nodded, he said, 'Ready, Melanie?'

'As I'll ever be.'

'Costumes?'

'Already in the car.'

Hutch took a deep breath and let it out slowly. 'Well, that's it, then. Wish us luck.'

Ruth, who had been dabbing at the corners of her eyes with a paper napkin, looked up. 'Break a leg!' Then erupted in a fresh episode of giggling.

Hutch leaned over, put a hand behind her head, and kissed his fiancé firmly on the mouth. 'There! That should shut you up, you silly girl.'

As we stood on the stoop and watched Hutch and Melanie drive away, I said to Paul. 'How are they going to dance without any sleep?'

Paul's arm snaked around my shoulder. 'Probably the same way you aced that paper on Stendhal.'

'How's that?' His face looked ghostly in the light from the porch light.

He pulled me close, his chin resting lightly on top of my head. 'Adrenalin.'

Eighteen

The Hippodrome – officially the France-Merrick Performing Arts Center – was a lovingly restored 1914 vaudeville theater and movie palace, the centerpiece of Baltimore's west side renaissance. Occupying an entire city block on Eutaw between Baltimore and Fayette Streets, the Hipp, as the locals called it, bordered on the Inner Harbor just four blocks north of Camden Yards where the Orioles had just played another losing season.

In restoring the Baltimore landmark, the developers had linked it to two adjacent nineteenth-century bank buildings. Now spacious lobbies, lounges and restaurants afforded impressive views of the city including, to the south, Baltimore's historic Bromo Seltzer tower modeled on the Palazzo Vecchio in Florence, Italy. Twelve letters advertising the famous antacid circled the clock's face rather than numbers. When we joined the line, tickets in hand, the face of the clock read 'L' o'clock exactly.

I'd seen *Prairie Home Companion* at the Hippodrome the previous October, and been dazzled by the facility. Bathed in soft golds, browns and beiges, the interior spaces of the theater glowed; each fresco, cartouche and medallion – flowers, corn husks, gryphons – had been so painstakingly restored that it was impossible to tell where the old ended and the new began. I was looking forward to seeing it again.

For half an hour our little party shivered outside the theater, watching as the line snaked out behind us, growing steadily by groups of four, six, ten until by seven thirty it extended all the way down Baltimore Street and disappeared around the corner of Paca. I remembered reading that the Hippodrome could seat 2,220; the line could reach all the way down to the Inner Harbor by now.

After a bit, a pair of bruisers dressed in chinos, muscles challenging the seams of their neon green T-shirts bearing the stylized *Shall We Dance?* SWD logo, moved down the line inspecting tickets.

When asked, Chloe presented her ticket solemnly. For the most part, my granddaughter waited patiently, sucking periodically on a straw stuck into a bottle of strawberry Yoo-Hoo. 'I wish I could sit in your wheelchair, Aunt Ruth,' she said after the guard moved away.

'Don't be silly, Chloe, you'll squish your aunt's sore leg.'

'Are they going to let us in soon?' she wondered.

'I certainly hope so.'

'I have to go to the bathroom.'

'It shouldn't be long now.' I could have used a chair or the bathroom myself, but the previous evening Hutch and Melanie had appropriated our camp stools. When we arrived at seven, we'd spied the pair hunkered down under the marquee with all the other shivering hopefuls. Over their heads, draped from one end of the marquee to the other was an enormous banner: Baltimore Welcomes Shall We Dance 2008! We'd given our team a thumb's up sign before hurrying around the corner to take our places in the audience line.

At seven forty-five, leaving Chloe in Eva's care, I decided to bop out front and check up on Hutch and Melanie.

I found Hutch dozing, his head leaning at an impossible, and most certainly uncomfortable angle against the wall. In contrast, Melanie seemed bright as a sparrow. 'We're fine, Hannah,' Melanie chirped when I asked. She extended her right arm, pulled up the sleeve of her parka. Circling her wrist was a white plastic wristband like the kind you get when they admit you to the hospital. Instead of name, date of birth, doctor's name and blood type, though, Melanie's wristband said '22'. 'Hutch is number twenty-one,' she told me, her face flushed with excitement. 'We could be in the first round!'

Curious about who had snagged spots one through twenty, I glanced up the line. Dancers one and two were no more than eighteen years old, sporting faux-hawk hairdos and dressed in baggy, saggy hip hop clothing. They guarded their number one slot at the plastic door of an elegant white tent with Palladian-style windows, the kind of tent one rents for wedding receptions and bar mitzvahs. Through the windows, rippled by the plastic, I could see other individuals working in their neon green shirtsleeves. Portable heaters in there, I bet. Lucky dogs.

Further down the line couples waited, some in costumes, some in street clothes, some in outfits so strange it could have gone either way. 'Are they going to let you change?' I asked Melanie, thinking of all the time and expense that would go down the drain if they couldn't wear their costumes.

'We'll have the use of dressing rooms, don't worry.' She flapped her arms like a scarecrow and laughed. 'Can you see me dancing a tango in this outfit? The Sta-Puf marshmallow girl meets the Michelin Man.'

I laughed at the image, too. 'Can I get you guys something to eat?'

'No thanks. After they gave us the wristbands and collected our forms, they said only one of us had to be in line at all times. So, when the sun came up, Hutch hiked up to Lexington Market – I was absolutely drooling for a Pollock Johnny's hot dog, all the way, you know, with chili, mustard and that secret stuff they put on it, but, darn it, the market doesn't open until eight thirty. So I ate some of the chips we brought along.'

She delivered this information in one long, breathless sentence. I felt exhausted just listening. It reminded me of the difference in our ages. Melanie was younger than my daughter, Emily. She probably even knew the names of Brittany Spears's babies.

My cell phone abruptly launched into 'Anchors Aweigh'.

Paul. 'Where are you, Hannah? They're about to open the doors.'

'Hold on, I'm coming!' I gave Melanie a hug, waggled my fingers in the direction of the still napping Hutch, and sprinted to rejoin my family.

By the time I got around the corner, green-shirted SWD staff had already opened the box-office doors and admitted the first group of ten audience members, counting heads as each person went in. When it was our group's turn, Eva pushed Ruth, and I held Chloe's hand, with Paul bringing up the rear.

Inside the lobby, adjacent to The Hipp Café (closed, alas, the muffaletta panini is to die for) the organizers had set up a sophisticated security screening station, like at the airport. Before we could enter the theater, we had to pass through a metal detector, beyond which I could see other uniformed staff seated at long tables pawing through audience members' bags. 'Are we flying Southwest to Dallas, or coming to see a television show?' I muttered to Paul as he joined me on the other side of the detector.

While a guard searched her wheelchair for explosive devices and her crutches for switchblade knives, Ruth hopped one-footed through the metal detector. Paul reached out for Ruth's hand, tucked it under his arm to lend support. 'Count your blessings, Hannah. If the doctors had needed to put pins in Ruth's leg, we might never have gotten to see the show.'

'Ha ha,' Ruth said. She turned to the guard who had just given the seal of approval to her crutches. 'Look, I can't bear messing with that blasted wheelchair in the auditorium. I'm just fine with these,' she said, adjusting the crutches under her arms. 'Can you stow the chair someplace until the show is over?'

The guard pressed a button on his walkie-talkie, and a green-shirted staffer arrived almost at once to give Ruth a receipt and take charge of the wheelchair.

We turned over our bags for inspection – even Angelina Ballerina – and after they had been blessed, we were moved along like cattle to a section of the lobby that had been cordoned off with velvet ropes. Once some sort of critical mass was reached – Twenty-five? Thirty? – another SWD staffer unhooked a rope, gave us a come-along sign, and escorted our group into the theater.

'Oh, wow!' exclaimed Eva as we traipsed single-file down the aisle behind the staffer. Like me, Eva must have been stunned by the lavish, art deco beauty of the place. Balconies with curtained box seats were stacked to our right and to our left. Behind and above us rose an ornate, multi-layered balcony.

'I'm glad we came early,' Eva said as we filed into a row of old-fashioned, red velvet seats. 'If I'd been in charge of the scheduling, we'd be back in row FF instead of up front in row K.'

Ruth settled into a seat at row's end, her cast extending into the aisle like a turnstile. 'Look at this,' she said as she adjusted her leg. 'The seat ends are wrought iron. What do they remind you of, Hannah?'

I leaned over for a closer look and smiled. It didn't take much imagination to see what Ruth saw. 'The legs on Grandmother's old Singer sewing machine!'

Paul sat next to Ruth, then came Eva, Chloe and me. 'Grandma, we have to move!' cried Chloe just as we were shrugging out of our coats and settling in. 'This seat already belongs to somebody. See?' She rubbed a chubby index finger back and forth over a brass plaque attached to the wooden armrest.

'We don't have to move, Pumpkin. That's the name of somebody who donated money to adopt your chair.'

'My chair is adopted?'

'Uh huh.'

'That's silly.'

'Do you have your notebook?' I asked, trying to distract my granddaughter from what was likely to be a discussion of every adopted child among her classmates and every pet we'd ever adopted from the SPCA. We'd taken Chloe out of school for the day on the condition she write a report on her experience. 'Look up, Chloe,' I said, and pointed toward the stage. 'Way, way, up.'

Above the stage was a classical mural – goddesses, muses and nymphs cavorting, or at the very least lounging about an Italian walled garden. The central figure bore a striking resemblance to Jackie O, if the former first lady had gone in for diaphanous robes rather than Oleg Cassini. 'Write a story about that picture,' I suggested.

'OK.' Chloe hauled out her notebook and a pencil and set to work.

The section of seats immediately in front of us nearest the stage seemed to have been reserved, and now I saw why. A boom camera sailed back and forth over the first several rows, like a grazing Brontosaurus. On the other side of the stage in front of the proscenium arch, a black-clad Steadicam operator appeared to be testing his equipment.

More quickly than I would have thought possible considering the security measures in place, the rows behind us became occupied. Soon, people began filling the balcony, too. The noise level steadily increased. The rustling of paper, the shedding of coats, the scuffling of shoes, the crackling of candy wrappers. Kids talking, parents hushing. Shouts of greeting. Coughing, sneezing. Even people breathing, multiplied by two thousand, contributed to the noise.

Just when I thought I'd be called upon to take Chloe to the restroom again, more for entertainment's sake than out of necessity, a man bounded down the aisle and up a short flight of steps to the stage, his green shirt bright as a traffic light as he paced in front of the Hippodrome's purple, gold-fringed curtain.

Some guys should never wear jeans, and this fellow was one of them. He was dressed in the same green SWD T-shirt as the rest of the crew, but he'd tucked it into his jeans and cinched it in with a belt riding several miles south of wherever a normal waistline might be. Clapped to his head was a serious pair of headphones with a wireless microphone attached to one side on a flexible stalk.

'Who is that guy?' Paul asked.

I shrugged. 'Some sort of technician?'

'Ladies and gentlemen, good morning!'

A few scattered 'good mornings' drifted stage-ward from the audience, including an enthusiastic one from Chloe, who had been well trained by Mrs Gottschalk, her third grade teacher.

On the stage, the guy cupped a hand over one ear. 'I can't *hear* you! Let's make some noise back there!'

'Good morning!' the audience roared.

'That's *much* better.' He took several steps forward. 'Welcome to our first casting call for *Shall We Dance?*' He raised both arms over his head and clapped his hands, which we took as a sign that we should do the same.

So we did.

As the applause died down, the guy continued, 'My name is Dave Carson, and I'm the stage director for this production. I'm the boss. I tell everybody what to do. I tell *you* what to do.' Up went the arms, and everyone clapped like crazy. Meanwhile, his T-shirt crept out from under his belt, revealing three inches of white, very hairy belly.

Dramatically shielding her eyes, Ruth said, 'Tell me they're not going to put that on TV.'

'Vomit girl was.'

'Oh, right. I forgot. This is *family* television.'

'Do you *mind*?' hissed the woman on my right.

Dave Carson apparently didn't notice any cool breeze caressing his midsection, so he forged on. 'A funny thing happened on my way to Baltimore today.'

Paul moaned. 'Lord, he thinks he's a comedian, too.'

'Shhhh.' The woman on my right was annoyed again.

'I walked into a bar down on Howard Street, and I sat next to this guy with a dog lying at his feet. And I said to the guy, Does your dog bite? . . .'

'Oh, no, not a bar joke.' I reached over and put my hands over Chloe's ears.

'Grandma, I know this joke,' Chloe whispered.

Thinking kids are growing up too darn fast these days, I removed my hands from her ears. 'You do?'

'Uh huh. It's not his dog.'

Up on the stage Dave said, 'I thought you said your dog didn't bite! And the guy says, Hey, it ain't my dog.'

'See?' Chloe scoffed as all around us the audience erupted in laughter. I should have put a hand over Chloe's mouth instead of her ears.

Encouraged, Dave pulled out another one. 'Say, did you hear the one about the circus owner who walked into a bar?' He paused, waiting for a response.

'No!' shouted someone directly behind me.

'Tell us, Dave!' somebody else yelled from the balcony.

Dave shuffled his feet in an aw-shucks sort of way, then

forged on with an old chestnut about a tap-dancing duck. I zoned out and watched Jackie O take shape under Chloe's pencil, looking a little like Minnie Mouse, but without the ears.

I snapped back to attention when Dave screamed into his microphone, 'Your duck is a rip off!' and spent another agonizing minute waiting for the punch line. 'So, asks the duck's former owner, did you remember to light the fire under the pot?'

I managed a modest titter at that, but the rest of the audience roared so loudly you'd think it was the funniest joke they'd ever heard.

'Well, I don't think we'll have to light any fires under the feet of the contestants here today, do you folks?'

Nooooh!

Dave made a time-out sign, cutting the audience off in mid-cheer. 'As you probably know, over the next few months, we will be conducting talent searches in New York, Chicago, Kansas City, Dallas and Los Angeles, so if you have friends in any of those cities, tell them to put on their dancing shoes and come on out! Email 'em. Text 'em. Call 'em on your cell.

'And speaking of cell phones . . . do you have a cell phone? Of course you have a cell phone. Everyone has a cell phone. My *goldfish* has a cell phone. Well, get them out now.' Dave waited for the deafening noise of everyone scrambling in his or her purse, bag or pocket to die down before continuing. 'Now, find the off button and push it. Done? OK? Now put those phones away. You won't need them any more today. OK, so you wanna know how it works?'

Oh, yes! Tell us, Dave. Tells us how it works!

'What we're going to do here today, and in those other cities I mentioned just now, is pick a total of sixty-five couples to compete in the finals in New York City. When they get to the Big Apple, they'll be told which six dances they will have to perform, and they'll be given just five weeks to prepare before the competition begins. One of the couples you see here today could very well be our next *Shall We Dance?* champions!'

Oh, yes! How cool is that!

'So, are we ready?'

The audience was so ready, hooting and hollering, that if Dave didn't get on with it, they were likely to storm the stage.

'But, first,' he shouted over the din of the restive crowd, 'first, you'll meet our three esteemed judges.' His arms shot skyward, followed by renewed clapping and hooting.

'They'll sit up here,' Dave Carson said, turning to his left and indicating with a sweep of his arm the curtain, which was slowly rising to reveal a starkly furnished stage. Wide and enormously deep, the Hippodrome stage could easily accommodate the most ambitious of Broadway shows, even those that required full-size helicopters to touch down in the center of it.

Now, however, it was furnished with a single, long conference-style table and three chairs, with their backs to us. Three microphones, one for each judge, sat on the table, and between the table and the back of the stage, was a standing microphone.

Eva leaned over and whispered, 'The judges will be facing *away* from us?'

'They face the contestants who'll be dancing back there, I suppose, behind the standing microphone.'

'Once we begin,' Dave continued, 'the contestants will be called out one couple at a time. Steve Owens here –' Dave gestured to the sound man on stage right – 'will cue up the music. Let's put our hands together now for Steve!'

Yay! Yay for Steve!

'Each couple will have ninety seconds to show the judges what they've got.' Dave leaned toward us, the audience. 'Ready?'

'Ready!' we all screamed, even me.

'Now, to meet the judges. First, all the way from Melbourne, Australia where he just finished filming *Paradise Bay*, Neville Grant!'

Neville appeared, gleaming white hair slicked straight back, bowing to acknowledge the thunderous applause. He was dressed entirely in black, including his shoes. The man was painfully thin, desperately in need of emergency ravioli.

Dave pumped Neville's bony hand. 'When will *Paradise Bay* be released in the United States, Nev?'

'Next year, Dave, and it's starring two of Australia's greatest exports, Mel Gibson and Nicole Kidman.'

The audience went insane with joy, while Neville, alternately waving and bowing, loped long-legged across the stage and eased into his chair.

'Next,' Dave continued, 'we have the beautiful and talented Samantha Purdy!'

The crowd went bonkers.

'Samantha's a former Miss America who wowed us in Atlantic City with her dazzling clog dancing. Come on out, *Sa-man-tha*!'

The beautiful and talented Samantha appeared from stage left, grinning hugely, did a quick double-toe-step, rock step, and waved to the audience. She wore a bright red sweater and slim, black jeans. Samantha's trademark waist-length auburn hair (she'd been a L'Oreal spokesmodel since 2001, and definitely worth it) was tied in a ponytail. She'd drawn the ponytail through the opening at the back of a Chicago Cubs baseball cap that was sitting on her head at a jaunty angle.

Dave grabbed Samantha's impeccably manicured hand and said, 'I understand you'll be joining the US touring company of Riverdance this fall, is that right?'

Samantha giggled. 'That's absolutely right, Dave. I'm so excited to be working with Marty Dowds and Maria Buffini and all the other talented individuals on the Riverdance team.' She took a deep breath. 'And I'm so excited to be here today, and to have this incredible opportunity to be part of discovering some astonishing new talent!'

Even from where we sat, it looked as if Samantha was capable of rattling on forever in a god-bless-all-the-poor-little-children-of-the-world sort of way, and Dave must have sensed it, too, because he raised Samantha's arm as if declaring her *dah winnah* in a boxing match and said, 'Let's hear it for Samantha Purdy!'

'*Cead Mile Failte!*' cried Samantha. '*Slan go foill!*' And she took her seat.

'What the heck was that?' Eva asked.

'Gaelic?' I suggested. 'In honor of Riverdance? They're Irish.'

'Shhhh,' said the sourpuss to my right.

'And last but certainly not least, Mr Jonathan Job, who with his partner Izabelle Kucharski, won the silver medal for ice dancing at the 2006 Winter Olympic Games. Jonathan, come on out!'

I am a major fan of ice dancing (Torvill and Dean are gods!) so I instantly recognized the handsome man emerging from stage right. Job was tall, muscular, and broad-shouldered – had to be to hoist Izabelle, a sturdy Polish lass, and sling her around the ice rink like he had done to win the silver. Job flowed, rather than walked, on to the stage.

'Welcome to *Shall We Dance?*, Jonathan.'

'My pleasure.'

'So, what's next for you?'

'I'm doing the choreography for Harry Potter on Ice, Dave. We'll be opening in New York City on November 1st, then touring the United States and Europe. We'll be in Baltimore next Thanksgiving weekend, in fact.'

'Did you hear that folks? Harry Potter on Ice is coming to Baltimore!'

The audience was delirious with joy.

'And how about your partner, the lovely Izabelle. What's she up to?'

Jonathan combed his fingers through his curly, sandy locks, looking uncharacteristically shy. 'Izzy's touring with Potter on Ice, too. And I suppose it's only a matter of time before *Entertainment Tonight* spills the beans, so I might as well announce it right now, Izabelle and I were married on New Year's Eve!'

The audience erupted in a frenzy of congratulatory delight.

'Well, congratulations, Jonathan. We wish you and Izabelle all the best. Now, if the judges will take their seats. Let's get on with it. Your job is to decide which of these talented contestants goes on to the finals in New York City this April.'

As Jonathan glided toward his place behind the table, Dave

approached the edge of the stage and spoke directly to us, the audience. We were such good friends by now. 'The auditions will start in just a few minutes, ladies and gentlemen, but first, a special treat! To get everyone into the *Shall We Dance?* spirit, and to demonstrate how it's done by the pros, *Shall We Dance?* has arranged for some amazing dancers to perform for you. First, from right here in Baltimore, Merryland are Ron and Janet Benrey dancing . . . the waltz!'

We sat enthralled while Ron and Janet, elaborately costumed as colonial Americans complete with powdered wigs, performed a gorgeous, perfectly coordinated Viennese waltz to the tune of the 'Love Theme from Romeo and Juliet'.

After their final bow and curtsy, Ruth muttered, 'Wait a minute. The waltz wasn't invented until the 1800s, am I right?'

Ruth was, but the woman on my right was glaring at us again, so I simply nodded and tried to ignore them both.

'So why aren't George and Martha Washington dancing a minuet, for Christ's sake?'

'Ruth!' I hissed.

Meanwhile, on stage, the auditions had begun. We had no idea what time Hutch and Melanie would perform, only that we had to sit through ten other contestant couples before we got to them. We watched a hip hop routine, a country western line dance for two, a pas-de-deux from *Swan Lake* – 'competent' (according to Jonathan), 'straight out of high school' (Neville) but 'boring, boring, boring' (Samantha) – and a couple dressed as characters from the *Phantom of the Opera* who leaped, pranced and stumbled their way though a waltz largely because she kept tripping on the trailing hem of her dress and he couldn't see very well through the eyehole of his mask.

Ruth frowned. 'Is that what Dave meant when he said that contestants should stand out?'

Unbelievably, by a two to one margin (Samantha being the lone dissenter), the judges decided to put the Phantom and Christine through to the finals.

'What a crock,' Ruth growled from the end of the row.

It was hard for me to believe, too, but I said, 'They've got to have somebody to make fun of, Ruth. Better Christine and her Phantom than Hutch and Melanie.'

I turned away from my sister when Dave reappeared on stage, flapping his arms like a wounded goose. 'Everybody up! On your feet! Arms in the air! Touch your toes!'

For a large man, Dave was surprisingly graceful as he danced on tiptoe, jiggling his arms to demonstrate how easily one could avoid the risk of deep vein thrombosis. 'Shake out those kinks!' he instructed as Steve slotted 'Rock Around the Clock' into his CD drive.

My kinks were quickly dispatched, so I sat down and amused myself by watching everyone shake, rattle and roll all around me.

'And now,' Dave continued, 'before we meet our next group of contestants it's time to bring out some more of our pros. Here they are, all the way from Annapolis, Maryland, dancing the paso doble, let's hear it for Jay and Kay Giannotti!'

I nudged Paul with my elbow. 'This is going to be great!' And all of us clapped like crazy.

Steve cued up the Giannotti's CD and the music began, a sultry *malagueña* with Spanish guitar and castanets.

Clothed in iridescent black, his shirt slit to the waist and wearing what looked like an ivory tusk on a chain around his neck, Jay backed out of the wings, heels tapping like a flamenco dancer, his shoulders arched and wide, his chest high, his head thrown slightly back. Next came Kay, following, her eyes locked on his, her white-blonde hair slicked back and held high with a Spanish comb. As she progressed, twirling her ruffled skirt like a matador's cape, Jay backed away, puffing his lips as if mouthing '*olé*'.

'Is Miss Kay the bull?' Chloe asked, almost picking up on the symbolism of the dance.

'No, she's the cape,' I said. 'Just watch.'

Suddenly Jay turned his back on his partner, tap, tap, tapping in place while Kay approached stealthily from behind. She pasted her body against his, wrapped her arms around his chest, fingers splayed. As the music grew in intensity, Jay peeled Kay's hand from his chest, and spun her away. She dropped to the floor, her legs sliding into a graceful split, while Jay continued his increasingly frantic tapping, dragging Kay around by her arm, as if he were mopping the floor with her body.

Jay released Kay's hand, turned away, as if in scorn.

Kay collapsed in despair, her cheek resting against the floor-boards, but only for a moment. In one fluid movement she leapt to her feet, arched her back, raised her arms toward the ceiling and pumped them up and down, as if picking apples.

Jay turned, as if he'd only just noticed his partner. She stopped picking apples, locked eyes on him and started to run. He spread his arms and caught her, she draped herself around his neck, nestled her head under his chin.

Unexpectedly, Jay's knees buckled, and he staggered side-ways. I gasped. Who would have thought Kay was so heavy? As I watched in astonishment, Jay's arms dropped to his sides, Kay along with them, dumping her in an unceremoni-ous heap on the floor, like a colorful bundle of laundry. Jay clutched his chest, staggered backwards, then collapsed.

The music played on.

First we heard an 'ooooo', the intake of thousands of breaths.

The music stopped abruptly.

Then silence.

By that time, Kay had crawled over to Jay where he lay on the floor. As we watched in horror, scarcely daring to breathe, she put her cheek to his face, then laid her head on his chest.

Dave hustled over from the wings, his ragged breathing amplified a hundredfold by the mike, the judges were on their feet, and Kay was screaming, 'Somebody call 9-1-1. My husband's having a heart attack!'

Nineteen

Chloe bounced on tiptoes, trying to see the stage over the heads of the people standing in front of us. 'What's wrong? What happened to Mr Jay?'

I wrapped my arm around my granddaughter and pulled her close. 'It's going to be all right, Chloe. Somebody's calling a doctor for Mr Jay.'

After seeing that there was nothing he could do to help Jay, Dave turned to the audience, arms raised, except that this time nobody clapped. 'Please, everyone, stay calm. Take your seats. The paramedics are on their way.'

The audience sat, but restless murmuring washed in waves through the theater.

The paramedics must have been standing by because they arrived almost immediately, two men in uniform carrying a stretcher upon which sat an instrument I recognized, a portable defibrillator. Paul stretched his long frame across Eva and Chloe's laps to grab my hand and give it a comforting squeeze. He had to know I was thinking about the day my mother had a heart attack while standing in our kitchen.

Up on stage, the paramedics went to work on Jay while Kay's brave face dissolved into a mask of panic, and she started to sob and shake.

I shot out of my seat. 'I need to go to her.'

Paul, always the voice of reason, jerked his head toward the stage where well-trained, green-shirted staffers had materialized, blocking all access from the orchestra to the stage. 'Sit down, Hannah. They're not going to let you anywhere near the poor guy.'

Reassuringly for me, Samantha Purdy had already reached Kay, wrapped both arms around her and was rubbing her back and rocking, soothing her as one might a child. After a few moments, Samantha led Kay off-stage where she could wait in the comfort of the star lounge or green room I figured must be backstage somewhere.

The problem must not have been with Jay's heart; after fussing about for several minutes, the paramedics put the defibrillator away. Together they lifted Jay on to the stretcher, made sure he was comfortable, strapped him in, and started to carry him away. Just before the stretcher disappeared into the wings, Jay raised a hand and managed a wave.

'He's going to be all right!' somebody shouted.

A sea of mighty, thunderous applause.

'Where do you suppose they're taking him?' Eva wanted to know.

I knew the answer to that question. The University of Maryland Medical Center was right around the corner. That's where they'd done all they could for my mother, the place where she'd died.

'What's wrong with Mr Jay?' Chloe asked again.

'Probably nothing serious, Pumpkin. But they're taking him to the hospital just to make sure.' Chloe didn't look convinced, so I added, 'Remember when you were very little and I was in the hospital?'

Chloe nodded. 'Sort of.'

'And they fixed me all up, right?'

Chloe had been clutching her notebook to her chest, but she opened it and spread it out on her lap, apparently reassured. 'Can I write about Mr Jay?'

'Honey, you can write about anything you want.'

'Chloe,' Ruth added, 'don't worry about Mr Jay. He's probably just exhausted. He's been practicing very hard on his dancing.'

'How do you spell egg-zausted, Aunt Ruth?'

While Ruth helped Chloe with her spelling, I said, 'Melanie told me Jay was feeling achy, thought he might be coming down with the flu. Wait a minute . . . look.'

Samantha Purdy had reappeared on stage, smiling hugely as if she'd just saved the entire Third World from war, poverty and disease. She approached the standing microphone, bent at the waist, put her plump, glossy lips close to it and said, 'He's going to be fine, ladies and gentlemen. Backstage just now, Jay was smiling and talking to me, ready to get right up off that stretcher. They're taking him to the hospital to have him checked out, but he's going to be fine, just fine.'

While Samantha was delivering the good news, Dave bounced as bouncily as a three-hundred-pound man could bounce back to center stage. 'That's great news, Samantha. Great news indeed. And wasn't that a fabulous paso doble, ladies and gentlemen? Let's give a big round of applause to Jay and Kay Giannotti, and we certainly hope to see you back on your talented feet real soon, Jay.'

Although I remained worried about Jay, and wondered how Kay was holding up over at the emergency room, I was anxious for the show to go on, so when it did, I clapped until my hands began to sting just like everyone else.

We sat through the next two auditions – neither of them worth writing home about, either in my opinion or the judges – before Hutch and Melanie were introduced.

I'd seen only the early practice sessions, never a dress rehearsal, so when the couple appeared on stage, I was stunned by their costumes. Melanie had transformed herself into a beaded, glittery flapper, her hair hidden under a sparkling cloche, spit curls caressing her cheeks. Hutch wore a black and white striped three-piece suit, a black shirt with a white tie, and spats. When the dance began, he was sitting on a chair, his head bowed, a fedora tipped over his left eyebrow.

A mobster and his moll.

'And now, dancing the tango, I give you Gaylord Hutchinson and Melanie Fosher, from Annapolis, Maryland! Cue the music, Steve!' ordered one of the judges. From the Down Under accent, I figured it was Neville.

Immediately, the familiar tune of 'Hernando's Hideaway' boomed out of the speaker banks.

Strolling, strolling, strolling, eyes downcast, Melanie approached Hutch. He glanced up languidly, slid the hat to the back of his head, seized her hand, rose from his chair, pulled her to him . . . and from that moment they moved as one, connected cheek to cheek, chest to chest, thigh to thigh.

I know a dark secluded place . . .

Circling, circling they stalked left. Whirling, whirling, they slithered right, their footwork so intricate it was hard for the eye to follow.

A flick of the foot here, a snap of the head there.

I tore my eyes away long enough to glance down the row to Ruth, wondering how she might be taking it, and was surprised (and relieved!) to see her beaming with pride.

You will be free, to gaze at me . . .

Back on stage, Melanie paused as if her shoes were glued to the floor. When Hutch backed away ever so slowly, Melanie's feet stayed where they were and she began a gentle slide into his arms. He turned, she bobbed up, they whirled and swiveled and spun until before anyone knew it, Hutch was back in the chair where he'd begun, with Melanie sitting on his lap. On the last *olé* of the song, Melanie snatched the fedora off Hutch's head and plopped it down on her own.

The audience sprang to its feet. They screamed, they hooted, they cheered.

I jumped up and down, cupped my hands around my mouth and shouted 'bravo' so many times that I made my throat sore. I hadn't yelled so long and so loud since the Orioles won the World Series back in 1983.

We couldn't see the judges' faces, but they must have been smiling, too.

A voice I recognized as Jonathan Job's said, 'Wow. I haven't seen anything so well coordinated since Torvill and Dean electrified the world with Bolero back in the 80s! How long have you two been dancing together?'

Melanie sprang from Hutch's lap, and the two of them made their way over to the standing microphone where Melanie breathed into it, 'Three months.'

Samantha gushed, 'You are just so amazing! Three months! You are blowing my mind. I am speechless!'

Hutch and Melanie's routine had blown Neville's mind, too. 'That, ladies and gentlemen, is what the tango is all about! A walking seduction. What can I say? Judges, this couple goes on to New York City. Am I right?'

'Oh, yes, definitely,' Samantha cooed.

'Too right.' This from Jonathan.

I was in real danger of choking on the lump in my throat. As the audience erupted into applause all around us, Chloe squealed, 'They won? Uncle Hutch won?'

Eva patted her head. 'Yes, indeed. Your Uncle Hutch won.'

At the end of the row, I noticed Paul fanning Ruth with Chloe's notebook. She'd slouched in her chair, broken leg half blocking the aisle. I recognized the symptoms; she was hyperventilating, but nothing a few minutes of in-with-the-good-air, out-with-the-bad-air couldn't cure.

Somehow we managed to sit through the next seven auditions, but the judges could have been watching dancing bears or boxing kangaroos or maypole dancing for all we cared. When Dave Carson came out at the end of the set to help us relax with 'seated sun salutations' – apparently the big man was into yoga, too – we half carried, half walked Ruth out of the auditorium, retrieved her wheelchair, and hurried out to the street.

We'd agreed to meet Hutch and Melanie at the Cheesecake Factory for lunch, no matter what, so we walked, rolled (and some of us floated) down to the Pratt Street Pavilion on the waterfront, arriving just as the restaurant opened.

A grilled eggplant sandwich was in my future, I knew, but when Hutch and Melanie showed up, I planned to treat everyone to a round of Godiva chocolate brownie sundaes. We would celebrate their triumph in style.

Twenty

B ut Jay was not all right. Far from it.
He'd rallied in the ambulance, but by the time the
EMTs rolled him into the Emergency Room, he felt nause-
ated and was complaining of pains in his abdomen. Before
the staff could check him in, he began vomiting.

This report came to me directly from Chance.

Early on Saturday, when nobody answered my repeated
calls to the Giannotti home, I'd stopped by J & K to see if
anyone had news. It was before business hours, the studio
was locked, but I could see Chance through the window,
so I pounded on the glass until he looked up from whatever he was doing on the office computer and unlocked the
door.

'Sorry to interrupt your work,' I apologized as Chance
stepped aside to let me in.

'Not a problem. When it comes to juggling Excel spread-
sheets, I actually welcome interruption.'

'Working on the books?'

'For my sins. I've got an associate's degree in accounting,
so guess who gets tapped to send out the past dues?' He
slipped his hands into the rear pockets of his jeans, the
denim stretched so tight over his adorable buns that I was
amazed he could get a toothpick into the pockets, let alone
his fingers.

'I've got Jay's gym bag in the car,' I told Chance. 'After
the EMTs took Jay away, Hutch retrieved it from the dressing
room at the Hippodrome. Hutch had a couple of meetings
today, so I volunteered to take care of it.' I waved in the
general direction of the parking lot. 'Should I leave the bag
here, do you think, or take it to their home?'

Chance shrugged his muscular shoulders. 'Your call.'

I shrugged my bony shoulders back. 'There could be something valuable in the bag, I suppose. Don't want Kay to worry about it.'

Chance seemed uninterested. 'Whatever.'

In point of fact, I'd already searched Jay's gym bag, and found nothing inside that I'd consider valuable, unless you count a pair of black denims, a white T-shirt, several pairs of socks, a can of talcum powder, a comb, and a jar of Dippity-Do hair gel. 'I guess I'll just take it up to Kay at the hospital, then. Is Jay still there, do you know?'

'They kept him overnight for observation,' Chance informed me. He checked his watch. 'Kay called this morning to ask me to check Jay's schedule and let his students know he won't be coming in this week. She said the doctors would decide by noon whether to release Jay or not. It's twelve thirty now and I haven't heard, so I figure they're still poking and prodding.'

'Kay must be frantic with worry.'

'I'd say so. She spent the night on a sofa. She sounded exhausted when we talked.'

'You have to admire Jay, going on stage in front of all those people when he felt so sick. Their paso doble was stunning, even if it ended a bit prematurely.'

'Jay's a showman. It was a really big deal to be asked to perform for the *Shall We Dance?* audience. No way he'd miss the opportunity. He was nervous about it, for sure. Jay kept telling me he was afraid he'd screw it up, but you probably noticed how Kay kept stroking his ego, pushing him in practice.'

Frankly, I hadn't, but I didn't say so. Before their exhibition at the Hippodrome, the only thing I'd seen Kay throw at Jay was drop-dead looks.

'Kay's quite the competitor. Always was.' Chance looked thoughtful. 'I think Kay and your friend Hutch would have been champions if Hutch hadn't dropped out of dance to focus on law school. It took Kay three years to find another partner.'

'Jay?'

'Not Jay. She met Jay at the Internationals. They were

both dancing with someone else. Have you ever seen a competition?'

I shook my head. 'I was hoping to attend the Sweetheart Ball tomorrow to see how it works, and to watch Tom and Laurie perform, but I already had a commitment to watch my grandkids.'

'Well, between heats there's general dancing. Jay asked Kay to tango, and the rest as they say, is history. Ironic that the partners they ditched hooked up and went on to beat Jay and Kay out of the US championships two years in a row. Ha ha ha.'

'Is Kay bitter about that?'

'Nah. They're both too wrapped up in running the studio now to worry about competitions. I think Kay's accepted the fact that Jay's much more interested in the business end of things. Recently he'd been saying he plans to hang up his shoes, that he's too old to compete.'

'Those who can, do. Those who can't, teach,' I quoted.

'Yes, except Jay can and does. He's an inspirational teacher.'

'Does Jay have many private students?' I asked, recalling how much time he'd taken with Ruth before she'd been sidelined by the parking lot attack.

'Quite a few. Melanie and Don, of course, then when Don shipped out, the time he spent working with Melanie and with Hutch.' He rolled his eyes. 'Then there's always little Tessa Douglas and her dreadful mother.'

'Preparing Tessa and little what's-his-name for *Tiny Ballroom*?'

Chance snorted. 'Next thing you know it'll be *Dancing in Diapers*.' He shivered. 'I don't know about you, Hannah, but seeing manic grins pasted on orange-colored ten-year-old faces is pretty creepy.'

I laughed out loud. 'Wearing Ken and Barbie clothes from the 1960s? I agree. Unnerving.'

I glanced around the empty studio. 'It's rather quiet today, isn't it? This is the first time I've been here when Tessa and her mother weren't. I was beginning to think they had an apartment out back or something.'

'It'd be more convenient, that's for sure. Tessa gets a

lesson of some sort almost every day. Ballet, tap, ballroom.'

I thought about the price list Ruth had showed me, did some quick multiplication in my head and said, 'That must cost Shirley a fortune.'

Chance's eyes widened. 'You kidding? Shirley gets a deep discount. Nudge-nudge-wink-wink.'

'Are you implying . . .' I began, thinking that if Jay and Shirley were having an affair, surely they wouldn't have been as openly friendly around the studio as I'd recently observed.

He arched an eyebrow. 'And he was working with Ruth Gannon for free.'

I froze. 'Ruth is my sister. She's not . . .'

Chance stopped me with a raised hand. 'Sorry. Forget I said anything.' He managed a boyish grin. 'Bit of a late night last night. Not functioning on all cylinders, I'm afraid.'

I wondered if Chance meant to imply that Ruth was getting a nudge-nudge-wink-wink special rate from Jay. I'd just seen Chance tapping away on the office computer. He could have been whiling the time away playing Free Cell, of course, but since Chance had access to the studio's computer files, including its financial records, he had to know how much students were paying and for what. *I* knew why Jay had been working with Ruth for free, and Chance should have known it, too: Ruth's good showing on *Shall We Dance?* would have been a major coup for the studio, a bullet point on any franchise prospectus Jay might be mailing out. It still was, but the name Melanie Fosher would be getting set in Times New Roman font alongside of Gaylord Hutchinson instead of Ruth Gannon.

Did Chance suspect Ruth of having an affair with Jay? And if so, had he mentioned his groundless suspicions to anyone else?

'Things are not always what they seem,' I said, both in defense of my sister and, in spite of how much the woman annoyed me, Tessa's mother, Shirley.

Chance shrugged his massive shoulders again, causing his neatly tucked T-shirt – 'I Do All My Own Stunts' – to inch upwards. 'Whatever.'

'Look, Chance,' I said, gladly changing the subject,

'I'm going up to the hospital. Are there any messages for Kay?'

Chance adjusted the belt that encircled his impossibly narrow waist. 'Just tell her it's all under control. We're closing the studio on Monday and Tuesday, but starting Wednesday, I'm taking Jay's students, and Melanie will be filling in with my classes, so we're completely covered.' He checked his watch again. 'She should be here by now, in fact. Melanie, that is. We've got the Swing and Sway Seniors coming in on the van at two. Always a lively bunch, but Melanie can handle them.'

I made a mental note to mention the Swing and Sway Seniors to my father and Neelie, bid goodbye to Chance, and pointed my car west on 665 and north on I-97.

When I got to the hospital, a cheerful woman at reception informed me that Jay had been moved to a private room on the sixth floor. She pointed me in the direction of the elevator.

I found the room, and entered it quietly. Kay was sitting on a chair pulled up close to Jay's hospital bed. On the bed, Jay seemed to be resting peacefully. An oxygen tube was strapped to his nose and an IV snaked into his arm. 'Kay,' I whispered.

Kay turned a worried, tear-streaked face to me. 'Hello, Hannah.'

'How's he doing?' I asked.

'They've sedated him. He's exhausted from throwing up.' She got up from the chair, took my arm gently, and guided me into the hallway. 'Let's go somewhere where we can talk.'

Kay led me down the corridor to an upholstered settee in front of a picture window that let in the bright winter sunshine. Her eyes looked tired, the lashes still heavy with dark clumps of the make-up she'd worn for the previous day's performance.

'He seems better today, Hannah. At least the vomiting has stopped. But he's really sick.'

'What's wrong?'

'They don't know.' She twisted her hands in her lap. 'They're testing him for everything under the sun.'

'So it's not flu?'

Kay looked away from me, and stared out the window. 'No.'

After a long moment she said, 'Isn't it amazing how life goes on?' She pointed. 'Those people down there in the street; those cars. My world's tumbling down, and I feel like they should stop and share my pain. But, no. They go on and on as if nothing's happened.'

'I know how you feel,' I said to Kay, confident that being familiar with my medical history because of Dance for the Cure, she'd realize that I wasn't mouthing empty platitudes. After my cancer diagnosis, I remember being surprised to see the flowers still blooming in the planters outside the doctor's office, people still driving along busy Bestgate Road, rushing to the mall on important errands. Later at the 7/11, someone had been arguing with the Vietnamese clerk because he'd had the bad judgment to run out of copies of the *New York Times*. 'This is not a crisis,' I remember telling the loudmouth jerk as I waited in line behind him to pay for my half and half. 'You could be diagnosed with cancer. *That* would be a crisis.' He'd given me a drop-dead look and stalked out, while the rest of the people in the line applauded. Maybe I'd given him something to think about.

Kay turned her attention from the activity on the streets of downtown Baltimore, blinking rapidly, saying nothing.

'So, if it's not the flu, what? Food poisoning?' I prompted.

'They're not sure. He's been complaining for weeks that his legs felt funny, like rubber, you know? But he danced through it, focusing on the routine. We almost made it, didn't we, Hannah?'

I laid my hand over hers. 'Your paso doble was brilliant. You'll be back on the dance floor in no time.'

She arched a single darkly-penciled eyebrow. 'Do you think they're going to put that on television?'

From Kay's expression, I couldn't determine whether she hoped they would televise a clip of their performance, or prayed that they wouldn't. I could picture it now, news at five, six and eleven – Kay's leap, Jay's catch and their fall – in slo-mo, over and over. I squeezed her hand reassuringly.

'Don't worry, Kay. There wasn't anything on the evening news last night.'

Cameras hadn't been allowed in the theater, but I wondered how many people had sneaked them in anyway, and how many views of Jay and Kay's routine had been posted to YouTube by day's end. I decided not to mention it.

Kay's brows drew together as if I'd asked her a particularly difficult question, then just as suddenly, the look of concentration vanished. 'I'm expecting the doctor in a few minutes. Guess I better get back to the room.'

I'd been dismissed. 'Perhaps he'll have good news for you, Kay.'

She rose from the chair and said, 'It's not botulism, at least. And since he's not eaten any fish, they can pretty much eliminate ciguatera poisoning. But it could be lupus, Hannah, or porphyria,' she rattled on, her voice rising. 'Or Guillaine-Barré syndrome? My friend Ellen's husband had Guillaine-Barré *years* ago and he still has to walk with a cane!'

I stared at Kay for a moment, taking it all in. I knew from sailing charter boats in the Virgin Islands that ciguatera was a nerve poison one got from eating large, tropical reef-feeding fish. Lupus was an autoimmune disorder. Porphyria rang a bell, too. 'Porphyria? Isn't that what King George III was supposed to have had?'

'Did you see the movie?' she asked, her eyes wide. 'I'm scared, Hannah.'

She was referring to *The Madness of George III*, where Helen Mirren had to watch while her husband, Nigel Hawthorne, descended into madness. 'Kay, that was in the eighteenth century! They have treatment for porphyria these days.'

'I know, but it's just so scary, not knowing.'

I urged her along the hall gently. 'Go back to the room and wait for the doctor. I'm sure he'll have good news for you soon. And don't worry about a thing.' I delivered the message from Chance.

'I don't know what I'd do without Chance and Alicia,' she said, tearing up again. She gave me a hug, catching me slightly off guard. 'And my friends.'

'If there's anything I can do . . .' It was a cliché, but heart-felt. 'I used to manage an office in Washington, DC. I can push papers with consummate skill.'

'Thanks, Hannah, but Chance can handle the business end of things for me, at least for a while.' She slipped her arm through mine, and drew me down the hallway along-side her while continuing our conversation. 'He's even expressed interest in buying into one of our franchise oper-ations,' she said, smiling.

I thought about Chance as I'd last seen him, heading back to the office computer: erect, graceful, confident. 'I'm sure that'd work out great for everyone,' I said, adding paren-thetically (particularly for Chance).

Kay brightened. 'And think of all the publicity we'll get from *Shall We Dance?* when Hutch and Melanie move on to New York City!' She froze in mid-step and turned to me. 'When Hutch called yesterday afternoon with the good news, I thought Jay would hop off the gurney and do a happy dance right there in the Emergency Room.'

'I wish you had seen their performance,' I said as we moved past the nurses' station. 'Absolutely stunning.'

'I know. I helped Jay with the choreography. I watched them practice.'

'And Tom and Laurie will no doubt do you proud in DC this weekend.'

Kay froze. 'Yikes! The Sweetheart Ball Championships!' She flushed. 'With all that's happened since yesterday, I nearly forgot.' She touched my arm. 'Don't tell Tom and Laurie.'

'Tell them what?' I grinned.

I left Kay at the door to her husband's room with a promise to let her know the minute I heard the results from DC.

As it turned out, we'd have a whole lot to celebrate.

Twenty-One

'First, first and first!' It was late Sunday night, and Laurie was calling me from inside an elevator at the J.W. Marriott Hotel. 'Stop that, now! Not you, Hannah, Tommy. Naughty boy is nibbling on my ear, messin' with my chandeliers. Ooooh!' she squealed.

'What are you laughing at, Hannah?' Paul closed his paperback novel and looked at me suspiciously.

'Shhhh.' I flapped my hand to quiet him, then used the same hand to cover the receiver. 'Apparently Tom and Laurie have done well at the championships. Hold on.'

'Tell you all about it when we see you,' Laurie bubbled. 'Oh, glory! We can show you the videos.'

'Cause for celebration,' I said, making a snap decision. 'No classes on Monday and Tuesday, so how about tomorrow night. Dinner?'

'Let me consult with my social secretary here.' Much giggling and rustling of fabric followed before Laurie came back on the line. 'He says we'll be delighted. You've got a big TV screen over there? This girl's so blazing no regular little twenty-four incher's gonna handle it.'

'Count on it,' I laughed, and with a shriek of delight, Laurie broke the connection.

The following morning when I polled the usual suspects, so many said 'yes' that I had to call everyone back and move the dinner to Daddy's.

I arrived at Daddy's sprawling home in the Providence neighborhood north of Annapolis more than an hour early to help set up. Neelie was already in the dining room putting out glasses, plates and cutlery. 'How many do I need?' she asked, clutching a stack of my mother's best china plates.

Mentally, I ticked off the guests. Three already there, Paul to come straight from an extra instruction session at the Academy, Hutch and Ruth, Melanie, Chance and Alicia, Tom and Laurie, and my friend, Eva. 'Twelve,' I told her, suddenly thankful that, much as I loved them, Emily and Dante had declined, citing Monday being a school night and too late for the children.

Neelie counted out the plates and set them in place on a white tablecloth decorated with baskets of flowers in delicate blue cross-stitch; my late mother's handiwork. The large watercolor over the buffet, the pillows on the living-room sofa, the pottery vase holding a bouquet of fresh flowers, Mom's work was all around me, never failing to remind me of how much I missed her.

'Where's Daddy?'

'In the kitchen,' Neelie grinned. 'Says he's cooking.'

I pressed a hand to my chest. 'Words to strike fear into my heart.'

In point of fact, my father was the world's worst cook. Not his fault, I suppose, because a succession of women – first his grandmother then his mother and finally his wife – had shooed little Georgie out of the kitchen.

Or, it could be genetic. Paul's sister, Connie, was a terrible cook, too. Eating at Connie's house was always a nostalgic stroll through the 1960s. Noodle casseroles featuring Campbell's cream of mushroom soup; salads thrown together out of boxes of Jello, fruit cocktail and miniature marshmallows.

Daddy's problem was that he refused to follow directions, winging it through meal preparation with no knowledge base. No wonder he stayed thin. One time, not long after my mother's death, I had arrived for a visit in the late afternoon to find my father in the kitchen, squinting at a faded and spotted recipe card, attempting to duplicate Mom's lasagne. He abandoned the card and stubbornly refused my help, so I poured a glass of wine and watched while he put the noodles on to boil. Daddy went on to collect an assortment of canned tomato products from the cupboard, which he opened and dumped into a pot for the sauce. 'Needs spices,' he'd said (meaning herbs), and began rummaging through the spice rack.

After fifteen minutes, I'd said, 'Daddy, I think the noodles might be done by now,' to which he'd replied, 'Oh! Is the water gone already?'

Needless to say, when I entered the kitchen, it wasn't with any great sense of optimism.

I found my father leaning over the kitchen counter thumbing through a pile of carryout menus that he kept in a see-through plastic folder next to the telephone. A good omen. I walked up behind him and wrapped my arms around his waist. 'How are the eyes?'

He turned and kissed my cheek. 'A little sensitive to light, but otherwise, it's a verifiable miracle.' He held a Curbside to Go menu at arm's length and read, 'Tomato bruschetta, mozzarella fritta, shrimp and artichoke dip . . .'

'Sounds like a plan,' I told him, snatching the menu from his fingers. 'You get the ice out of the freezer and set up the bar. I'll take care of ordering dinner.'

Daddy clucked my chin. 'You just want to make sure I don't forget the eggplant Parmesan.'

I slapped his face lightly with the menu. 'Busted!'

After Daddy left with the ice, I made a quick call to Paul's cell phone asking him to stop by the Macaroni's on Jennifer Road to pick up our dinner, although it was more than a bit out of his way to do so, then called Macaroni's and turned cooking our dinner over to them. In less than five minutes, I was back in the family room where I found Daddy presiding over the bar, as instructed. 'A Bloody Mary for me, please, light on the vodka,' I said, and lobbed him a pair of limes, which he caught one at a time with his left hand, like a juggler. His bad eyesight was, quite obviously, history.

When the doorbell rang, Bloody Mary in hand, I sang out, 'I'll get it!'

I found Hutch standing on the doorstep, carrying Ruth who was still encumbered by her ungainly cast. I had to laugh.

Hutch was beaming. Ruth, too. 'Over the threshold,'

Hutch said, entering the house, being careful not to bang Ruth's leg on the door frame.

Ruth giggled like a teenager and kissed him on the mouth. I hadn't seen her so bubbly since her engagement was announced. 'Honestly, Hannah,' my sister said as Hutch swept past me, 'I'm so proud of him I could just about burst.'

And I was proud of her, too. When Hutch entered the *Shall We Dance?* competition with Melanie, I'd expected jealousy from my sister, but there appeared to be none. Perhaps this was how a childless couple felt when they welcomed the birth of a child via a surrogate mother. Happy to have the child, and grateful to the person who made it all possible.

Hutch installed Ruth on Dad's favorite red leather BarcaLounger, waited until she got comfortable, then hustled off to fetch her a Martini.

'Three olives!' Ruth reminded his departing back, and then turned to smile at me. 'We're still pinching ourselves.'

I told her again how amazing I thought Hutch had been.

'Hutch thinks there was a definite advantage to going on early. The judges didn't have a lot to compare them to, so they stood out.'

'Ha-ha! Like the belly dancer who partnered with the guy wrapped around a plush boa constrictor?' I grinned. 'Don't know about you, but I thought that act showed promise.'

'They were supposed to be Adam and Eve,' Ruth informed me.

We were still dissecting the competition like bad-mannered judges when Melanie arrived with Chance and Alicia, followed almost immediately by Tom and Laurie, flushed with excitement, and by Eva, looking sophisticated in her brand new Judi-Dench-as-M-style hairdo.

As I was showing everyone to the bedroom where they could put their coats, Laurie pressed a DVD into my hands, introduced herself to Eva and said, 'Girl, you're smokin'! Love the hair.'

Even in the darkened hallway, I could see Eva blush. 'You look pretty hot yourself, Laurie.'

'Oh, do you like the scarf?' Laurie fluffed up the bow. 'It's Thai silk. Tom had business in Bangkok last year and brought it back for me.' Laurie ran her hands down her narrow hips, smoothing the peacock blue fabric. 'And aren't we glad that Capri pants are back? Thank you, Mary Tyler Moore!'

Underneath her short lambswool jacket Laurie wore a white silk shirt with a plunging V. The toes sticking out of her strappy black heels were painted the same bright blue as her pants. She peeled off her jacket, tossed it on the bed and tripped down the hallway trilling, 'Tommy! A vodka Martini!'

How she managed to totter up the icy drive from her car to the house in those heels, I'll never know. And surely Laurie was too young to remember Mary Tyler Moore, but maybe she caught the reruns of *The Dick Van Dyke Show* on Nick at Night.

I heard Paul's deep baritone announce, 'Hello, everyone! Where do you want the food?' and moved to go out and meet him, but was waylaid by Melanie just entering the bedroom, removing her hat.

Eva, bless her, said, 'I'll go help Paul,' and bustled past.

'Hi, Hannah. Nice to see you.' Melanie handed me her coat, so I laid it carefully on the bed. As she stood in front of the mirror repairing the ravages of winter hat hair with her fingers, I congratulated her once again on Friday's stunning performance, and her footwork in particular. 'That was all Jay,' she sniffed. In the mirror, her face crumpled.

'I called the hospital this morning,' I told her, 'but they wouldn't tell me anything. Is there any word on his condition?'

Looking at me through the mirror, Melanie sucked in her lips, and shook her head. 'He's out of intensive care, but they're still trying to figure out what's wrong with him.' She turned around. 'Kay texted it could be something called GBS. I was afraid to ask. What the hell is *that*?'

Since talking with Kay on Saturday, I'd done some research on the Internet, so I explained about Guillaine-Barré Syndrome, its symptoms – weakness and tingling in the legs, muscle pain, respiratory difficulties, dizziness – and its possible side effects. If Jay was suffering from GBS, there was a chance he'd never dance again. But I didn't tell Melanie that. 'Is Jay still allowed visitors?' I asked, hoping to sail into less treacherous waters.

'I guess so,' Melanie said, tearing up again.

I grabbed a tissue from the box on the bedside table and handed it to her.

'But not me,' she sniffed. 'I just can't bear to see him that way.' She pressed the tissue into the corner of each eye. 'You know, *sick*.'

'I'm sure he'll be back on his feet very soon,' I said with more confidence than I felt. I had one-hundred percent faith in the UMMC doctors, nurses and support staff, but they didn't know everything, and sometimes, as with my mother, even the best isn't enough.

Melanie looked around the bedroom, spotted the wastepaper basket, and tossed her used tissue into it. 'Jay is going to choreograph our routines for *Shall We Dance?* you know.'

'Hold that thought, Melanie.'

As we walked down the hall to join the party, I was surprised by Eva coming back the other way. She grabbed my arm, pulled me toward the guest bedroom on the street side of the house. 'You need to see this.'

Thinking my friend had lost her mind, I followed her into the room, instinctively reaching for the light switch.

'No!' Eva gently batted my hand away. 'Keep the light off.'

'Eva,' I whispered. 'What's gotten into you?'

She dragged me over to the window, and pulled aside one of the linen drapes. 'Look. There. Across the street.'

Following her instructions, but wishing she'd be more specific, I said, 'A bunch of parked cars?'

'No,' she said. 'The silver Prius by the corner. There's a guy in it.'

I squinted into the dark. Sitting behind the wheel was a man with a square head, square chin and no neck, like he'd grown up in a box.

'That's Jeremy Dunstan,' she said.

'Are you sure?'

'Positive. A Prius Hybrid. You know, the answer to the question, What would Jesus drive?'

'He followed you here?'

'Evidently. He certainly doesn't live in the Providence community.'

'So where does he live?'

'Admiral Heights, near the stadium. I had Therese look it up in the church records.'

'I thought you said he was leaving you alone, Eva.'

'I did, too. Even when I thought I caught sight of him outside of Graul's Market the other day, I decided it was my imagination.'

We sat down together on the foot of the bed, in the dark, the light from the hallway just illuminating her face. 'What am I going to do, Hannah?'

'Do you want me to go out there and talk to him?' Then thinking better of it, I added, 'Or Paul? The Midshipmen say Paul can be pretty intimidating.'

If I hadn't known Eva so well, I might even have questioned the existence of this shadowy man; yet there he was, just as Eva had described him. I couldn't tell about his height, of course, but the body shape was right, and as he turned his head toward my father's front door, light glanced off his glasses.

'You need to call the police,' I said.

'That's what the bishop told me when I sent him copies of Jeremy's emails.'

'Well?'

'I said I had to think about it.'

'Eva!'

'The man thinks he's in love with me, Hannah. I'm afraid of what he might do if they slap him with a restraining order.'

I was going to say that the man wasn't likely to make a scene during a church service, what with all the congregation there as witnesses, and then I remembered that nut job who went postal at two churches out in Colorado. I took a deep breath. 'You can't be responsible for every troubled soul in the world, Eva!'

'You sound like the bish. He reminded me that Jeremy Dunstan's spiritual health doesn't depend on me, and that I can't help everybody.'

'The bish is right.'

We sat in silence for a moment, until my father's high, clear tenor sang down the hallway, 'Suppertime, suppertime, suppertime, suppertime!'

I took Eva's hand and pulled her to her feet. 'C'mon. If Jeremy's still out there when the party breaks up, we'll call the cops. In the meantime, I believe your services will be required at the table, Rev Haberman.'

Although a lush Cabernet Sauvignon would have been nice with the penne rustica, Daddy had opened two bottles of New Zealand Sauvignon Blanc, and was walking around the table, filling wine glasses before taking his place at the head of the table opposite Neelie.

Before he could say anything, Alicia raised her glass. 'Here's to Melanie and Hutch, *Shall We Dance?* finalists!' She turned to her left, where Tom sat next to Laurie. 'And to Tom and Laurie! Three firsts! Deserving champions all.'

As we clinked glasses all around, I thought I heard Melanie mutter, 'Some more deserving than others.'

I nudged Melanie gently with my elbow to get her attention. 'I beg your pardon?' I wasn't sure I'd heard her correctly.

Melanie sipped her wine and smiled. 'Oh, nothing. I was just talking to Chance.'

Daddy scowled at me and cleared his throat. 'Eva. Will you say grace?'

It was our custom to hold hands around the table for grace. Daddy gathered up mine, I took Melanie's. At the far end of the table, Paul winked at me, and I smiled as Eva blessed our food.

> Give us grateful hearts, our Father, for all your mercies, and make us ever mindful of the needs of others. We ask you to bless those whom we love, now absent

from us, and we especially remember your servant, Jay. Be present with him that his weakness may be banished and his strength restored, through Jesus Christ our Lord. Amen

'Amen to that,' said my father, hardly pausing to take a second breath before spearing a shrimp with his fork.

All the time I was crunching my tomato bruschetta, I wondered about Melanie's remark. Was she implying there was something wrong with Tom and Laurie's win, some rule that they'd unwittingly broken that might disqualify them from competition? As I ate, I kept one eye on Melanie; with everyone talking at once, her eyes were getting a workout. I don't know how she kept it sorted.

After the last morsel of tiramisu disappeared, I helped clear the table. I was rinsing the dishes and stacking them in the dishwasher when Chance came in to thank us for dinner, and say his goodbyes. Sensing an opportunity to ask him about Melanie's remark, I followed him to the bedroom where we'd put the coats. 'Say, Chance. What do you think Melanie meant at dinner when she said that some are more deserving than others?'

Chance slipped his arms into his jacket, and zipped up the front. He shrugged. 'I think you'd better ask her.'

By the time we got out to the living room, though, I couldn't find Melanie anywhere.

As I waved Chance out the front door, I noticed that Jeremy Dunstan's Prius had disappeared from the street – thank goodness – but so had Melanie's KIA. Sometime while I was doing the dishes, Melanie Fosher had slipped quietly away.

Twenty-Two

With help from Ruth, I managed to track Melanie down on her cell phone. Without saying why I wanted to chat, I arranged to meet her for lunch at Galway Bay, the Irish pub and restaurant around the corner from our house on Prince George street that had long-ago become the regular Ives family hang-out.

When Melanie arrived, the hostess, Peggy, seated us in an alcove just inside and to the left of the vestibule, handed us green, leather-bound menus, and took our order for iced tea with extra lemon.

'Everything's good here,' I told Melanie as I opened my menu to check out the insert that described the daily specials. 'I'm particularly fond of the salad Kinsale and the seafood pie, but don't let that influence you.'

Melanie studied me over the top of her menu. 'Thanks for inviting me. After all the excitement running up to *Shall We Dance?* it's been a little too quiet around our apartment.' She laid down her menu with a sigh. 'Don isn't due back from Iraq for another ten months. Sometimes I'm so lonely I want to scream.'

As the tables around us began to fill up – with dark-suited legislators from the Maryland State government, rumpled professors from St John's College, and smartly uniformed naval officers from the Academy – she reminisced about the previous summer spent with her husband and his family on Martha's Vineyard. Melanie, as it turns out, was an only child from Lawrence, Kansas, and she'd bonded at once with Don's boisterous, fun-loving brothers and sisters, two of each.

The waitress made a timely arrival with our tea just then, and we both ordered the seafood pie with a side order of soda bread. 'Paul's never been away from home for more than two weeks,' I said, slipping the paper wrapper off my straw. 'I can't imagine being separated for more than a year.'

'I'll have plenty to occupy my time once Hutch and I start preparing for the competition in New York, of course.' Melanie paused to sip her tea before continuing. 'I just hate to think of Don having to watch the program on television rather than in person, but what can you do?'

'He must be busting the buttons clean off his uniform.'

She grinned. 'I texted Don right away, and you should have seen all the smiley- and kissy-faces he sent back.'

Melanie was tapping the contents of a pink Sweet'n Low packet into her glass when a cell phone began to play 'Anchors Aweigh' at the adjoining table. A naval officer – from the stripes on his sleeves I knew he was a lieutenant commander – silenced the ring, apologized to his table-mates with a hasty 'duty calls', and rushed past us out of the restaurant.

'Can't even let the poor boy eat,' I muttered, noticing the plate of half-eaten corned beef and cabbage the officer had left behind.

'When duty calls, Hannah, we are obliged to go.'

I felt my face flush. If I'd hoped to distract Melanie from thoughts about her husband's situation in Iraq I was failing miserably. Talking about Jay certainly wouldn't lighten the mood, so I decided to steer the conversation back to the previous weekend's triumphs. 'I would have liked to see Tom and Laurie compete in DC,' I said. 'Laurie showed me one of her costumes, and it was simply gorgeous.'

'Nobody from the studio was there, I guess.' Melanie spread butter on a slice of soda bread.

'So what did they win, exactly?'

Melanie shrugged, looking bored. 'Who? Tom and Laurie?'

'Yes,' I said, biting my tongue, thinking, Who else could we possibly be talking about?

'Plaques and vouchers,' Melanie said. 'The plaque is an engraved, Plexiglas kind of thing you receive for participating, then you get vouchers for first, second, and third places that are worth dollars off at next year's competition.'

Plaques and vouchers didn't seem like much of a return for all the time and money that Laurie told me she and her partner had invested in the Sweetheart Ball Championships. 'At least you and Hutch stand to win a substantial prize,' I commented, thinking about the New York apartment, the cash and the car.

Melanie smiled. 'Well, yeah.'

Suddenly the waitress appeared at my elbow with two hot mashed potato-topped casseroles and set them down in front of us. I poked a fork into mine to help the steam escape. While I waited for the dish to cool, I said, 'Tell me something, Melanie. Last night at dinner, you made a comment that some folks were more deserving than others. What did you mean by that?'

Melanie scooped a bit of mashed potato on to her fork, swirled it around in the light tomato gravy. 'I feel strongly that people ought to abide by the rules.'

'What rules are you talking about, Melanie?'

'It's really none of my business, but sometimes I overhear things that I'm not supposed to.' The potatoes disappeared into her mouth.

'Like what?'

'I'm not sure I should say.'

The way Melanie looked at me then, blandly and without blinking, made me want to scream, but I decided to try a bit of light-hearted bribery. I rustled up a super-sized grin and said, 'Bread pudding with extra rum sauce for dessert?'

Melanie stared thoughtfully at the county map of Ireland etched on the window glass behind me before answering. 'I guess it's OK. I already told Jay.' She put her fork down, folded her hands on the edge of the placemat in front of her and leaned across the table toward me. 'One evening when I was waiting for Hutch, I overheard Tom and Laurie talking. Do you know what SRS is?'

I thought for a moment, running through a myriad of possibilities. Sound Retrieval System? Student Record

Services? Scoliosis Research Society? I gave up. 'Do I have to play twenty questions?'

Melanie didn't smile. 'It's sexual reassignment surgery.'

I took this information in, turned it around a few times, but it didn't go anywhere. 'So?' I took a sip of my iced tea, waiting for Melanie to answer. She was taking her time.

'Laurie is a man.'

I sucked iced tea into my lungs, and began coughing so violently that nearby diners turned their heads and whispered to one another behind their hands as if deciding who'd be the first to get up and save me with the Heimlich maneuver. When I finally regained control of my lungs, I laid down my napkin and croaked, 'That's impossible.'

'You can think that, but you'd be wrong.'

My mind reeled with images of Laurie, svelte, glamorous Laurie, gliding around the dance floor, sharing beauty tips with me in the dressing room. 'But I've seen Laurie in her underwear! She's got bigger boobs than I do! Are you sure that you heard correctly?'

Melanie nodded. 'This was a bit more serious than my mistaking "where there's life there's hope" for "where's the lavender soap", so before going to Jay with what I suspected, I confronted Laurie. She admitted it.'

I must have managed some sort of gasping denial because Melanie continued, 'Laurie has been living as a woman for three years, Hannah. She's supposed to have SRS next month in Singapore.' Melanie leaned closer. 'But SRS or no SRS, nothing will change the fact that *she* is still a *he*.'

I took a deep breath. 'I simply can't believe it. Laurie's so feminine. How . . .?'

'Depilatories, hormones, surgery. You know.'

Hormones and hair removal products aside, what really blew my mind was I'd seen Laurie in the raciest, laciest panties in the Victoria's Secret catalog. If Laurie were a man, and she hadn't yet had her surgery, where did she hide her, oh gawd, privates? When I got home, I'd have to ask Paul. Maybe he'd know.

When I eventually remembered my seafood pie, I was amazed the dish was still hot. After toying with my entrée

for a few minutes, I looked up and said, 'Excuse me,
Melanie, but I don't see where you're going with this. So
what if Laurie is actually a man living as a woman. What
harm is there in that?'

'"It's an abomination before the Lord." Deuteronomy 22,
verse 5. "The woman shall not wear that which pertaineth
unto a man, neither shall a man put on a woman's garment."'

The words of a song from *Porgy and Bess* swam immediately to mind: 'The things that you're liable to read in
the Bible, they ain't necessarily so.' Up until a few moments
ago, I'd always liked Melanie, but then our conversations
had never strayed into the landmine-strewn territory of polit-
ics or religion. Now I was having wickedly unchristian
thoughts, like suggesting to Eva that she introduce Melanie
to Jeremy Dunstan.

'Melanie,' I said at last, trying not to let my exasperation
show. 'Surely you recognize that there are laws in the Old
Testament that simply don't apply to modern life. How to
sacrifice animals, for example, or sell your daughter into
slavery. And for some silly reason, we're not allowed to
stone people any more.'

Melanie speared a shrimp and popped it into her mouth.

'And contrary to Deuteronomy, you are wearing pants
today.'

'The men in ancient Israel didn't wear pants.'

Oh, Lord. Where was Pastor Eva when I needed her?
She could quote chapter and verse with the best of them,
using the Bible to prove or disprove just about any point.
This conversation with Melanie was going nowhere fast.

I pushed aside my seafood casserole, no longer hungry.
'OK, so let's take it as a given that Laurie Wainwright is
biologically a man. So what?'

'The Sweetheart Ball Championships that Tom and Laurie
just took several firsts in?'

'Yes?' I'd read all about it. The results were already posted
on the Sweetheart Ball website: First place. Waltz, Tango
and Quickstep. International Standard Advanced. Thomas
Wilson with Laurie Wainwright. Second in foxtrot and
Viennese.

'The championships are sanctioned by the National Dance Council of America,' Melanie continued. 'They have very strict rules, and one of those rules is: "a couple is defined as a male and a female." Page four.'

I was beginning to think that Melanie could tell me on what page of the white pages my telephone number appeared. But I could see what she was getting at. According to the NDCA rules, Tom and Laurie were not qualified to dance as a couple. Oh-oh. 'So, what will the Sweetheart people do if they find out? Take away their vouchers and plaques?'

Melanie shook her head. 'It's probably too late for that now, but they'd certainly be barred from future competitions, if they continue to dance with each other, I mean.'

'Maybe after Laurie has the surgery—' I began, but Melanie cut me off.

'As I said earlier, it's really none of my business.'

'But you told Jay.'

Melanie shrugged. 'He didn't believe me, either. So I suggested it might be something he'd like to look into, that's all, if he was concerned about protecting the reputation of the studio.' She took a deep breath, then let it out slowly. 'But it's a moot point, now, isn't it?'

'It is?'

'Apparently Jay never said anything to the organizers, or to the judges. Tom and Laurie danced. End of story.'

I sat back, stunned, thinking, You self-righteous little fool. Do you think you can open a Pandora's box of trouble, and simply walk away? End of story? No way.

I managed to finish my seafood pie, but when the waitress came by to refill our tea, I asked for the check. In spite of the tempting treats on the menu – crème brûlée cheesecake? – Melanie took a rain check on the bread pudding. Neither one of us was in the mood for dessert.

Twenty-Three

'Well, that explains the scarf,' Paul said when I told him about Laurie.

'It does?'

'Adam's apple,' he said, touching his throat. 'Women have them, too, but they're far less prominent. Laurie wore the scarf to hide it.'

'Right,' I said, feeling stupid. I took a few deep breaths. 'OK,' I continued. 'Adam's apples, I get. But how on earth did she hide . . . you know?'

'Her sexual organs?'

'Exactly.'

'Well, the testicles could be tucked up into the body where they originally came from, I suppose. Whenever they get cold, they tend to migrate northward anyway.'

'They do?' In spite of sex education classes in high school and decades of marriage, this fact was news to me. 'And the penis?'

'Having little experience wearing ladies' underpants, I really haven't a clue.'

'That's reassuring, darling, but not particularly helpful.'

'That's why God invented the Internet.'

Logging on to the Internet in our basement office a few minutes later, I discovered that what Paul told me about the testicles was true; they could easily be persuaded to disappear within the body. As for what 'transwomen' did with their inconvenient penises, well, let's just say that I now know one hundred and *two* uses for duct tape.

I also learned about breast augmentation, facial feminization surgery, tracheal shaves, androgen blockers, and laser hair removal, not only on the face, but on the chest and arms as well.

Ouch!

I clicked around a bit after that to read about sexual re-assignment surgery, but when I landed on a south-east Asian site featuring colorful before and after photos, I decided Too Much Information, and switched the computer off.

'I still can't believe it,' I told Paul that night over dinner. 'Laurie is feminine in almost every possible way. We were comparing fingernail polish, for heaven's sake!'

'She's had a lot of practice, Hannah. She's been passing for, what did you say, two years?'

'Three.' I served myself some green beans. 'I'm still flab-bergasted. If you put ninety-nine women and Laurie in a room and told me to pick out the one who's a guy, I never would have picked her, not in a million years. The teller at the BB&T drive-through, maybe, or that woman who makes the sandwiches at the snack bar in Dahlgren, but not Laurie.' I plopped some mashed potatoes on my plate and garnished them generously with butter. 'Truth or consequences. You danced with Laurie. Didn't you pick up any vibes?'

Paul blushed. 'Not even a hint.' He chewed thoughtfully on a piece of his tuna steak. 'Are you sure Melanie's being truthful?'

'Why on earth would she lie?'

Paul shrugged. 'Jealousy?'

'Of what? Besides, Melanie told me she confronted Laurie, and that Laurie admitted it.' I shook my head. 'No, it's probably true.'

We ate in silence for a while until with a contented, well-fed sigh, Paul laid down his fork and leaned back in his chair. 'Frankly, I admire the hell out of her. Imagine all she's endured just to get this far. And after the surgery, it'll be too late to change her mind.'

I thought about what I'd learned about SRS from the Internet and said, 'Pretty drastic, and needless to say, irre-versible.'

Paul rose from his chair and started to clear away the dishes. 'Melanie's probably one of those fruitcakes who believes all it takes to be 'cured' is constant prayer and a hefty dose of theologically-based reprogramming.'

Carrying the wine glasses, I followed my husband into the kitchen. 'How could Melanie possibly understand? Melanie wasn't born a man in a woman's body.' While Paul rinsed the plates, I tipped the wine glasses over pegs in the dishwasher. 'Why would anyone go through all that heartache, soul-searching, counseling, pain and considerable expense involved in a permanent sex change if they didn't deeply believe that they were born into the wrong body?'

'Did you notice,' I said after the dishwasher began surging away, 'how we keep referring to Laurie as "she"? Even Melanie didn't use male pronouns when she was talking to me about Laurie.'

Paul smiled. 'I would say that Laurie's made a success of being female, wouldn't you?'

'Completely.'

'Then I wouldn't worry about her.'

'But I do. I really like Laurie and Tom. And I hope Melanie's big mouth doesn't make trouble for them.'

Paul gave the kitchen counter a final swipe with a damp sponge and tossed it into the sink. 'You said she told Jay Giannotti?'

I nodded.

'And he didn't do anything with the information?'

'Not that I know of.'

Paul gathered me into his arms. 'Hannah, you worry too much. Give it a rest.' He kissed the top of my head.

So I stopped worrying.

For a whole minute.

'I wonder what Laurie's name was before it was Laurie?' Next to my nose, his shirt smelled freshly of Tide.

'Hannah!'

I looked up. 'Lawrence? Laurent? Luke? Leonardo?'

'Laurie can be a boy's name, too,' Paul reminded me as he released me and headed in the direction of the living room. 'Remember *Little Women*?'

'Oh, right.' I was addressing his broad, navy T-shirt-covered back. 'The boy next door. The one who marries Amy when Jo jilts him.'

I was still mulling over names – a totally pointless exercise – when Paul and I settled down in the living room to watch a new episode of *Law and Order*.

He pointed the remote at the screen and began clicking through the channels, searching for the station in hi-def. 'You know what, Hannah?' he said as the screen pulsed with quick-cut images and the familiar theme began to play.

'What?'

'Male or female, Laurie Wainwright is prettier than most, and a damn fine dancer.'

The next day I called ahead, and since Jay was still in the hospital, I decided to visit. I doubted that the subject of Laurie's gender would come up, but if it did, I planned to mine the opportunity. If Jay planned to use the information Melanie had provided to make trouble for Laurie, at least I could be a good citizen and give the girl a head's up.

When I got to Jay's room I found Kay standing by the bed, picking food off an insulated, compartmentalized plate with her fingers. 'How about a green bean, Jay? It's overdone, just the way you like it.'

Jay was propped up on three pillows, looking terrible. His eyes were dull and sunken, jittery in their sockets. His luxurious eyebrows had thinned, giving him an oddly surprised expression. In spite of the tan, his face looked ashen.

I knocked lightly on the door frame. 'May I come in?'

Kay turned away from the food tray and said, 'Hi, Hannah. We're just having lunch.'

From the amount of food left on his plate, it didn't look like Jay was having much to do with lunch. I entered the room, and set a gaily-wrapped box of candy on the foot of the bed. 'Maybe this will do for dessert?'

Jay winced, then smiled wanly. 'Thanks, Hannah. Maybe later.'

'You were out of it last time I visited.' I managed to dredge up a smile. 'I'd come by to tell you how much I enjoyed your paso doble.'

Jay raised a hand, waved it feebly, then let it fall on to the covers. 'I really screwed it up big-time, didn't I?' He turned his head, trying to catch his wife's eye. 'I keep telling Kay I'm too old for this, but she doesn't listen.'

'Old, *schmold*! You guys were great. And the choreography you arranged for Hutch and Melanie knocked everyone's eyes out.' I patted Jay's hand, and was surprised when he winced again, and jerked it away.

Kay shot me a warning glance. 'His skin's really sensitive.'

'Sorry. I didn't know.'

Jay managed a feeble grin. 'Seems I'm always causing trouble.' He turned his head on the pillow. 'Kay, could you pour me some ginger ale, please?'

While Kay filled a plastic glass with ice, popped open a can of ginger ale and began to pour, I filled them both in on the party a few nights previously. 'And did you hear that Tom and Laurie won several firsts at the Sweetheart Ball? They were over the moon.'

Jay nodded and replied with obvious effort. 'Tom called to tell us. I'm pleased, very pleased. They're hard workers, and super serious about dance. I'm referring them to Paul Pellicoro and Eleny Fotinos in Manhattan. I've done about all I can for them here.'

'Pellicoro? Is that the guy who taught Al Pacino to tango in *Scent of a Woman*?'

Kay answered for her husband. 'Right. You may have seen them interviewed on TV.' She popped a flexible straw into the ginger ale and held it for Jay while he took a sip, then another, then another. Swallowing seemed to be a problem. Jay held up a hand, and Kay moved the ginger ale away.

'And while we're talking about talent, do you think your future brother-in-law will give up the law for dance?' Jay asked me.

I grinned. 'I doubt it. Ten years out, and he's still paying off his student loans. But he's gung-ho, full-steam-ahead for the *Shall We Dance?* competition.' I explained as well as I could about the arrangements Hutch was making so that his firm could function for the months they'd be without him.

Kay held out the glass. 'More ginger ale?'

'No thanks, sweetheart. I think I'll take a nap now.' He exhaled slowly and closed his eyes.

'I've tired you out, Jay. I'm sorry.' I started buttoning my coat and headed toward the door.

Kay set the ginger ale down on the bedside table, leaned over her husband, adjusted his pillows, and smoothed a long, lank lock of hair out of his eyes. Suddenly she gasped, withdrawing her hand as if she'd received an electric shock.

'Kay!' I whispered. 'What's wrong?'

Kay turned to me, her eyes wide and frightened, like an animal caught in the headlights. Tears welled up, spilling over on to her cheeks. Silently, she held out her hand. In it lay a hank of her husband's handsome, blue-black hair.

'He's losing his hair?' I glanced at the pillow where Jay's head rested and noticed other strands that had separated from his head when he moved it. It can happen suddenly, just like that, with chemo. One night you've got hair, the next morning you're standing in the shower and it's falling out in clumps, swirling around the drain at your feet.

But Jay wasn't on chemo.

As I stood there looking from Jay's littered pillow to Kay's ravaged face, I remembered something I'd read in an Agatha Christie novel written late in her career and not one of her best – *The Pale Horse*. Mark Easterbrook, the writer-hero realizes that somebody's been poisoned with thallium. 'But one thing always happens sooner or later,' he says. 'The hair falls out.'

I took Kay by the shoulders, soothing her, trying to calm her down, although under the circumstances saying, 'There, there, it's going to be all right,' seemed pretty hollow.

At least she'd stopped shivering. 'Kay, have the doctors tested Jay for heavy metal poisoning? Arsenic? Or thallium?'

'I don't know,' she bawled, clutching the lock of her husband's hair to her bosom with both hands.

I located Jay's call button on the end of a cord clipped to the bed rail, and punched it repeatedly. 'When the nurse comes, you have to tell her about the hair.'

Kay sucked in her lips and nodded silently, but I wasn't sure my words were getting through.

'Honey?' It was Jay calling to his wife from the bed. 'What's wrong?'

She rushed to his bedside. 'Oh, Jay! Your beautiful hair is falling out. Hannah thinks it could be heavy metal poisoning.'

With some effort, Jay raised a hand and rubbed it across his brow and over his temple, coming away holding a few strands of hair. 'I'll be damned.' Under the circumstances, he was surprisingly calm.

A nurse appeared in the door. 'How can I help?'

Kay stared, and pointed to me.

I told the nurse what I suspected.

The nurse, young, freshly-uniformed and scrubbed, considered me with cool, green intelligent eyes. 'Of course. I'll call the doctor right away.'

'Heavy metal?' Jay asked after the nurse had left. 'Isn't that how they murdered that Russian guy?'

At the mention of murder, Kay gasped.

'For heaven's sake, Kay. Who the hell would want to murder me?' Jay turned back to me. 'Thallium, wasn't it?'

'Alexander Litvinenko? They thought so at first, but it turned out to be polonium-210. Much more toxic,' I hastily added, although from what I remembered of the newspaper accounts at the time, thallium poisoning could be pretty deadly, too, especially if you didn't diagnose it in time.

'Ha! Seems I've been poisoned by spies!'

As sick as he was, the man hadn't lost his sense of humor.

Twenty-Four

'*Thankyouthankyouthankyou,*' Kay gushed into the phone the next day. 'You were absolutely right, Hannah.'

'Jay has thallium poisoning?'

'Once they knew what they were looking for, they found traces of it in his urine. The blood work was complicated and took a bit longer, but it's come back positive, too, so there isn't any doubt.'

I smiled into the phone. 'It's amazing the useful facts you can learn from reading mystery fiction.'

'An Agatha Christie novel, you said? Who would have thought it?'

'Christie was a smart old dame. A lot of research went into her books.' Before we could drift off on a literary tangent à la Oprah's Book club, I asked, 'What do the doctors say, Kay? Is Jay going to be all right?'

'No guarantees.' Kay rushed on, breathless. 'No one here is underestimating the seriousness of Jay's condition, but they're forcing fluids, and have started him on the antidote, a course of Prussian Blue. Fingers crossed he'll respond and turn the corner . . .' She paused. 'He's in such pain now that the simple weight of his hospital blanket is agony.'

'I'll keep you both in my prayers,' I said, thinking that I needed to update Eva so she could add Jay's dicey condition to her prayer list, too. Unlike some pastors, Eva never claimed to have a direct line to God, but it seemed to me that previous problems I'd referred to her had had a good record of being rubber-stamped 'solved', so why knock a good thing?

'We hope they don't have to do dialysis,' Kay continued, 'but Jay says he'd happily let them cut off his left arm if it'll take away the pain.'

'Does Jay have any idea where he picked up the thallium?'

I'd been doing some research since my visit to the hospital, and I knew that thallium wasn't that easy to obtain. Having been banned in the US since the mid-1980s, unless you worked for a company that manufactured thermometers, optical glass, semiconductors or green fireworks, it wouldn't just be lying about.

Colorless, odorless, tasteless, thallium rapidly deteriorates in the body after death. It's such a perfect poison that some wag had nicknamed it 'inheritance powder'.

The other day Jay had jokingly dismissed the idea that anyone would want him dead, but perhaps he was wrong. Should Jay be out of the picture, Kay would get everything, including the studio. But, when all was said and done, who knew how much the business was actually worth, and whether it would be worth killing for. Except maybe Chance . . .

'Rat poison,' Kay snapped, jolting me out of my reverie.

'What?'

'Thallium used to be an ingredient in rat poison, they tell me. Ant poison, too. It's illegal now, but there might be some old cans of it lying around somewhere.'

I thought about the moldy boxes with unreadable labels cluttering the shelves of the tool shed behind my father's house, about the dented, rusting cans stacked on the concrete floor in the basement, each containing who-knows-what, and said, 'Did Jay garden?'

'Are you kidding? Jay grew up in the desert. He wouldn't know a geranium from a tulip.'

'Hold on a minute, Kay. Even if you had a whole vat of contraband rat poison out in your garage, how would it have gotten from the vat and into your husband?'

'That,' Kay said, 'is the million-dollar question.'

I pondered Kay's comment with growing dread. It seemed to me there were three possibilities.

One: accidental ingestion. Easy to do with a chemical that's colorless, odorless, and tasteless. I remember reading that attempts had been made to add bittering agents or 'adversives' to thallium products to make them less palatable and therefore safer, but it seems that rats had turned up their whiskers at bittering agents, too, so manufacturers had scratched that plan.

Two: somebody slipped the thallium to Jay, in which case we were looking at a particularly vicious case of murder.

Or, three: he took the poison himself.

But even if Jay had been suicidal – and I'd seen nary a sign of that – I couldn't imagine him, or anyone, ingesting thallium on purpose. Swallowing a bottle of sleeping pills, jumping off the center span of the Chesapeake Bay Bridge, shooting yourself in the head with an antique rifle, all would be quicker and less painful ways to bid 'goodbye cruel world' than going through the agonizing, long-term torture of thallium poisoning.

'What do *you* think happened, Kay?'

Kay sighed, sounding weary, resigned. 'Oh, I don't know, Hannah. I'm so worn out, I can't think straight.'

'Go home and get some sleep, Kay. You must be exhausted.'

'I am. Thank God Jay's sister is flying in from Texas tonight to help out. We've never gotten along particularly well, but under the circumstances, I'll just bite my tongue and put up with her fussiness.'

'If you need me . . .'

'Thanks, Hannah. I'll remember that.'

A phone call after midnight is rarely welcome, even if it brings good news, so I wasn't overjoyed when the bedside telephone jolted me out of a deep sleep at 2:17 the following morning.

Next to me Paul snorted, 'I'll get it,' knocked the phone off the table with a flailing arm, then tripped over the handset when he swung his legs out of bed to look for it. While he answered with a bleary, 'Hello,' I checked the digital clock and groaned.

'It's for you, honey,' Paul said, cradling the base of the phone in one hand and handing me the receiver with the other. 'It's Kay, and I don't think it's good news.'

I sat up, fumbled with the receiver, pulled my knees up to my chin, and took several deep, steadying breaths while trying to gather my thoughts. 'Kay?'

A word here, a ragged gasp there. I could barely understand what she was saying, and then: 'He's gone. Jay's gone.'

'Oh, Kay, I'm so sorry!'

'They started the treatment, but it was too late. All too late!' she wailed.

Over the next five minutes, alternating between hysterics that segued into gasping hiccups, punctuated by two short conversations with Jay's sister, Lorraine, I learned that by the time the antidote kicked in, the damage to Jay's liver and kidneys had been too severe. His body gave out on him, he slipped into a coma and died of massive organ failure.

'The sons of bitches have ta-ken Jay a-way!' Kay sobbed.

I knew what that meant: an autopsy. The office of the Chief Medical Examiner in Baltimore was going to be deeply interested in exactly what had sucked the life out of Mr Jay Giannotti, dance instructor, of Annapolis, Maryland. And I would bet my new dancing shoes that Baltimore's homicide detectives were already on the case, too.

'Idiots! The doctors are idiots!' Kay screamed. 'They screwed around with test after useless test until it was too late, and now they won't even tell me when I can bury him!'

In the background I could hear Lorraine's soothing voice, trying to calm her sister-in-law whose rant now included the words 'malpractice' and 'lawsuit'. Eventually Lorraine was able to pry the cell phone from Kay's grasp, and I learned that funeral arrangements would be handled by Kramer's, an Annapolis funeral establishment tucked away at the bottom of Cornhill Street in a grand Georgian mansion once belonging to a colonial tea merchant. I hadn't been to Kramer's since my friend, Valerie, died, and I wasn't looking forward to visiting it again. Funeral services held in funeral homes always struck me as odd, like sending a loved one off to heaven from the lobby of a Holiday Inn, so I was relieved when Lorraine added that Jay's funeral mass would be held at St Mary's Catholic Church on Duke of Gloucester Street, 'at a later date'. I thanked her, reiterated my offer to help out in any way I could, jotted down her cell phone number on my bedside pad, said goodbye and left Kay and Lorraine to mourn Jay's passing together.

Then with Paul's comforting arms around me, I buried my face in my pillow and bawled.

Twenty-Five

I was up early that morning, eyes red, lids puffy. Paul had already made coffee – fresh ground Columbian, I love that in a man – and I inhaled the first cup gratefully.

As I stood barefoot at the kitchen counter shivering in my pink-flamingo nightshirt, pouring cream into a second cup, Paul came up behind me, wrapped his arms around my waist, and nuzzled my neck. 'I have to go to class, sweetie. Are you going to be all right?'

'I'm going to lay low today and busy myself with a little research. Maybe some righteous indignation will keep the tears from coming back.'

Paul reached over my shoulder, lifted the mug out of my hand, turned me around and pulled me close, resting his chin against the top of my head in a way that always gives me goose bumps. 'Promise me you won't do anything dangerous or foolish.'

I promised. I didn't plan to take the face I'd glimpsed in the mirror that morning out anywhere; it would startle the pedestrians or frighten the horses.

After the phone call, I had talked to Paul about my growing suspicion that Jay had been murdered, and in a cruel, calculated way. I could almost understand strangling someone, I'd said, or shooting them, or clobbering them with a baseball bat in a fit of jealous rage, but what kind of monster feeds someone a poison so lethal that it slowly, ever so slowly, shuts down all the body's organs? So painful that even touching the hairs on the back of the victim's hand can cause exquisite pain? Disfiguring, too, and by the time your hair falls out, and you go bald, it's almost always too late. Even if you survive past that point, you can have paralysis or neurological problems for life.

'Jay could have been poisoned accidentally,' Paul suggested, continuing our conversation of the night before precisely where we left off when he started snoring and I, comfortable in his arms, eventually dropped off to sleep. 'There was the recall of pet food from China, remember? Where the manufacturers added melamine to artificially up its protein content and ended up killing a lot of dogs and cats.'

'Jay wasn't eating cat food, you dope.'

'That's just an example. Who knows where our food comes from these days.'

'Or our medicines,' I added. 'I wonder if Jay was popping any Chinese herbal remedies. I read an article—'

Paul clamped a playful hand over my mouth. 'Hannah, if I've told you once, I've told you a thousand times, but do you ever listen? You do not. Butt out, and let the police do their job.'

'Yes, Mother,' I teased.

Years ago, when my younger sister, Georgina was in a spot of trouble, I'd had my first encounter with the Baltimore homicide detectives made famous on the HBO series *Homicide: Life on the Street*. I own all seven seasons on DVD – 122 episodes plus a made-for-TV movie. Don't know why I always got the serious, no-nonsense-ma'am ones rather than the callous, smart-mouthed cops who always made me laugh, but maybe cops were only funny and irreverent on television. Maybe this time it'd be different.

'I'm serious.' Paul tipped my chin up so I was looking right into his dark, luminous eyes. 'But you're *not* going to listen to me, are you?'

'If I hadn't been an avid reader of mystery fiction, Jay's doctors would still be scratching their heads and saying "huh?".' I started to cry. 'But he'd be just as dead, wouldn't he?'

Using his thumbs, Paul wiped away the tears that began trickling down my cheeks again. 'I'm glad you're staying home today.'

'I don't know. Maybe I'll visit the kids,' I said, changing my mind. 'I can wear dark glasses. Take Coco for a walk in Quiet Waters Park. That always clears my head.' Coco is a labradoodle, the sixth member of the family living at my daughter's on Cedar Lane in Hillsmere Shores, a quiet water-front community of modest homes that adjoined the popular county park.

'Do that.' He kissed me gently on the forehead. 'And don't bother to cook tonight. I'll take you to Galway Bay.'

I like that in a man, too.

Paul had taken my LeBaron for an oil change, so I had to drive his Volvo to Cedar Lane. The kids were still in school and Emily and Dante at the spa, so I used my house key to let myself in. I cheerfully fended off Coco's energetic, slobbery, face-licking leaps, attached her to the lead and took her outside.

It was a bright sunny morning, one of those rogue February days where the temperature soars into the seventies and the crocuses, totally confused, pop up their tiny yellow heads and say, 'Hello spring!' only to be smothered by snow and frozen to death the following morning.

With a friendly wave to the park ranger on duty, Coco and I jogged by the gatehouse, past the pavilions, all the way to the South River overlook, scene of many an Annapolis wedding. On the return loop, I took Coco off the lead and let her frolic free within the fenced-in area of the dog park. At the dog beach – no humans allowed – Coco sniffed hopefully at the water's edge, tried the mushy ice with a tentative paw, then gave it up as a lost cause, bounding back happily when I called. Before she could show her appreciation by decorating me with muddy paw prints, I washed her feet at the pet rinsing station, then headed back to Emily's, both of us in much better spirits.

By mid-afternoon, back home, I decided it would be friendly-neighborly to take dinner to Kay's. I kept a supply of home-made casseroles in the freezer, so I was always prepared for unexpected guests, like when Paul took pity on a homesick midshipman and invited him or her to our place for dinner. We'd sponsored two plebes a year in the recent past, but the new regime at the Naval Academy had cracked down on off-campus time with a humorless draconian hand – 'we are a nation at war on terror' – so I hadn't seen as much of 'our' mids as usual. The new admiral's seriousness of purpose was illustrated by renaming all the sandwiches in the Dahlgren Hall snack bar after weapons systems, rather than professors or coaches. Can your stomach handle a 'Sidewinder' or a 'Tomahawk?' Jeesh.

For the mids, too, it was something of a joke. 'Well,' one had commented to me on a rare evening out, 'at least we can still order a submarine.' We'd had a good laugh, and I fed the famished boy a steak.

Still thinking about silly sandwich names, I peered into the basement freezer and selected a nine by thirteen pan of turkey tetrazini I'd made during a marathon cooking session before Thanksgiving. I'd never been to the Giannotti's, so I looked up Kay's address in the telephone book and found that they lived in the upscale Gingerville community a half mile south of Annapolis Harbor Center, just off Route 2.

I set the casserole on the floor of the Volvo, drove out Rowe Boulevard to the Route 50 exit, took the Route 2 cut-off, whipped into Whole Foods for a loaf of Tuscan bread and some salad, then drove south to the Giannotti house, squinting at house numbers as I drove through the quiet neighborhood.

The Giannotti's turned out to be a neat Dutch colonial nestled on a well-landscaped corner lot where Tarragon crosses Thyme. Several cars were already in the drive, including Jay's Audi, I noticed with a pang, so I parked on the street.

When I rang the bell, Lorraine answered the door. She was olive-skinned like her brother – statuesque, attractive, full-lipped, and impeccably groomed in a Miss Texas of 1985 sort of way.

'You must be Lorraine,' I said. 'I'm Hannah Ives. We talked on the phone early this morning.'

She brightened at this, like a well-mannered Southern woman should. 'Oh, yes,' she drawled. 'Do come in. Kay will be so glad to see you.'

'I don't want to disturb her if she's resting.'

'She's up and about.'

'Did she get any sleep at all?' I asked as I held out the casserole and the plastic bag containing the bread and the salad.

Lorraine took the dish from my hands and smiled wearily. 'Not so you'd notice. I imagine she'll crash tonight. Jay's doctor gave her a blister pack of Ambien to help her sleep, but she's refusing to take any. Always was a stubborn little miss.'

'I'm so sorry about your brother,' I said, as I followed her into the sparkling, sunlit kitchen.

Lorraine put the casserole on the counter, popped the bag into the side-by-side, and then turned to face me. 'Thank you. It's been quite a shock. Daddy died several years ago, but Mom's still with us. I haven't decided whether to tell her or not.' I must have looked puzzled, so she explained, 'Mom's in a nursing home in Corpus Christi. Her memory kind of comes and goes, if you know what I mean.'

I nodded. 'That's so hard. Were you and Jay their only children?'

'Yes.'

'I have two sisters, and I can't imagine what it'd be like to lose one of them.' I reached out and touched her arm.

Lorraine smiled sadly. 'Would you like to see some family photos while you're waiting for Kay? I brought some picture albums from home, helping get things together for the funeral.' She smiled. 'It's a Catholic tradition, you know, at least where we come from. Pictures of the deceased on display at the mass.'

I smiled back. 'I'd like to see them very much.'

Lorraine led me from the kitchen through a swinging door into the dining room. Spread out on the polished mahogany table I saw a half-dozen photographs, mostly of Jay, but some included other family members. What drew my attention, though, was an 18 x 24 color photograph of Jay and Kay propped up on the table like a centerpiece. It had apparently been taken at a dance competition; the couple posed in mid-banderilla wearing the same stunning paso doble outfits they'd chosen for their exhibition at the Hippodrome.

'They look gorgeous,' I commented. 'And so happy.'

'That was taken at the Internationals,' Lorraine told me.

Other pictures showed Jay as a much younger man, posing in dance costumes with a woman I didn't recognize. When

I asked about her, Lorraine said, 'That's Jay's first partner, Deborah Drew.'

'Oh, right. One of the instructors at the studio told me that Jay had started out with another partner before he teamed up with Kay.' Still holding the photograph of Jay with Deborah Drew, I glanced up at Lorraine. 'Was Jay always interested in dancing?'

'Oh my, yes. Mother taught dance, you see. She converted our two-car garage into a studio. She had quite a few students, too. There isn't much else to do in Hard Bargain, Texas.'

'Do you mind if I ask you something?'

When she nodded, I said, 'I've always wondered about the name Giannotti. It sounds Italian. I don't usually associate Texas with Italy.'

Lorraine laughed, a husky, resonate sound that would have made even the sourest of pusses smile. 'Believe it or not, Italians are the sixth largest ethnic group in our state. We originally came from Sicily, settled down in the Brazos Valley to grow cotton and corn on the bottom land that nobody else wanted. After the Galveston flood, a number of our forebears moved to west Texas and eventually ended up working in the oil fields.'

'Where exactly is the glittering metropolis of Hard Bargain?' I smiled at the name.

'About halfway between Odessa and Pecos, a little town about as beautiful as the name sounds.'

'I've never been west of San Antonio,' I told her.

'What would be the point?' she replied with a mischievous grin.

I set the photo down and picked up another one of Jay posing with a trophy several inches taller than he was. Looking over my shoulder Lorraine said, 'Jay was twelve when that picture was taken.'

'Did you dance, too, Lorraine?'

'I tried ballet, but I just hated it. Not like Jay. Practically from the day he was born, he loved all dance . . . ballet, tap, ballroom.' She turned to the buffet and picked up a 5 x 7 size photo album that had been lying there, balanced it on her left forearm while she leafed through it. 'Here it is!' She slid a photo out of its protective plastic sleeve and handed it to me. 'Isn't he the cutest thing?' she cooed, slipping back to her roots and pronouncing the word 'thang'.

The photograph showed a teenage Jay dressed in dancing tails, his dark hair trimmed short all over, with the exception of a rat-tail – a few strands braided in the back, like a Star Wars Jedi knight. Posing with him was a younger girl dressed in a Chiquita Banana costume. 'You?' I chuckled, tapping the elaborate headdress.

'Guilty!'

There was something strangely familiar about the face of the young Lorraine in the picture, but I couldn't put my finger on it. 'You're a couple of years younger than your brother, right?'

'Two.' She smiled sweetly and sadly. She handed me the photo album. 'Here. Make yourself comfortable, Hannah. I'll go look for Kay, then maybe I'll rustle up some tea. Kay may be hiding out in the hot tub. She was all spun up this morning. The police showed up with a search warrant looking for the source of the thallium that killed Jay. They scooped everything out of both medicine cabinets and dumped it all into baggies. They rummaged under the sink. They even searched the tool shed, and went away with a bunch of stuff in paper bags.'

'That must have been upsetting.'

'Damn right!' Kay appeared out of nowhere wearing a white terry-cloth robe, her fair hair nearly invisible under a turban-like towel. 'They even took away my bath salts. Neanderthals!'

'Lorraine was just showing me your family pictures,' I explained. 'I didn't realize that Jay started dancing at such an early age.'

'It was his passion,' Kay said. 'And mine, too. Now I have to figure out a way to go on without him.' She pulled out a dining-room chair and lowered herself into it. Her eyes caught mine and stayed there, unblinking, as if challenging me to come up with an instant solution.

'I really admired Jay,' I said after a moment. 'He made

dancing lessons seem like fun. I'm glad I got to know him.' As Kay watched, I paged backwards in the album, observing as Jay and his sister grew progressively younger. 'Seeing these photos, I wish I'd kept up with my dancing when I was little, but my dad was in the navy and we moved around a lot, so dancing lessons and piano lessons were kind of catch-as-catch-can.'

I glanced up from the album to see Kay still looking at me intently, so I babbled on. 'In my first dance recital – we were stationed in San Diego then – I danced the role of William Tell's apple. I was only six, but I looked in a mirror at myself wearing that stupid apple costume, and I knew even then that some people don't belong in leotards no matter what color they are.'

Kay managed a smile.

I paused at a picture of Jay and his sister dressed in dance tuxedos and top hats, leaning theatrically on canes, their fresh-scrubbed, pre-teen faces wreathed in smiles. Young Jay resembled the handsome man he had become, but little Lorraine had changed since then, metamorphosing over the intervening years from cute-as-a-bug child to Junior League matron with a dark helmet of Lady Bird Johnson hair. Nine-year-old Lorraine (or so the handwritten caption said) had an unruly tumble of dark curly hair, bright blue eyes, a slightly tip-tilted nose just like . . . my heart did a quick rat-a-tat-tat in my chest.

Little Lorraine was the spitting image of Tessa Douglas.

I swallowed hard, hoping Kay didn't notice, and kept my eyes down. Had Kay ever seen these early family photos? If so, she could hardly have failed to notice Lorraine's resemblance to the young Douglas girl. I leafed back a few more pages, casually, very casually, struggling hard to keep my voice even, my face blank. 'I'll bet,' I said brightly, 'that if I turn to the beginning I'll see little Jay dancing a rumba in his diapers!'

Kay laughed. 'Believe it or not, there are home movies something like that. Jay dancing a tarantella for St Joseph Altar. I think he was four. Jay's mother dragged the movies out the Christmas just before we were married.'

'St Joseph Altar? Help out a poor Episcopalian.'

'Sorry. March 19, St Joseph's feast day. It's an old Sicilian custom. You decorate a table in the church and lay out pasta, cakes and breads to thank God for His blessings.'

I closed the little album, rubbed my hand over the embossed flower on the cover, and set it back in place on the buffet. 'Do you find looking at the photos comforting or upsetting, Kay?'

'A bit of both, I suspect, but I'm going to let Lorraine take care of it. I'm just too tired, and my brain isn't functioning properly.'

'I'm sure the police visit today didn't help.'

'You know what the cops told me? As little as a quarter of a teaspoon of thallium can kill a person. Did you know that?'

I did, but I wanted Kay to think that apart from what I read in Agatha Christie's works, I didn't follow the thallium issue all that closely. 'My gosh.'

She nodded with authority. 'It can. That's why they took everything away, even the itsiest-bitsiest canister. I don't know what I'm going to use to clean my sink because they even took away the fucking Comet.'

'You can buy more Comet,' I said reasonably.

'I know, but it makes me so damn mad! Anyone would think the cops suspected me of giving Jay the poison myself! And if I did, it's not likely I'd have left the evidence lying around the house, now, is it?'

With my blood beginning to gel in my veins, I agreed that it wasn't.

'I don't want you to think that I don't *want* to know where Jay picked up the poison, Hannah. Until we find out, other people could be in danger, too. Remember the Tylenol poisonings back in the eighties? Somebody filled Tylenol capsules with cyanide and put them back on the store shelves.'

I stopped breathing. Really, I did. Was Kay a copycat killer? Had she papered Walgreens and CVS with adulterated drugs that she later fed to Jay in order to set up her alibi?

Then I remembered the last box of SinusTabs I'd bought and began to breathe again. A legacy of the Tylenol scare – the year we lost our innocence – was tamper-proof packaging so secure that I had to use a pair of scissors, an ice pick and some extremely bad language in order to extricate the capsule from its container.

'It's after the fact now, anyway,' Kay continued, 'and it's not going to bring Jay back, is it?'

Again, I agreed.

At that moment, Lorraine reappeared looking very Betty Crocker in a floral apron and carrying a tray with the wherewithal for tea. 'Will you join me in the living room?'

I left the dining room and its accusing photos, followed Lorraine into the living room where I sat on the sofa and gratefully accepted a hot cup of Earl Gray. I needed reviving.

'Cookie?' Lorraine asked, offering the plate up in my direction.

I selected a chocolate bourbon crème and bit in. From an armchair opposite me, Kay refused a cookie, but sipped her tea. I hoped it was just my imagination, but she seemed to be staring at me suspiciously.

I'd been to Catholic funerals before, and if Jay's ran true to form, one of two things was going to happen. Shirley would attend the funeral with her daughter Tessa, and Lorraine would see Tessa, recognize the resemblance, and suspect, as I had back there in the dining room, that Tessa could be Jay's daughter. Everyone else in the congregation might notice it, too.

But, Lorraine had brought the photo album from Texas with her, and Kay had been busy, so there was a slight chance that Kay hadn't seen the early photographs, and wasn't aware of the resemblance between Tessa and the young Lorraine. But she'd seen Jay dancing in diapers, so Mom had most likely showed her the photo album, too.

Had Kay suspected all along that Tessa was Jay's daughter, or had she just found out and killed him for it?

Any way I turned it around and looked at it, I figured that all hell was about to break loose.

Twenty-Six

After a restless night, with Paul insisting that my imagination was running away with me when I knew darn well that it wasn't, I showed up early at Hutch and Ruth's to ask Hutch for advice.

Ten minutes before the police.

Ruth and I were having coffee in the sun room at the back of the house, and I'd barely said, 'Hi,' when the doorbell rang.

Hutch went to answer it. 'Come in and sit down, officers,' I heard Hutch say. 'We're just having coffee. Would you care for some?'

'Yes. Thanks. It's a long drive from Baltimore,' the older of two detectives said as he followed my future brother-in-law into the room.

While Hutch got everyone settled on the chintz-covered furniture he'd inherited from his grandmother, I gracefully fetched the coffee.

When I returned to the sun room from the kitchen and introductions and mugs were passed all around, the older detective fixed his attention on Hutch and said, 'We understand you were at the Hippodrome at the time Mr Giannotti collapsed, is that correct?'

'Yes it is. My partner and I were auditioning for the *Shall We Dance?* TV show. Jay and his wife, Kay, are our teachers. They had been invited to dance an exhibition . . .' Hutch paused. 'But you're probably well aware of that.'

The young detective had taken a notebook out of his breast pocket and flipped it open but so far, he hadn't written anything down, so I figured they already knew what Hutch had just told them.

'Yes, sir.' The detective set his mug down and continued,

'When you were at the theater, did you share a dressing room with Mr Giannotti?'

Hutch looked thoughtful. 'Not a dressing room, exactly. They had several generous spaces cordoned off in the rehearsal area backstage – one for the men, one for the women – where contestants could change, put on their make-up and so on. Jay and I shared that space with a lot of other guys.'

With a glance from his superior, the younger officer finally spoke up. 'Did Mr Giannotti have anything with him, like a clothing bag, or a suitcase, or a duffel?'

'Yes, he did. He'd brought his costume in a plastic garment bag, but when he changed, he stuffed his jeans and toiletries into a gym bag.' Hutch got up from his chair, walked to the window, then turned around to face the officers again. 'I presume from your questions that you've interviewed the staff at the Hippodrome, and that you're aware that I took the bag away from the Hippodrome after Jay was taken ill. But you'll have to ask Jay's widow about the bag. It's been returned to her.'

From my seat by the window, I began to squirm. I'd completely forgotten about Jay's bag. Bright red, with a blue International Dance Sport logo, it was still in the trunk of my LeBaron. With Hutch's and my fingerprints all over it.

'Uh, Hutch?'

'Not now, Hannah.'

'Can I see you in the kitchen for a minute?'

Hutch fixed me in a steely glare, guessing (correctly) why I wanted to speak to him. 'Jesus Christ, Hannah! You didn't return the bag to Kay?'

'I'm sorry, no. I put the bag in the trunk of my car, then Paul took the car in for an oil change. With all that's happened, I simply forgot.'

Suddenly I became the unwelcome center of attention.

'Do you still have the bag, ma'am?'

I glanced quickly from the detective to Hutch, and when Hutch nodded, I said, 'I think it's still in my trunk. Shall I get it for you?'

'Please.'

'It's got our fingerprints on it,' I added helpfully.

'That's to be expected,' the detective said. 'Look, none of you are under suspicion at this time. We appreciate your cooperation with our investigation.'

Across the room, Ruth let out an audible sigh of relief.

When I returned with Jay's bag and handed it over to the senior detective, he thanked me and said, 'We've been asking everyone if they knew anyone who had a reason to want Mr Giannotti dead.'

I do, I thought, but decided for the moment to keep it to myself.

After yesterday afternoon, I was deeply suspicious of Kay, but somewhere in the middle of the night, Paul had convinced me that an old photograph constituted the flimsiest of evidence, everyone is supposed to have a doppelgänger, and that if the proverbial jury wasn't still out, it sure as hell ought to be.

After Kay, Tom and Laurie's fear of exposure sprang immediately to my devious mind, but no way was I going to out them unless I had to.

Then there was Shirley, but I hadn't worked out exactly why. I disliked the woman intensely, so it was probably just wishful thinking on my part.

Were there thugs in the dance franchise business, I wondered? According to Google, Saddam Hussein had favored thallium to rid himself of potential rivals. Maybe a rival studio head had taken Jay out.

Suddenly I realized that everyone had stopped talking and were once again staring at me. Hutch's elbow shot into my ribs. 'Your turn, Hannah.'

'Everyone loved and respected Jay,' I added helpfully. I felt my face grow hot. 'Except for his killer, of course.'

'Yes, ma'am.' The detective and his sidekick rose to go. 'Thank you for coming forward with the bag, Mrs Ives.'

'You're welcome. I'm sorry that I didn't think of it myself, but I really and truly forgot.'

The detective passed Jay's bag to his associate. 'It happens to the best of us,' he said. 'If necessary, we'll be in touch.'

For some reason he handed *me* his business card. 'And if you think of anything else . . .'

After the police left, I apologized again to Hutch. 'I'm sorry if I embarrassed you in front of the police.'

'Not a problem.'

'You know,' I said, 'it's probably a good thing I didn't give the bag back to Kay before Jay died.' I described what had happened at the Giannotti home in Gingerville the previous afternoon. 'If we *had* returned the bag and there *was* evidence of thallium poison in it, and Kay *is* involved, like O.J.'s bloody knife, that bag would have been history by now.'

Hutch sighed and reached for his mug, sipped the liquid, probably cold by now, and made a face. 'The cops won't be happy about chain of custody issues – anybody could have added to or taken from that bag between the time it left the Hippodrome dressing room area and today. But it's better than nothing.'

From her chair across the room, Ruth bristled. 'You two are taking this awfully calmly. Kay is supposed to be doing your choreography for *Shall We Dance?*, Hutch. What if she gets arrested? What if *you* get arrested?'

Hutch smiled benignly. 'Cool your jets, Ruth. This is still February. The competition isn't until April. Surely things will be settled by then.'

'Maybe you need a lawyer, darling.'

'I don't need a lawyer, I *am* a fucking lawyer!' Hutch raised a hand. 'I know, I know. You don't have to say it. A lawyer who represents himself has a fool for a client.'

'I'm just worried, that's all.' I recognized the tone. Ruth was struggling to remain cheerful. 'This is your big chance, sweetheart. Maybe we should hire another choreographer to work with you and Melanie.' Ruth patted the arm of her chair, and Hutch, like an obedient little fiancé, closed the distance between them, settled his lawyerly buns on the spot she'd indicated, and snaked his arm behind her shoulders. Hutch examined the top of Ruth's head, located a spot where the gelled-up spikes might prove less lethal, and planted a conciliatory kiss there. 'And here I thought I was going to make my name in wills, trusts and estates.'

I blinked. 'Surely you're not giving up the law?'

Hutch chuckled. 'Of course not. But I've been scrambling to settle what I can settle, and reassign ongoing matters to my long-suffering associate so I can be free for a couple of months. She hates me now, but it'll be character-building for her to fly solo.'

'What happens if that Market House thing blows up?' I asked. 'There was something about it in the *Post* again this morning.'

Hutch represented one of the heirs in a never-ending battle over the historic Annapolis market, built in 1784, and deeded to the city on the condition that unless the property be used 'for the reception of sales and provisions' it would revert to the heirs of the original owners. The gourmet market sat on valuable property at water's edge and was now being run, unprofitably it seems, by an out-of-town management company. There was talk – again – of tearing it down.

'That market's been putting shoes on the children of lawyers for three hundred years, and it's not going to stop now. Any attempt to tear it down will be blocked by Hysterical, er, Historical Annapolis,' he said with a grin. 'I'm not worried.'

'To change the subject for a moment,' Hutch continued. 'I have information for you, Nancy Drew.'

'You do?'

'I talked to my buddy up at the Medical Examiner's . . .' He paused, I swear, just for the dramatic effect.

'Stop it! You are making me crazy!'

He raised his free hand. 'OK. The autopsy's done.'

'So soon?'

'Homicide put a rush on it. The report won't be official for a couple of days, not until it's typed up and the M.E. signs off on it, but they did a segmental analysis of Jay's hair, and it turns out that his exposure to thallium had been going on for quite some time, perhaps more than a year.'

'Oh my God! Well, that shoots my thallium in the Tylenol capsules theory all to hell.'

'Exactly.'

Hutch drained his mug and set it down on the end table. 'What was in Jay's gym bag, Hannah? Do you remember?'

'You didn't look into it?'

'I didn't see any reason to.'

I stared at the bright floral drapes and tried to picture the bag's contents. 'Clothing, running shoes, socks, hair goo, talcum powder, bottled water . . .'

Hutch looked thoughtful. 'Could have been in the water, I suppose, the dose that sent him over the edge.'

'Or . . .' Several thoughts were niggling the back of my brain: Jay's powdery footprints on the floor of the studio, and something I'd read on the Internet. I sent my cerebral messenger down to retrieve them, and a few seconds later, the little fellow came up trumps. 'I think I know how it could have been done!'

Hutch stopped toying with Ruth's fingers, and sat up straight. 'How?'

'Thallium is a white powder. Somebody put it in Jay's talcum powder.'

Ruth made a face. 'You don't have to swallow it?'

I shook my head. 'Thallium can also be absorbed through the skin. Even more quickly, I would think, through hot, sweaty dancer's skin.'

'How would anybody know that?' Ruth wondered.

'The same way I do, from reading about it on the Internet.' I leaned forward, resting my forearms on my knees. 'Two articles come to mind. Back in the sixties, the CIA hatched a plot to discredit Castro by putting thallium in his shoes when he set them outside his hotel-room door for a shine. They didn't want to kill him, just embarrass him silly by making his trademark beard fall out.'

'Makes me proud to be an American,' Hutch quipped.

'The other side in the Cold War wasn't so bright, either. Not long ago, a group of Russian soldiers discovered an unlabeled bin of the stuff lying around a dump in Siberia, so they said, what the heck, rolled it up in their cigarettes and used it to powder their feet.'

'Not much in the way of entertainment in Siberia, I'd guess. No USO.'

Ruth punched her fiancé on the arm. 'Be serious for once.' She turned to me and asked, 'Did the soldiers die?'

I shook my head no. 'They became desperately ill, but eventually recovered.'

Hutch regarded me seriously. 'It's an interesting theory, Hannah, but it's simply that, a theory.'

Personally, I thought my theory was brilliant and fit the facts as I knew them, but far be it from me to say so. 'Will the cops let us know if they find anything suspicious in Jay's bag?'

Hutch snorted. 'We'll probably read it first in *The Sun*, but I have a couple of contacts in Homicide who owe me favors, so perhaps we can get a head's up.'

I smiled at the two of them snuggled up like teenagers and said, 'Well, for what it's worth, lovebirds, I'm betting all my money on the grieving widow.'

Twenty-Seven

Jay's departure from this world had been agonizing and slow, so it was only right that he be carried off to heaven in a proper, gentler way.

The *Capital* obituary was laudatory and long, highlighting Jay's raised-by-his-own-bootstraps journey from oil rig roustabout to ballroom dancing star. The obit in the *Sun* had been edited with a heavy hand, but both papers invited friends and family to a rosary service at Kramer's Funeral Home on Monday night at seven, followed by a funeral mass at St Mary's at ten the following day.

'C U @ kramer's,' Melanie had texted. 'Something 2 tell U.'

When Paul and I arrived at Kramer's, it was just as I had remembered it. Rich oriental carpets, a mahogany highboy, a massive circular table supporting a flower arrangement – fresh and very real – the size of a Volkswagen Beetle. To our right, a carpeted staircase led upstairs, but I had never seen it anything but roped off. To our left was the receiving line, and beyond that, an easel and a table decorated with flowers where Giannotti family photographs were on display.

As my husband and I were passed down the receiving line, offering condolences to tanned, rugged Texans who, with the exception of Kay and Lorraine, I did not know, I wondered which photographs Lorraine had chosen. When I got to Lorraine – who wore a suit of in-charge navy blue with bold brass buttons – she greeted me like a long, lost sorority sister, then handed me over to Kay.

Kay looked serene and fragile in a St John's knit jacket and matching flared skirt that couldn't have cost a penny less than twelve-hundred dollars at Neiman Marcus. The black color complimented her hair, and emphasized her paleness. 'I'm so sorry about Jay,' I told her sincerely as I squeezed her hand. Silently, I admired her notched collar, flap pockets and the elegant gold buttons that marched down her front and thought, Is this what a murderer looks like?

Who was it who said that poison was the weapon of choice for a woman? Dame Agatha Christie again, I suppose. Roman matrons certainly had a field day with it, possibly inspiring those modern-day women who rid themselves of burdensome husbands with loving doses of 'inheritance powder'. If I crossed her, Kay might not come after me with a gun, but I'd better watch what I ate.

Moving away from the line, I looked around for Melanie, but didn't see her. We said hello to Chance, and to Tom and Laurie – who had jettisoned her scarf in favor of a violet, scrunch-neck turtle. Under her overcoat she wore a short A-line skirt in a deep, dark purple that matched her heels. Tom, on the other hand, appeared in neat jeans and a collarless shirt. As the four of us dawdled at the photo display I couldn't resist teasing Laurie, 'You couldn't dress down if they paid you to do it!'

She rattled her bracelets at me and said, 'Girl, if you've got it, flaunt it!'

When the pair moved on to the Blue Room to find seats, I examined the photographs more closely. Lorraine had chosen a retrospective picturing Jay alone, acknowledging, I suppose, who was actually the star of the show.

Silently, with his hand on my elbow, Paul nudged me forward.

No open casket, I was relieved to see, and the service, once it started, was short and sweet. In preparation for saying the rosary, I'd rummaged through my jewelry box at home and located the rosary I'd bought from a street vendor in the shadow of St Peter's in Rome. I brought it to the funeral home with me, hoping as I prayed my lap around the beads that its origin would give them extra oomph.

While an electronic organ played softly, two cousins from Odessa and an uncle from San Antonio stood up to deliver remembrances of Jay. The old guy stuttered and stumbled, and got so involved in a chronological catalog of Jay-isms, punctuated by snuffling and dabbing at his nose with a napkin-sized handkerchief, that he'd only reached age ten before Lorraine took him gently aside, copiously weeping, or we might have been there all night.

Hutch attended, but not Ruth. Shirley and not Tessa. If Tessa *was* Jay and Shirley's child, it must have galled the woman when the immediate family traipsed around the corner after the service for a quiet dinner at Maria's Sicilian Ristorante. Shirley could hardly expect them to include her, of course, especially if they didn't know how she was 'related' to Jay. In the lull between the eulogies I studied Shirley's grief-ravaged face and wondered, now that Jay was gone, what she was going to do.

Daddy slipped in at the last minute, taking a seat in the back that Neelie had been saving for him. Alicia breezed in late, missing the service altogether. Surprisingly, Melanie never showed at all.

But, I was sure I'd see her in the morning.

Jay's funeral was smack dab in the middle of a class day, so Paul begged off on the Mass. Eva called and said she wanted to go, so we agreed to meet on the steps of St Mary's at 9:45.

Occupying acres of prime real estate on the banks of Spa Creek, St Mary's Catholic Church, red-brick and imposing, boasted a tall white spire, one of four with St Anne's, the Maryland State House, and St John's College that dominated the Annapolis skyline.

I walked to the church from home, cutting down private alleys, around the controversial Market House, across Main and down Green, arriving there a bit early. Eva arrived early, too. I caught sight of her chugging down Duke of Gloucester, not coming from the direction of St Anne's as I expected, but around the corner from the St Mary's parking lot.

I waved, and she hustled over to give me a hug. 'Your family here yet?'

'Not yet. Whoever got here first is supposed to save a pew.'

Eva checked her watch. 'Good. We've still got time. Come with me.'

She grabbed my upper arm and practically dragged me down the driveway and behind the church to the parking lot. 'I have to show you something.'

The back window on the driver's side of her little gray Corolla was open a couple of inches, and I was about to say, 'Hadn't you better lock your car?' when she wrenched the back door open. 'Look at that.'

Resting on the back seat was a brand new, two-toned, high-class pet carrier. Inside the cage, head on paws, staring morosely out the door with bright, golden eyes was a plump, gray cat.

'Let me guess,' I said, noticing the elaborate red bow tied to the carrier handle. 'Jeremy.'

Eva folded her arms across her chest and nodded.

'I thought you had a restraining order!'

'I do, but apparently that only applies to Jeremy Dunstan and not this beautiful animal. Whose name, by the way, is Bella de Baltimore.'

Eva reached into the pocket of her overcoat, pulled out a legal-size envelope with a piece of masking tape still attached to a corner, and handed it to me.

'I can hardly wait,' I said, opening the flap and pulling out the paper inside.

> Dear Eva (I read).
> Even though you won't go out with me, you can
> hold this sweet kitty and feel GOD's love
> (and mine!) that way. But you can't fight LOVE
> forever!
> Yours always,
> Jeremy
> P.S. Her name is Bella de Baltimore and she is a PURE-BRED Chartreux

My eyes darted from the cat, to Jeremy's letter, to the face of my friend, and back to the cat again, and for some reason, I started giggling. 'It's unbelievable! If you wrote this in a book, nobody'd believe it!'

I was glad to see Eva giggling, too, but after half a minute of silliness her face grew serious. 'What am I going to do, Hannah?'

'With the cat?'

'That, too.'

'I'm at a loss at what to do about Jeremy. The man's clearly deluded. As for the cat, it's pedigreed, you can take it back to the breeder.'

'And just who might the breeder be?'

I admired the gorgeous animal, marveling at its woolly gray-blue fur and unique golden eyes. 'We have the cat's name, so there'll be records. You can check with the Cat Fanciers' Association.'

'And in the meantime?' Eva's eyes were as pleading as the cat's.

'Oh, oh. I have a feeling there's a litter box in my future.'

'As a guest, I can't possibly bring a cat into a house with two dogs! I can't keep the cat, Hannah. Particularly not now. Maybe when I move back into the parsonage.'

We hadn't owned a cat for years, not since Emily left home and Marmalade, age twenty, died. I couldn't see any reason not to, so I agreed to host the cat temporarily. 'I'll have to ask Paul, but I think he'll be OK with it.'

Eva hugged me. 'Thank you, friend!' She closed the door and locked it, leaving the window cracked as before. I was grateful that the day had dawned cloudy and cool, so there was no danger of little Bella What's-her-Name overheating while we attended Jay's funeral service.

Inside the church a few minutes later, the organ prelude had already begun, a ponderous and solemn hymn that I didn't recognize. On the left-hand side of the aisle, about halfway down, I could see Emily discreetly waving. Eva and I hurried past the photographs of Jay that were on display at the back of the sanctuary, accepted a program from a young second cousin, blue-suited, scrubbed and polished within an inch of his young life, and slid into the wooden pew next to my daughter.

I leaned across Emily to plant a kiss on Chloe's cheek, gave one to Emily, too, then sat back to examine the program: *Mass of the Resurrection for Jerome I. Giannotti, 1958-2008*. So, Jay had been fifty. He looked much younger. Centered on the program cover, in full color, was a picture of Jay taken at the same event as the 18 x 24 I'd recently seen in Kay's dining room. In this pose, however, Kay was facing away from the camera, while Jay looked over her shoulder, smiling directly into the lens.

Sadly, what was left of that gorgeous man lay in a polished rosewood coffin, sitting on a bier just in front of the altar, surrounded by flowers.

I pulled a handful of tissues out of my purse. I was going to need them.

'Swing Low, Sweet Chariot' played softly as the sanctuary gradually filled up around us. Hutch arrived, pushing Ruth in a wheelchair, her leg extended stiffly in front of her. Although I caught their eye and waved them forward, they took an easier route and sat in the back. When Daddy and Neelie arrived, they took the pew immediately behind us, sliding all the way over to the wooden divider to make room for Alicia and Chance when they arrived. I caught sight of Tom and Laurie, sitting together near a bas relief plaque depicting the seventh station of the cross and waved. Melanie I didn't see anywhere.

A mystery tune segued into the more familiar 'Morning Has Broken', and then it was time for the opening hymn. We stood, and the congregation managed – just – to muddle through the next hymn:

> Be not afraid.
> I go before you always.
> Come follow me,
> And I will give you rest.

'I'm not familiar with this hymn,' I whispered to Eva somewhere in the middle of the verse about raging waters and burning flames. 'It's not very singable.'

'Another legacy of the Folk Mass debacle,' she whispered back. 'Some of that St Louis Jesuit crap, written by priests whose mothers were struck in the head with guitars while pregnant with them.' She raised her eyes to the blue, star-studded sanctuary ceiling and added, 'May God forgive me for saying so.'

I missed the next half stanza while biting my tongue and concentrating on the stained glass windows in order to keep from laughing.

During the eulogies, I located Shirley and Link sitting with Tessa in a pew near the front, and a block of graying heads that I suspected belonged to the Swing and Sway Seniors since I'd seen their Ford Econovan parked outside. By mid-service I was intimately familiar with the backs of several hundred heads of people I didn't know, but no Melanie.

Before I knew it, the priest was holding up the host and saying, 'This is the Lamb of God who takes away the sins of the world . . .' and we were responding, 'Lord I am not worthy to receive you . . .' and I'd still not located her.

'Have you seen Melanie?' I asked Eva as members of the congregation began filing up to the altar rail to receive communion.

'Is she Catholic?'

'I'm pretty sure. Of the evangelical persuasion.'

'If she's a faithful Catholic, she'll go up to receive. Keep watching.'

We sang the communion hymn 'I am the Bread of Life', repeating the refrain 'I will raise them up' so many times I thought I would scream, and still no Melanie.

Not at the rosary service.

Not at the funeral.

I was getting seriously worried.

The Mass ended, we were directed to go in peace, and the congregation recessed silently while a soloist sang the Prayer of St Francis of Asissi, 'Make Me an Instrument of Peace', in Spanish, in a clear, high soprano voice that tore at my heart.

Rather than following my family and friends out of the sanctuary, I loitered at the back, listening, all the while studying the photographs of Jay, silently mourning the man who, against all odds, had taught my lead-footed husband how to waltz.

Oh, Señor, hazme un instrumento de Tu Paz . . .
Porque es:
  Dando, que se recibe;
Perdonando, que se es perdonado;
Muriendo, que se resucita a la
Vida Eterna.

It'd been years since I took Spanish, but with what I knew
of French, I translated the words silently as she sang:

Lord, make me an instrument of peace.
Where there is hatred, let me sow love.
Where there is injury, pardon.
Where there is discord, vision.
Where there is doubt, faith.
Where there is despair, hope.
Where there is darkness, light.
Where there is sadness, joy.
O divine Master,
Grant that I may not so much seek to be
Consoled as to console;
To be understood as to understand;
To be loved, as to love;
For it is in giving that we receive,
It is in pardoning that we are pardoned,
And it is in dying that we are born to eternal life.

One day, I thought as I stood there quietly sobbing, we'll
all be gone and forgotten. The HIA monogram on my towels
faded, their edges frayed, the terrycloth cut up into squares
for polishing whatever passes for cars by then.

As the last notes of the song died away, I was startled
out of my reverie by a voice behind me. 'He was the love
of my life, you know.'

I turned to find Kay regarding me with puffy, red-rimmed
eyes. Behind her stood a priest. With a light touch of her
hand on his surplice, she indicated that he should go ahead
without her.

'The pictures you selected are wonderful,' I said after the

priest had disappeared through the doors that led to the narthex.

A corner of her mouth twitched. 'Lorraine went a bit overboard, so I had to pare it down a bit from what you saw at the house the other day, but I think it's representative, don't you?'

I scanned the photographs, a dozen or so, that were arranged on the table just as they had been at Kramer's the night before. As then, there were none that featured little Lorraine. Once again, I wondered if Kay had noticed Lorraine's resemblance to Tessa or if, as Paul kept suggesting, my overactive imagination was running away with me.

I blew my nose, carefully considering my answer. 'I didn't know Jay as a youth, so it'd be hard to say, but seeing him looking so happy in these pictures makes me wish I did, and feel even sadder that such a promising career was cut short.'

'He set his goals very high,' she said. 'Sometimes I thought he'd bitten off more than he could chew.'

I froze. Was she talking about Jay's plan to franchise J & K? His crushing workload? His personal life?

While dabbing at my eyes I studied his widow's face, looking for clues. It was as if she'd drawn a line in the sand and was waiting – composed, and lethal – for me to cross it.

I knew I'd have to force her hand.

Even though I stood in a church sanctuary only inches from the holy water, the devil made me do it.

I took Kay's pale, too-cool hand in both of mine, looked straight into her ice-blue eyes and said, 'By the way, Kay, sometime when you're not so busy, and all this is over, I need to return Jay's gym bag to you. From the Hippodrome? Hutch retrieved it simply ages ago and gave it to me, but with all that's happened, golly, I'm sorry, I simply forgot about it. There's probably nothing of value in there, but I'd like to get it back to you sometime. At your convenience, of course.'

As I rattled on, I noticed that Kay's chest had stopped rising and falling – appropriate for a funeral, I suppose – but it told me more or less what I wanted to know. If she had been going about the business of widowhood feeling secure, I sure as hell wanted to give her something to worry about.

I dropped her hand, tossed a cheery, 'Just give me a call, will you?' over my shoulder as I turned and headed for the door.

Leaving Kay standing alone amidst the photos of her victim, I fled the church and joined my family who were waiting for me on the sidewalk.

'Mother! Where have you been?'

I kissed her cheek. 'Later, Emily.' With a conspiratorial wink at Eva, I rounded up the stragglers and said, 'Come with me to the parking lot. There's somebody there that I'd like you to meet.'

Twenty-Eight

I tried to reach Melanie for two days, texting repeatedly to her cell, but my messages were never returned. No one answered her land line either.

I drove to the Fosher apartment in Laurel, near Fort Meade, but no one was home. Melanie's silver KIA Rio wasn't parked in its assigned spot in front of the complex either.

I sat in my car and stewed, listening to Mozart on the radio and staring up at the drapes pulled across Melanie's living-room window until it occurred to me – at long last – that something might have happened to Don. That he'd been wounded or killed, and that the army had called Melanie away. There had to be some good reason why she wasn't picking up messages.

If she had to leave so suddenly, though, it was odd that she hadn't told me. On the other hand, if somebody called me with the terrible news that something had happened to Paul, I might rush out without notifying anyone, too.

Three days later, the *Capital* reported the body of a woman between the ages of twenty-five and thirty had been found floating in the South River near Church Creek. The identity of the victim was being withheld pending notification of next of kin, but with a cry of anguish, I told Paul I knew it had to be Melanie.

I had to find out for sure.

Plan A was to call Dennis, my long-suffering brother-in-law slash policeman. But talk about not sharing information with anybody, when I called the station, I learned from an associate that he and Connie had taken advantage of an unexpected break in Dennis's caseload by shouldering their skis and hightailing it off to Vail.

I was on my own.

So I waited.

I texted Melanie every day.

Five days later, I was still waiting and worrying when my cell phone rang with a caller ID I didn't recognize.

'Hello?'

'Mrs Ives?' His voice was deeply masculine, but tentative. 'This is Don Fosher.'

'Thank God! I've been so worried. Is Melanie OK?'

There was a pause. I waited, but heard only breathing, followed by a long sigh. The moment I heard it, I knew what had happened. Don only confirmed my worst suspicions when he said, 'Melanie's dead, ma'am. That's why I'm calling.'

I felt like I'd been punched in the solar plexus. I couldn't say anything; I couldn't even breathe.

'Ma'am?'

'I'm here,' I gasped. 'What on earth happened?'

In halting voice, Don Fosher confirmed what I had suspected all along. It *was* Melanie's body the crabber had found while checking his pots in the South River the previous week. 'Melanie gave me your email address and telephone number,' Don continued. 'She told me that you could be trusted.'

Trusted? My thoughts were in a jumble, and I tried to sort them out.

When I didn't say anything, Don said, 'There's something funny going on, Mrs Ives. The county police think she fell from the South River Bridge, hitting her head on a piling as she fell. But I don't believe that, do you? What would Melanie be doing on the South River Bridge? Driving over it, maybe, but not jumping off.

'Melanie texted me every night,' Don continued in a lifeless monotone, 'even when I was out on operations. But when I got back from the field this time, the last message I had from her was dated two Sundays ago.'

I took that in. *The day before Jay's funeral.*

'She didn't drown, Mrs Ives. Melanie died of head injuries. I think somebody hit her over the head and pushed her in.'

Frankly, I was beginning to think so, too. Had Melanie

shared something she'd overheard with Kay, or with somebody else, unwittingly putting her life in danger?

First Ruth, then Jay, and now Melanie. Taking lessons at
J & K was turning out to be dangerous.

I needed more information. 'I went looking for her car,'
I told the grieving husband. 'Did the police find it?'

'Someplace called Yellow Fin,' Don told me, his voice
breaking. 'I've never heard of it.'

I had. Yellow Fin was a waterfront restaurant at the north-
west end of the South River bridge, within walking distance
of Gingerville. A little too close to Kay Giannotti for
comfort.

'Where are you now, Don?'

'BWI.'

'Do you need someone to pick you up?'

'No, ma'am, but thanks. I'm just getting into a cab. I
should hit town in about thirty minutes.' His voice wooed
and wowed and I thought I'd lost him until he said, 'I have
to go to the funeral home. Kramer's. Do you know it?'

Unfortunately, I knew it all too well.

'I do. I'll meet you at Kramer's, then. Will an hour and
a half give you enough time?'

'Without my Melanie, ma'am, I've got all the time in the
world.'

Like the well-trained mother I was, I added, 'And you're
coming home with me for dinner.'

Like the well-bred boy he was, he couldn't refuse. 'Yes,
ma'am.'

When I got to the funeral home at three, Don was waiting
for me on the steps. I recognized him at once. It wasn't
hard. Like most returning soldiers, Don was dressed in desert
fatigues. A duffle bag leaned against the steps at his feet.

'Don?'

'Ma'am?' He removed his cap with one sweep of his
hand, crushed it in his huge fist, and extended the other
ham-sized hand to me.

Even though we had just met, I gave him a hug, rubbing
my palms comfortingly across the massive expanse of his

back. 'I'm so sorry about Melanie. She was a lovely girl, and we were just getting to be good friends.'

'Melanie liked you, too,' he said sadly. 'She'd been emailing me about you. Taking her to lunch and like that. That was nice of you.'

Wandering tourists and pedestrians passing on urgent business had to swerve off the narrow brick sidewalk and on to the street in order to get by us so I suggested we move inside Kramer's. 'Let's find a place where we can chat more comfortably.'

Back again, way too soon, in the funeral home's House Beautiful lobby, I looked around for Kramer, Jr. and his impeccable three-piece suit, but didn't see him. 'Have you talked to the funeral home people yet, Don?'

Looking miserable, he nodded.

'Then they shouldn't have a problem about our sitting in here.' I turned to my right and opened the door of a miniature meeting room (the brochure would describe it as 'intimate') containing a small desk, three upholstered chairs, a backlit stained glass window, soundproof walls to mask the wails, and uplifting music like 'You Light Up My Life' and 'Wind Beneath My Wings' drifting in at low volume over the intercom.

After I sat down, Don closed the door, dumped his duffel, and slumped in the chair opposite, sending it jittering back a few inches on the carpet. 'This has been the worst week of my life!'

I smiled sympathetically, feeling like a shrink. 'Do you want to tell me about it?'

Don looked relieved, and it all came tumbling out. 'I'm out on a five-day operation, see. I come back to base, I'm fresh off the truck and all I want is a cheeseburger and a hot shower. On my way to the shower, I'm stopped by my first lieutenant and this other officer I don't recognize, but he identifies himself as a chaplain, and asks if we couldn't go someplace quiet. So he takes me to the canteen, buys me a cup of coffee and sets me down. "Sorry, son," he says. "I have some bad news for you."

'I knew right then that somebody'd died, but I thought

it'd be my grandmother. She's ninety.' His fingers brushed vigorously over the stubble on his head as if he were trying to drive the bad memories away. 'When the chaplain told me it was Melanie, my whole world crashed and burned. An hour later I'm sitting on a Medevac plane in a seat they'd saved for me, and now here I am, talking to you in a freaking funeral home. Totally unreal. Like punch me, it's a bad dream, I *gotta* wake up.'

'I'm so sorry, Don.'

'Melanie's going to be cremated,' he continued. 'She'll be buried in the family plot up in Chilmark on Martha's Vineyard.'

I was surprised to hear that. 'Didn't Melanie tell me she was from Kansas?'

'She was, but her parents died when she was way young. My parents loved her like she was their own.' A tear as big as the Atlantic Ocean slid down the big man's cheek. 'It's Abel's Hill, the same cemetery where they buried John Belushi. She'll like that.'

'Everyone loved Melanie,' I said. 'She was enormously talented. It's a big loss for all of us.'

'Yes ma'am. Except for the son-of-a-bitch who killed her. Begging your pardon, ma'am.'

'Please, call me Hannah,' I insisted, taking my time, not wanting to push the grieving young man, or cut him off prematurely.

Don blushed. 'I'll try, but they sort of drill the "ma'am" into us, if you know what I mean, ma'am.'

Don opened his duffel, rooted around for a minute, came up with an unopened bottle of water and held it out.

I raised a hand. 'No, thank you.'

'May I?'

'Of course.'

He twisted off the cap, and took a long drink, draining half the bottle in the process. 'OK . . . Hannah. I gotta tell somebody or it's gonna drive me freaking nuts. I think I know who killed Melanie.'

Resisting the urge to leap out of my chair, I said calmly, 'Tell me about it.'

'We were very close, Melanie and me. She told me

everything. Her worries, her fears. A couple of weeks ago, she picked up something at the dance studio, so she asked me about it. "What do I do, Don? Do I keep quiet about it, or do I tell?"'

I reached out and patted his hand. 'When we had lunch that day, Melanie told me about it, too. I know she told Jay, but I think he died before he could tell anyone else, even if he'd wanted to, which I don't think he did.'

Don looked puzzled. 'What do you mean, she told Jay? No way she'd tell Jay! She told Kay.'

I sat up straight. Something wasn't computing. 'She told Kay?'

Don nodded vigorously. 'Melanie picked up on something, I don't know what, but whatever it was she was totally convinced that Jay was having . . .' He paused, swiping at his glistening brow with the sleeve of his uniform. 'I guess it's what you'd call an "unnatural relationship" with this little girl he was teaching. Tessa Douglas.'

While I stared in disbelief, Don charged on. 'Melanie suspected that Jay was just being nice to Tessa's mother so that he could be near the little girl.' He shook his head, screwed up his mouth as if being forced to eat something particularly horrible, like liver with onions, or haggis.

I sat back, shocked to the tips of my toes. I'd been convinced that Tess was Jay's daughter, when all along . . . My gut twisted. Suppose Jay was a pedophile, attracted to the child because she *resembled* his sister. I felt ill.

Don blinked rapidly, fighting tears. 'Melanie asked me what she should do, to protect Tessa and the reputation of the studio and all, and I told her to tell Kay. The wife is always the last to know, I said. Oh, sweet Jesus,' he wailed. 'It's all my fault. What a rotten piece of advice that was! Now Kay's up and killed my sweet little girl, too.'

Too. Don and I were definitely on the same wavelength.

'Don, do you still have copies of those emails?'

'Yes, ma'am. On my cell phone, and on the server, too.'

'You need to print them out and share them with the police.'

If Jay had been abusing Tessa, that threat was now gone.

But if Kay had killed Jay to protect the studio, and killed Melanie to keep her from her spilling the beans about Jay, what would keep Kay from silencing a nine-year-old girl?

'Don,' I added, laying a hand on his arm for emphasis, 'you need to do it soon. If what you suspect turns out to be true, that little girl's life may be in danger, too.'

Twenty-Nine

'On the other hand,' I mused to my patient husband from the comfortable depths of our living-room sofa after we'd fed Melanie's husband dinner and sent him up to our third-floor guest room for the night, 'as much as I like Laurie, you have to agree she has a pretty good motive for wanting Melanie out of the way, too.'

'Why don't you ask her?'

'Oh, right, sure. So I meet Laurie for lunch, ask her point-blank if she murdered Jay and Melanie, and would you like French fries with that?'

'I think you know Laurie pretty well, and you're good at reading body language.' He wrapped an arm around me and pulled me close. 'Before you do, though, make sure it's in a public place and that Laurie knows you told me you were meeting.'

I took Paul's advice, and arranged to meet Laurie the following day at the food court in the mall, the Johnny Rocket's end. 'Coolness,' she said over the telephone. 'Afterwards we can go shopping!'

I rang off, thinking that after our little chat Laurie might not be much in the mood for shopping.

At the appointed time, Laurie caught sight of me first. She stood on tiptoe near the escalator that led up to the movie theaters, waving and 'yoo-hooing'. Judging from the bags from Ann Taylor Loft and Claire's Boutique that she carried I figured she'd got a jump start on the shopping.

I visited Panda Express while Laurie went to Hibachi-San and we joined up again at a table near the escalator. 'At least we're on the same continent,' Laurie commented (incorrectly), eyeing my shrimp-fried rice as she sat down.

Between bites, Laurie showed me the blouse she'd bought

at Ann Taylor, and I described the shoes I was looking for to go with my new red skirt. I'd eaten my last shrimp, and she'd finished up her tempura, but I'd still not found a way to work SRS casually into the conversation, so I thought, screw it, and dove in with both feet.

'Laurie,' I said as I twisted my napkin to shreds on my lap underneath the table. 'Before she died, Melanie told me something about you, and I'm just going to come right out with it and ask you if it's true.'

As I spoke, a smile began tugging at the corners of Laurie's mouth, and by the time I'd reached the end of my convoluted sentence, it had turned into a full-blown grin. She moved her tray aside, leaned across the table toward me and said, 'She told you I used to be a guy.'

My breath flew out of me in a rush. 'Yes!'

'And you worried that I might have bumped Melanie off to make sure she kept quiet about it, is that right?'

'I'm ashamed to say that the thought had flitted across my mind.'

'Honey, I've been living RLS, real life experience, for three years, my SRS is next month, and I couldn't care less who knows it!' She retrieved her handbag from the floor, plopped it on the table, pried it open, and drew out her wallet. 'Look at this,' she said, showing me her driver's license. It was from Illinois, her name was Laurie R. Wainwright, it pictured Laurie as she sat before me now, and there, in the critical box reserved for 'sex' was the letter 'F'.

'Isn't that the most beautiful thing you've ever seen?'

'I guess it is,' I said with a laugh. I slid the tangible proof of her new identity back across the table, relief flooding through me. 'I look like a convict on my driver's license,' I added, but I knew it wasn't the picture to which Laurie was referring when she used the word 'beautiful'. It was the letter 'F' for 'female'.

'I've got a temporary passport in my name, too, but that's so precious I leave it at home.'

I felt my face grow hot. 'I'm thoroughly embarrassed.'

'Don't be! It may be some sort of secret down here in

Maryland, but it's just because Tom and I don't talk about it much. Everybody knows back in Chicago!'

Still thinking about the license I asked, 'Is it hard to get all the paperwork changed?'

'Honey, it's a freaking nightmare, and Illinois is easier than most. To get the license changed, I had to see a shrink and babble on about how much I hated myself, yada yada yada, until he got totally bored listening to me boo-hoo and he filled out the report I needed. Then my doctor had to do a report. After SRS, it'll take an affidavit from the surgeon saying the operation is complete, but it won't be long before I'll have a brand new birth certificate, social security card . . . you name it.'

Laurie picked up her Diet Coke, leaned back in her chair, inserted the straw between her glossy, cherry-red lips and sipped thirstily. She smiled around the straw, as if something amusing had just occurred to her. 'And if the Social Security Administration thinks I'm a girl, who's going to argue with them?'

'Will you be able to dance professionally?'

There. I'd asked the million-dollar question.

Laurie didn't skip a beat. 'You bet'cha. The organizers have the right to demand verification of anything I write on my application, but if I put down an 'F', and I've got the documentation to back it up . . . no problem.'

'I'm really glad about that.'

'One thing I can't do, though, is run in the Olympics.' She threw her head back and laughed out loud. 'Not until they figure out a way to get rid of my Y-chromosome, anyway.'

We sat quietly for a moment. Laurie was first to break the silence. 'You know what your friend Melanie said when I told her I used to be a guy?'

I shook my head.

'Deuteronomy 23:1.'

I rolled my eyes. Deuteronomy again. 'Since Pastor Eva's not here, you'll have to help me out a bit, Laurie.'

She stared up, as if reading the words off the ceiling. '"He that is wounded in the stones, or hath his privy member cut off, shall not enter into the congregation of the Lord."'

'Oh, for heaven's sake.' Frankly, I was getting sick and tired of Deuteronomy. Surely there was some book in the Apocrypha we could replace it with. The Book of Judith, for example. I made a note to ask Eva about it.

Laurie placed her empty cup on her tray. 'That Melanie was one crazy, mixed-up little bitch, but she sure as hell could dance.'

I grinned. 'My husband says the same thing about you, Laurie, but not the crazy, mixed-up part.'

'He does? Sweet boy. I probably should thank him.'

To my amazement, Laurie raised an arm and began jangling her bracelets. I twisted my head to see Paul ambling in our direction, carrying a tray of half-eaten barbeque. 'I didn't want to interrupt the gab fest,' he said, pulling out a chair and sitting down to join us. 'But, have you picked out a fresh, spring color for your hair yet, Hannah?'

I popped him one on the side of his head with the flat of my hand. 'You were spying on me. Admit it.'

'Never.'

I gave him a peck on the cheek. 'Thank you.'

'Well,' Laurie said, rising from her chair. 'Are we going to go look for shoes or not?'

'We are.' I stood up, too, and looked at Paul. 'Will you take care of our trays, *sweetheart*?'

'Of course, *darling*.'

I waggled my fingers at him. 'Toodle-loo!'

As Laurie and I strolled up the ramp from the food court in the direction of Nordstrom at the opposite end of the mall, Laurie said, 'Your Paul's a great guy. You should keep him around.'

'I intend to,' I said with a grin. We paused for a moment in front of Borders's window to check out a display of cookbooks. 'Do you mind if I ask you what your name was before?'

'You'll laugh,' Laurie said as we moved on.

'No, I won't.'

At Hot Topic Laurie stopped to admire a spaghetti-strapped black dress with white polka dots and red buttons. After a moment she said, 'Oscar.'

I stared at my friend, sputtered, giggled, and finally laughed until tears ran down my cheeks.

'I told you so,' Laurie said. 'Now, stop laughing, girl, and let's go get those shoes.'

Thirty

I'd hoped for a quiet day, but it wasn't to be.

I fed Don Fosher breakfast, supplied him with a house key, then waved him off to the police station where he had an appointment to turn over the printouts I'd helped him make of Melanie's email. After he finished at the police station he had an even sadder mission: reporting to Kramer's where he would pick up Melanie's ashes and carry them home with him to Massachusetts on a flight out of BWI later that evening.

With no evidence to the contrary, the county police were treating Melanie's death as accidental. At least that's what was reported on the front page of the *Capital*. I hoped the information Don provided would help the police reconsider.

Ruth called at ten, in tears. Hutch had officially withdrawn from the *Shall We Dance?* competition. A stand-in for Melanie was against the rules. 'Maybe next year,' the producer growled. Ruth downed two Excedrin and took herself to bed.

Hutch stopped by at eleven on the way to his office. I gave him some coffee and half a pan of home-made cinnamon rolls. He seemed remarkably unruffled about *Shall We Dance?*, perhaps even relieved. 'Since I've blocked out the time,' he said mysteriously, licking sugar off his fingers, 'perhaps I should do something constructive with it.'

Ten minutes after Hutch left, Paul popped home for a tuna fish sandwich, then headed back to the Academy to teach a one thirty class.

I was just thinking about Kay when she rang through on my cell. 'Hannah? Is this a good time to talk?'

Fearing the conversation might be a bit tricky, I took a minute to stall. 'Can I call you back in ten minutes? I've got somebody with me right now.'

I hung up the phone and called Paul, but I could hear his cell phone chirping away on the entrance hall table. Absent-minded professor had forgotten it again. I left a message on his office phone, then called Eva, who picked up on the first ring.

'Eva, Kay called. I may need you. Where are you right now?'

'Standing in the checkout at Safeway.' I could hear the *beep* as each item passed over the scanner. 'As soon as I'm done here, I'll be right over. Can you store my chicken in your freezer?'

'First your cat, now your chicken! I'll store a whole side of beef, if you have it.'

I returned Kay's call. She must have been waiting by the phone because she picked up on the first ring. She was leaving soon for Texas. Would I be a *dear* and bring Jay's gym bag over now?

While her tongue dripped with honey, mine was abject with apology. Mannered, stilted, overly-polite, like conversation in a bad novel. 'Golly, I'm sorry, Kay, but I'm dog-sitting this afternoon, and my car's in the shop. It's inconvenient, I know, but can you come to me?'

'I've got a very small window, but I think that can be arranged. Where shall we meet?'

'I'll be walking Coco at Quiet Waters Park. Do you know it?'

'Near Hillsmere. Where the symphony plays in the summer?'

'Exactly. I'll meet you at the Blue Heron Center. Is three o'clock good for you?'

'Ideal. See you then, Hannah. Goodbye.'

Then I made a second phone call and invited somebody else to the party.

While I was still on the phone, Eva let herself in the back door and leaned against the door jamb, listening to my half of the conversation.

'Are you out of your mind!' she cried when I hung up the phone.

'Maybe.'

'Shirley Douglas?'

'If Melanie's right about Jay abusing Tessa, maybe I've been barking up the wrong tree all along. Maybe *Shirley* poisoned Jay. If she found out about it, who would have a better motive for murdering an abuser than an enraged mother?'

I invited Eva to sit down at the table and shoved a plate of chocolate chip cookies at her. 'Thallium, the perfect revenge. A slow, agonizing poison, just atonement for the long-term sexual abuse of her little girl.'

Eva waved away the cookies as if they were laced with thallium. 'But why would she keep coming to J & K Studios, exposing her daughter . . .?'

'You'd have to be there to see it, right? To witness the man's deterioration inch by painful inch, to revel in the gradual loss of his ability to dance.'

'That's sick.'

'So's pedophilia.' The words tumbled out of my mouth before I could stop them, but Eva didn't flinch.

We sat silently for a while, listening to the icemaker shuck cubes into the bin. After a bit, I told my friend, 'I'm having a hard time processing the idea of Jay as a pedophile,'

Eva smiled grimly. 'They don't come ready-made with a big red "P" branded on their foreheads.'

'I know,' I said, remembering Eva's late husband who in his own way had been just as charming as Jay. But then, charm had to be an essential part of any successful pedophile's toolkit.

'Hannah,' Eva began in a tone she might use with a wayward child, 'what do you hope to accomplish by throwing Kay and Shirley together in the same pot?'

'I hope to stir things up a bit, and arrive at the truth.'

'An admirable goal, truth. But the path along the way could be dangerous.'

I smiled. 'That's why I invited you along.'

Eva frowned, apparently considering her options. When she spoke again, I knew I'd have her support. 'Who's going to be around Quiet Waters Park in the middle of February?'

'More people than you'd think,' I replied. 'I'm meeting them at the Blue Heron Center which adjoins the Visitors' Center, so the employees are there, and today – I checked

– they're opening an art show in one of the galleries. There'll be plenty of folks hanging around.'

I took Eva's grocery bag, moved aside some potatoes, and tucked it into the vegetable crisper. 'And another plus. Unless they have season passes, they'll have to check in at the gatehouse to get in. There'll be a record of that.'

Eva shook her head. 'I don't know, Hannah. It sounds pretty hare-brained to me.'

I rested my fists on my hips. 'What is anybody going to do to me in public with you standing by my side?'

'Probably nothing.'

'There you go.'

Eva checked her watch. 'How much time do we have?'

I checked the digital read-out on the microwave: two fifteen. 'About forty-five minutes. And Eva?'

'What?'

'I know where I can get the dog, but where the heck am I going to get the gym bag?'

In the end, we parked at Emily's, collected Coco and jogged to the park carrying a red gym bag that I'd picked up at a management conference six or seven years before and had stashed in the basement. I held the side with the AMAC logo next to me – it'd been so long, I'd forgotten what AMAC stood for – and prayed it would stand up to Kay's inspection, at least from a distance.

'What do you plan to do, Hannah?'

'Get one of them to confess, of course.'

'And how will you manage that, pray tell?'

I shrugged. 'If I make Kay mad enough, it might happen. She's going to be pissed off big-time when she finds out that I lied about the bag.'

'Can I ask you something, Eva?' I paused on the path while Coco strained after a squirrel, tugging at the leash, jerking my arm up and down. 'After Roger was outed on NBC by PredatorBeware, did you ever feel like *killing* him?'

Eva had jogged a few feet ahead, but she stopped and turned to face me. 'I felt sickened and betrayed, but I can truthfully say I never once thought about murder.' A bird sitting on a bare branch chose that moment to warble a greeting, and Eva smiled. "Vengeance is mine. I will repay, saith the Lord." Romans 12.'

'I know, I know,' I said as we continued down the path together. 'But sometimes I wish he'd hurry up and get around to it.'

'Hah!' said Eva. 'I'm going to steal that line.'

'I'm convinced the Baltimore cops are going to nail *some-body* sooner or later for Jay's murder,' I said a little breathlessly, thinking about the evidence that might have turned up when they analyzed the contents of Jay's gym bag. 'But, I am *not* going to let anyone get away with Melanie's, and the local cops seem clueless.' I told Eva about my conversation with Don, then added, 'Accident, my foot! A spot on *Shall We Dance?* A husband who adores her and vice versa? That girl had everything to live for.'

As we hurried on two cars drove by, but neither belonged to Kay. I had no idea what Shirley drove. We passed various pavilions named for trees – Red Maple, Sassafras, Sycamore, White Oak – trotted through the formal gardens, and up the stairs to the patio.

I checked my watch. It was two fifty-nine.

Kay was already sitting on one of the teak, Chippendale-style benches that surrounded an elaborate Victorian, three-tiered cast-iron fountain that looked like it should be flowing with wedding champagne rather than water.

Sitting on the bench next to Kay was Tessa's mother, Shirley Douglas.

'Well . . .' Kay flashed a smile like the snake in the Garden of Eden. 'I see you've brought a friend along, and so have I.'

Shirley glanced nervously at me. 'Kay and I are not friends, not exactly. I'm not sure why she asked me here.'

I fessed up. 'Kay didn't invite you here, Shirley. I did.'

Kay turned a cool eye on her 'friend' Shirley. 'Hannah probably wants me to tell you about Jay and about Tessa.'

Oh, oh, I thought. Now the shit is really going to hit the fan.

Shirley laced her fingers and flexed them nervously. 'I don't know what the hell you're talking about, Kay.'

The look Kay sent Shirley dripped with malevolence. 'Of course you do, Shirley. Melanie told me all about it.'

'Melanie? What does Melanie have to do with anything?'

'Melanie noticed Jay talking to Tessa. She watched them for a long time.' Kay's eyes narrowed dangerously. 'That's how Melanie found out that Jay was abusing your daughter.'

Shirley leapt to her feet, her back rigid. She loomed over Kay, still seated on the bench, hands primly folded in her lap. 'Abuse Tessa?' Shirley screamed. 'You are out of your fucking mind, lady! Jay wasn't an abuser.'

'Pimp,' Kay snarled.

'What?' Shirley paled.

'You disgust me. Don't you have any pride at all? Using your daughter like that. It's despicable. You're no better than those so-called parents who allowed their kids to spend the night at Neverland and then sued Michael Jackson for the hanky-panky they *knew* was bound to take place.'

'I . . .' Shirley began, obviously reeling from Kay's full-frontal assault.

Kay seized the advantage. 'Chance clued me in on the hush money Jay's been paying you.'

'I don't know what you're talking about.'

'Does the name Michael Lombardo ring any bells?'

Shirley shook her head, genuinely puzzled.

'He's Jay's cousin, currently serving five to seven in the Texas State pen at Huntsville for robbing a pawn shop.'

'So Jay's cousin is a crook. So what?'

'So why is Michael Lombardo on the J & K Studio payroll, and why is his paycheck being automatically deposited to a trust account in Tessa's name at Bank Annapolis?'

Shirley's eyes widened. 'Jesus.'

Kay puffed air out through her lips, and turned to me. 'You watch, Hannah. She's going to pretend she didn't know about it.'

Either Shirley was a consummate actress, or she really didn't know. She took a step backwards, a strategic retreat, as if to gather her thoughts.

But Kay wasn't finished with Shirley yet. She stood up,

too, so she could look Shirley straight in the eye. 'You must be blind. Either that, or an enabler. Melanie told me.'

If Shirley was intimidated by Kay, she certainly didn't show it. She stood her ground, puffed herself up and played her trump card. 'You're the one who's blind, Kay! Jay didn't abuse Tessa. Tessa was his daughter!'

I grabbed Eva's hand and squeezed. It felt good to be right about Jay. He wasn't a pedophile after all. He was a father.

Kay gasped, put a hand to her chest, staggered backwards, catching her heel on a brick. She would have fallen had she not reached out to steady herself on the rim of the fountain. 'You're lying!'

I was dumbfounded. 'Kay didn't know,' I whispered to Eva. 'I don't know how it's possible, but she really didn't know!'

Shirley took the offensive then, quickly closing the gap between Kay and herself. 'Why do you think we stuck with your studio all these years when there were other, better studios in the area? Loyalty, that's why. Jay always looked after Tessa.' She paused to draw a breath. 'Besides, he wanted to spend time with his daughter.'

She fixed Kay with a look of pure venom. 'It'll all come out in his will, you know. He's leaving his half of the studio to Tessa.'

Kay's face grew dangerously red. 'The hell he is!'

Shirley folded her arms and glared Kay down. 'You don't know anything. Jay loved me. *Me!* He loved Tessa. You were too selfish to give him kids.' She smoothed her hands over her narrow hips. 'Boo-hoo-hoo. Might spoil your figure for dancing.'

Kay stood galvanized, rapidly blinking.

'When I got pregnant, Jay was overjoyed. He wanted to tell the whole world, but I wouldn't let him. He's . . .' Her voice caught. 'He was one of the most unselfish men I've ever known.

Kay suddenly revived. 'I don't believe that Tessa is Jay's child. You'll have to prove it.'

A sly smile crept across Shirley's face. 'There's DNA.'

Kay laughed out loud. 'DNA? How? Jay's been cremated. In a couple of hours, I'm taking his ashes back to Texas.'

I was thinking that comparing Lorraine's DNA to Tessa's would probably do the trick when Shirley crowed, 'We had a paternity test done when Tessa was born. I was married to Link, so we had to be sure.'

Eva breathed into my ear, 'Sounds like Jay didn't trust Shirley much, either.'

Eva'd said it quietly, but Shirley must have overheard because her eyes darted in our direction. 'And before you ask, Link knew all about it, but agreed to raise Tessa as his own. Link had a severe case of mumps as a kid, so he could never father children. It was the perfect solution for all of us.'

The perfect solution? I thought back to the day I'd comforted Tessa as she huddled miserably on a cold tile floor, hunched over the commode. Tessa was the glue that held that marriage together, but at what cost?

Kay stumbled to the bench and lowered herself down on it. 'Melanie was wrong?'

I handed Coco's leash to Eva and moved closer to Kay's bench. 'I don't know what Melanie thought she saw, Kay, but whatever it was, it was clearly misinterpreted.'

Kay's eyes swung from me to the red bag and back again. 'That's not Jay's bag, is it?'

'No, it's not. The police have Jay's bag. They've had it all along.'

Kay rested her head against the back of the bench and closed her eyes. 'Jay was from a big Catholic family. He wanted children, *lots* of children.' Her eyelids fluttered open and, for some reason, she was looking again at me. 'I couldn't give them to him. It's complicated, but I just couldn't.'

'Kay . . .' Shirley began.

Kay waved a tired hand, cutting her off. 'About the will.'

Shirley went on alert. Had she been Coco, her ears would have quivered. 'The will? What about the will?'

Kay's head lolled slowly to the other side until she was looking directly at Shirley. 'Tessa's not getting the studio. The studio comes to me. *Everything* comes to me.' She drew a deep breath and exhaled it slowly. 'But I guess where I'm going, there won't be any need for a studio, or a house, or anything else.'

'But the will?' Shirley wouldn't let the matter drop.

Kay smiled blandly. 'Jay intended to make a will favoring Tessa, but I found a draft on his computer and put a stop to it. I thought you found out about the abuse and were blackmailing him.' Her head lolled back. 'I made a mistake there, too, didn't I?'

Something rustled the ornamental hedge behind me, and suddenly he was there: Don Fosher, a mountain in cammies, waving a dull gray pistol. 'Move away from her, everyone. I have no beef with you.'

I stood rooted to the bricks. 'Don . . .'

'I'm sorry, Mrs Ives. I came back for my stuff, and I overheard you arranging to meet this, this . . . murderess!' He steadied the weapon with his left hand, and pointed the barrel directly at Kay's head. At a distance, Don could probably shoot the eyebrows off a fly. At close range, Kay didn't stand a chance.

Tears coursed down Don's face, but his grip on the gun didn't waver. 'Why did you kill her? Why? Tell me why?'

I would have been petrified, but Kay didn't even blink. 'Melanie said . . . oh, what does it matter? It's a little late for me to be sorry about it now.'

That wasn't the right answer.

Deep down, the horrible scream began, rumbling up through Don's chest and out through his mouth, a cry of such agony, such desolation that my heart nearly broke. His finger twitched on the trigger.

'Stop!' someone yelled.

We all froze as a figure shot past, tripped over Coco's leash, and dived like a missile at the feet of the gunman. Big as he was, Don Fosher went down, his gun bouncing and skittering along the bricks.

'Thou shalt not kill!' Kay's rescuer shouted.

Over Coco's frantic barking, Eva yelled, 'Sweet Jesus, it's Jeremy!'

'Get the gun!' Jeremy screamed, but Don's arm clamped over his throat, cutting off his air. Don was trained in hand-to-hand combat; Jeremy was no match for him.

Yet somehow Jeremy squirmed free, and fell on Don's

back like a human cinder block. Don rolled over, throwing the smaller man off, while Coco nipped at his heels.

While the two men wrestled, I searched frantically for the gun, but it must have slipped under one of them. First Don was on top, and then Jeremy. Don roared, flipped Jeremy like a pancake, straddled him, and pinned him to the bricks.

'It's over,' said the big man, back in control of the gun and pointing it at Jeremy's head.

Jeremy squeezed his eyes shut. '"The Lord is my shepherd, I shall not want, he makest me to lie down . . ."'

'Shut *up!*' Don screamed, and clipped Jeremy in the temple with the butt of the gun.

Jeremy's glasses flew into the air, the Lord's Prayer silenced. Blood began to pour from a gash in his head and puddle on the bricks.

Don reared back in horror. 'Oh, God, what have I done?'

I took advantage of the lull to push firmly on Don's shoulder, catching him off balance and causing him to topple sideways, unresisting.

I knelt at Jeremy's side. He was still breathing, but his pulse was ropey. I found a wad of tissue in my pocket left over from Jay's funeral, and I used it to press against Jeremy's wound, staunching the flow. Time had slowed; seconds became minutes, minutes, hours.

Behind me, I could hear the beeps as Eva dialed 9-1-1.

I heard Shirley say, 'I've got the gun,' and didn't feel anything but relief, until a few seconds later when the explosion of a gunshot deafened me.

Keeping the tissue firmly pressed to Jeremy's head, I twisted around.

Kay lay slumped on the bench, a dark stain beginning to leak between the buttons of her camel hair coat. Don Fosher bent over Kay. First her mouth moved, and then his. I couldn't hear a word, but after a moment his body language said it all.

Kay Giannotti was dead.

It seemed obvious at first. Don had killed her.

Then I saw it was Shirley Douglas who held the gun.

Epilogue

It took a while for the dust to settle. First, I had to apologize to Paul a million times for pig-headedly (his word, not mine) undertaking a dangerous mission with only my spiritual advisor along for support.

Shirley Douglas got out on bail. Link's connections on Capitol Hill had netted Shirley a hotshot criminal lawyer with a win-lose record of sixty and nil, who wore his hair in a ponytail. Word was, she'd get off light.

Alas for Tessa, production of *Tiny Ballroom* was postponed indefinitely following a boycott of the show's sponsors by Citizens Against Childsploitation. As a diversion, Tessa's father enrolled her in a gymnastics class. Tessa excels on the parallel bars and hopes to be ready for the 2012 Olympic Games in London.

Shirley's victim's ashes were flown to Texas by a second cousin once removed, where they were interred in the Giannotti plot next to her husband of twenty-five years, Jerome Ignatius Giannotti.

Everyone agreed it was Don Fosher who'd brought the gun – unregistered – to the park, but the sergeant remembered nothing about the incident until he 'came to' and found himself scuffling with a total stranger for control of the weapon. Post-traumatic stress was mentioned. After counseling at Walter Reed Medical Center in Washington, DC, Sergeant Fosher was back in Iraq. He has extended for another year.

In March, Ruth's attacker, Kenneth Parks, a sixteen-year-old student from Annapolis High was apprehended. Fresh out of Ruth's cash, he attempted to use her cancelled VISA to buy a laptop computer on the Internet, asking that it be shipped to his home address. Needless to say, Kenny's parents' car didn't sport a 'My child is an honor roll student at . . .' bumper sticker.

Eventually, we learned that lab analysis had identified the formulation of the thallium contained in Jay's talcum powder as identical to Jardines Rat-a-Tué which hadn't been sold in the US since 1978.

I was thinking about this one day while staring at Eva across her kitchen table.

Eva raised any eyebrow. 'What? Do I have spinach on my teeth?'

'Not your teeth. Your hair. I'm remembering your roots.'

'Roots?' She tugged on a lock of silver bangs and stared up at it, cross-eyed. 'Thanks to Wally, I don't have any roots.'

'But when you did, wasn't it because you used some off-brand hair dye that was years past its sell-by date?'

Eva laughed. 'In Stanley, Utah, rotating stock was an alien concept. They never took stuff off the shelves in the stores. I saw thirty-year-old merchandise gathering dust, still wearing their original price tags.' She grinned. 'Never know when you're going to need a tube of Ipana toothpaste.'

'Maybe Hard Bargain, Texas has some old-fashioned farm supply stores, too,' I mused.

I made this suggestion to the nice detective who'd given me his card when he drove all the way down from Baltimore, Maryland to relieve me of Jay's gym bag. He'd said, 'Thank you, ma'am,' which I figured was nicer than 'buzz off'. Nevertheless, he called later on to report that a clerk at Finkel's Fair Store in Hard Bargain, Texas, had said yes-indeedy-do, Miss Kay Giannotti had bought some of that there Rat-a-Tué for her mother-in-law's mouse problem, why it must have been over a year ago now, and they only had two cans left at $2.95 and should he hold them?

I paid a call on my spiritual advisor at her home in the parsonage to report on this interesting development. Eva invited me into the kitchen, and together we rustled up some tea while the gray Chartreux watched with round, copper eyes from her basket near the stove. 'Hello, Bella,' I said, kneeling down to give the animal a good scratch behind the ears.

'I've changed her name,' Eva told me. 'She now answers to Magnificat.'

'Certainly appropriate for a church-going cat,' I said, getting to my feet, 'but quite a mouthful. I can't see you standing in the back yard calling, Here Magnificat, here Magnificat!, can you?'

Eva shook her head. 'That's why she'll be Cat for short, although her breeder in Fulton, Maryland might think the name's a bit undignified for such a fine, blue-blooded feline.'

As Eva poured hot water into our cups, she asked, 'I know you talked to Don recently, and I'm curious. What was it that Kay said to him just before she died?'

'It was a line from the movie, *Dirty Dancing*. "Nobody sticks Baby in a corner."'

Eva plopped a teabag into her cup. 'Poor thing. Thinking her husband was having an affair must have gnawed at her, but being told he was a pedophile would have sent anybody over the edge And I should know.'

'Jay didn't exactly win any prizes for faithfulness, but from everything I hear, he really loved her. And speaking of love,' I continued with a grin, 'how's Jeremy?'

'Fully recovered. He emails that during his hospital stay God came to him in a dream and suggested that he might not be cut out for life in the fast lane with a priest for a wife.'

Eva set the kettle back on the stove, and sat down. 'Looking for guidance, Jeremy opened his Bible, closed his eyes and stabbed his finger down at Solomon 2:16: "My lover is mine and I am his; he browses among the lilies." Believe it or not, Jeremy's now dating a lovely girl who works as a sales associate in the greenhouse at Homestead Gardens. God has spoken, what more can I say?'

'That reminds me.' I opened my purse and pulled out a narrow box. 'Now that you're back in the parsonage, I think you'll be needing this.' I slid the box across the table.

Eva tipped up the top and peeked in. 'Pastor Barbie! I don't believe it!' Tenderly, she withdrew from the box a Barbie doll decked out in full priest regalia. It had been made as an ordination gift for Eva by her sister. I'd rescued Barbie from the trash can where a despondent Eva had tossed her when she left St Cat's on sabbatical. For the past several months, Barbie'd slept on a bookshelf at my house.

Tears trickled down Eva's cheeks as she stroked the doll's hair. 'Poor Pastor Barbie, I treated you very shabbily.' She smiled across the table. 'Thanks, Hannah, for saving her for me.'

Eva tucked Barbie back in her comfortable bed of bubble wrap. 'It's back to the office for you in the morning.' And almost in the same breath, she said, 'Want to stay for dinner?'

'I can't tonight, sorry. Ruth's got her cast off, so Hutch has invited us to Dance Night at the Davidsonville Dance Club. Cast of thousands, but I haven't been dancing since . . . well, since Jay was still alive. I find I'm looking forward to it.'

Later that evening, seated in a family group at the end of a long table at the popular dance hall in Davidsonville, Hutch stood up, raised a glass of wine and shocked us all. 'A toast! To my wife, Mrs Gaylord Hutchinson.'

Hutch winked, and shot me a goofy grin. 'I told you I was going to do something constructive with the time I set aside for *Shall We Dance?*'

'What? When?' Daddy sputtered.

'Ruth and I were married this afternoon at the County Courthouse.'

Ruth beamed at her new husband, and then turned the brights on us. 'I said the hell with the flowers, the cake and the dress. Screw the hotel and the band! I have everything I need right here.'

Remembering the Bridesmaid's Dress from Hell that I was obliged to wear when Connie married Dennis, I couldn't have been happier about the dress part, either.

'And Maya Tulum was more than happy to move up our reservations, so in two days, we're off to the Yucatan!' Hutch added.

Hutch took Ruth's hand, raised her gently to her feet, and led her out on to the dance floor. I watched them waltz happily away.

I listened to the music for a bar or two. 'I don't recognize that tune. Do you, Paul?'

Paul slipped his arm around my shoulders. 'It's called 'Lost in the Darkness' from the musical *Jekyll & Hyde*. Come on.'

He grabbed my hand, tucked it under his arm, and led me out to join the others on the floor. While we waltzed, Paul hummed and dum-de-dummed along with the music as if he were unsure of the words, but toward the end of the song, he began to sing softly in my ear, 'I'll never desert you, I promise you this, Til the day that I die.'

I smiled up at him, and his lips found my mouth, and for one magic moment we danced completely alone.